Spark

HOMECOMING HEARTS
BOOK TWO

HJ WELCH

CHAPTER

One

JOEY

JOEY'S BACK SLAMMED INTO HIS FLIMSY APARTMENT DOOR, making it rattle. He laughed into the mouth he was currently kissing. "Someone's keen," he mumbled playfully.

His date bit his lower lip and hummed. "Hell yeah. You gonna let us in or are we doing this out here?"

Considering the dingy hallway they were in, Joey thought that might be unwise. "Keys," he uttered around the tongue being shoved into his mouth. He fumbled in his pocket and tried to fish the door key out.

His date wasn't really a date, more of a hookup. Dave or Dean or Derek? Something like that. He was big and buff and wore a leather jacket. He ticked all of Joey's bad boy boxes, and after one drink and awkward small talk, he was far more interested in getting naked than finding out anything boring like where the guy was from.

Dean. He was pretty sure that was it. Dean bit at his neck and groped his crotch as Joey turned around, jammed his key into the lock and opened the door.

They tumbled into his tiny apartment. Joey didn't bother flicking the light switches on. There was enough illumination coming from the multi-colored neon lights on the street outside to fumble their way along.

He'd at least intended to reach the bedroom, but Dean had other plans. He pushed Joey against the wall, crowding him with his whole body as he unzipped his fly and grabbed at Joey's cock.

He cried out. It was a little bit rough, but Joey didn't mind that so much. He liked big guys, and big guys generally liked being in charge. He focused on slipping his own fingers through the guy's jeans and briefs, finding his thick cock to squeeze.

"You like that, sweetheart?" Dean growled.

He spun them around so his back was leaning against the wall and kissed Joey again. Claiming his mouth, devouring his tongue. He yanked at Joey's cock, making him wince, then whipped his own dick out, stroking it provocatively.

"Like what you see?" Dean asked.

"Yeah," Joey said. It was big and red and probably just what he needed inside him to forget about his shitty day.

Dean pushed on his shoulder though. "Urgh, blow me, pretty boy," he begged. Joey wasn't entirely sure he knew his name.

That didn't matter. It was way weirder when guys wanted to fuck him because he was famous...used to be famous. People were already forgetting there was ever a band called Below Zero.

He angrily chased that thought away and allowed himself to be shoved to his knees. At least this way he could jack himself off the way he liked.

It never felt okay to ask guys to be gentler. Like, sex was supposed to be aggressive and fun and hot. But they did like to just grab and pull and slam most of the time. Even now, Dean seized his hair and guided Joey's mouth towards his cock. It was fine, he wanted to suck it. So rather than wish for, what? A cuddle? He got right to it.

It was warm and salty and slid easily down his throat. "Yeah, gorgeous, take it," Dean rasped, fucking into his mouth. "Oh Christ, gonna come down your pretty throat. You'll like that, won't you?"

Joey would. Rather than answer, he carried on bobbing his head. He used one hand to squeeze his fingers around the base, the other to tease his own prick just the way he liked, stroking the end with his fingertips.

Dean grunted and thrust faster, chasing his release. "Gonna come," he whined. "Are you ready? Want to watch you swallow me."

Joey nodded, looking up at him through his lashes, jerking himself off harder.

"Jesus, you're so pretty," said Dean, caressing his face. "Look at you, you little slut, you love it."

Joey moaned, feeling his orgasm building. All it took were a few more thrusts, and Dean was shooting down his gullet. Joey only flinched briefly before sucking it down, drinking every last drop as he came too, over his shirt and the wall.

Dean panted and slumped backwards, letting his cock soften between Joey's lips while he caught his breath. Joey wiped his mouth and struggled to his feet, tucking himself back in as he did.

"That was hot," he said, leaning in for a kiss.

Dean smiled and kissed him back. "It sure was."

He pulled away to rearrange his junk and zipped up his fly. "Um," said Joey. "Do you want a beer?"

Dean smirked and touched his thumb to Joey's lip. "Thanks for a fun time, honey." He checked his hair in the mirror then winked at him. "Catch you around."

He sauntered to the door, letting himself out. He threw Joey a kiss over his shoulder, then he was gone.

Joey stood dumbly in his hall for a moment then crossed the carpet to secure the lock, chain and bolt.

That was fine, he'd only been looking for a bit of sex. And anyway, he only had a couple of beers left. It would have been a shame to waste one on a stranger.

He sighed and turned on the lights. The apartment was merely a single room with both bed and kitchenette in the same square space. A bathroom big enough for just a shower and a toilet was the only other room.

He shrugged off his jacket and hung it on the back of the door. After kicking off his boots, he stripped off his spunk-covered shirt then headed to the fridge. He plucked one of the beer bottles out and a carton of milk, then grabbed the last of his cereal, a bowl and a spoon.

His body was still pleasantly thrumming from the orgasm as he nestled into his pillows and filled the bowl with off-brand Cinnamon Toast Crunch. As he poured some milk with one hand he pulled out his phone with the other. 11:53.

He sighed again, heavier this time, and looked around at his sparse apartment. He'd sold most everything of value, keeping hold of only sentimental things. A few photos were the predominate decoration on the walls. They were all old now though and looking at them made him feel sad rather than happy.

He shook his head and picked his phone back up. With a loud dance remix playing, he began munching on his cereal, trying to think about nothing but the melodies punching through the air around him. He tapped his foot to the beat and hummed along.

Sometimes life took you unexpected places. Sometimes life dragged you kicking and screaming where you didn't want to go. Six months ago, he would never have thought he'd be all alone on a Saturday night, no job, no prospects, eating cereal for the fifth meal in a row.

Things could be worse, he knew. He just wasn't sure how.

The song tapered out and he watched the clock on the phone tick down to midnight. As the numbers blinked over, the lights went out, plunging him back into the neon-bathed gloom.

Joey felt his throat constrict, but he refused to cry. He had no money left for bills, his rent was overdue, and he'd sold everything he could.

With a heavy heart, he ate the last bite of cereal and placed the bowl on the side. There was just one little stash of money he had left, the money that he'd held onto for the last five years, just in case. He'd always hoped he would never have to use it, but deep down, he knew he couldn't fight it anymore.

He stood and rested his head on the glass window, looking out at the little sliver of L.A. he could see. The milk and grain churned unpleasantly in his stomach, but there was nothing for it. That money had only ever been intended for one thing, and he was now desperate enough to use it.

It was time to buy a ticket home.

CHAPTER

Two

GABE

Gabe closed the front door and gently leaned his back against it, looking down the hallway of his home.

It was so quiet.

He inhaled very slowly, fighting the lump rising in his throat. This was for the best, he knew that. It didn't make it much easier. But if he kept reminding himself this was ultimately what he wanted, he might be able to keep it together.

Dusk was settling and the house was gloomy, so he turned on every light as he moved through the rooms. He thought it might bring some warmth, some life to the space. All it did was highlight what was missing.

Lewis hadn't taken much apart from his own, obvious possessions. His side of the wardrobe was bare, his tennis racket was gone from the spare room, his toiletries from the bathroom. They had agreed who would get what of their mutual items in emails devoid of personality over the past week.

Those messages had summed up their relationship in its dying days. No passion or anger or hurt. Just sad acceptance.

Lewis had always loved the Francesca DiMattio painting,

so Gabe had been happy to let him take that. Lewis had tried to buy his half from him, but Gabe had argued he was keeping so many other things it balanced out. Even if money was a bit tight, it felt petty to demand payment for a work of art that had once brought them both joy.

Money seemed so trivial as he sat on the bed, their bed. He ran his hand over the comforter and decided one of his first tasks tomorrow would be to replace the bedding. They hadn't had sex in so long, but there had been many happy moments between these sheets. He needed a fresh start.

Gabe let out a shaky sigh and looked at the ceiling, blinking back the tears that threatened to fall. He and Lewis weren't the same people they'd been in their early twenties. Over the past five years they'd changed to want different things, to have different dreams.

Gabe snorted and stood up, running his hand through his hair. That wasn't true. Gabe had always known what he'd wanted. It was Lewis that had outstripped him, reaching higher and higher with his career. There was only so much a town like Greenwich could offer him, and only so much even its biggest law firm could offer in interesting cases. Lewis was meant for greater things. It was no wonder the bright lights of New York City had lured him away eventually.

He'd been a fool to think their love would be enough reason to stay.

It made Gabe wonder if it really was love. Wasn't love supposed to be all-consuming? Move heaven and earth? Light up the night's sky and all that other poetic stuff? Gabe wasn't sure.

He had certainly loved being with Lewis. He was one of those guys that always had to be in a relationship. He didn't see the point of messing around with people if he didn't picture a future together. Lewis had been smart and hot and great in bed. He earned good money and was never shy about treating Gabe to dinner, concert tickets, weekends away, whatever he wanted. It had been so wonderful.

But...had there been something missing? That special spark? Was that why it hadn't been that hard to slip apart?

He touched one of their framed photos standing on the dresser in the landing. They had experienced so much together, and now it was over.

They didn't share that many friends. Also, the breakup had been amicable, so Gabe wasn't looking at a drastic reduction in his social circle. But his friends had all liked Lewis. Probably all assumed they would get married someday soon. He didn't really feel like reaching out to any of them that evening.

He didn't want to be alone either. He could always hit the gym or climb one of the walls at the community center. But that wouldn't entail much meaningful human interaction. There was Paddy's Irish Bar down town. He worried though that if he started drinking, his emotions might skew his judgment. He didn't fancy getting wasted or the hangover that would inevitably follow.

Scrubbing his face, he finally walked into the kitchen and looked at the empty spot on the floor. He knew exactly want he wanted to do, and who he was missing the most. At the lack of dog bed, he gave in and allowed some of the tears he'd been forcing back to fall.

All he wanted right now was to bury his face in Max's warm fur and take a walk around the park. But Max would be settled in his new home in Manhattan by now. He'd have the whole of Central Park as his backyard.

Gabe sat down on the cold tiles and leaned his head back against the wooden cabinet. How many hours had he sat here as a child and kept his mom company while she cooked and baked? Or his dad when he had enough time to make them his secret recipe ribs?

This house was made to be filled with love and laughter. But for the first time in thirty-five years, it was hollow.

"You're still here, dumbass," he growled at himself. He rubbed his eyes and pushed himself back to his feet.

It would be very odd indeed if he wasn't sad over the man he'd been with for half a decade leaving. They had shared so much together, and now Gabe had to remember the things that made him happy by himself.

He'd make more time to see friends now. He still had his job down the library and with all the volunteering gigs he did, he wouldn't be lonely.

Perhaps it was about time he tried being single for a while? One of the things that drove him and Lewis apart was that neither of them were ever home at the same time. Now there would be no one around to complain.

Deep down though he worried he just wasn't built to be alone. Maybe he'd get himself a cat? They were pretty self-sufficient, but that way he wouldn't be on his own when he came home.

He stretched his arms over his head and scratched his short beard. Yeah. Maybe he'd go to the shelter after he'd got the new sheets and see if they had any kitties who needed a good home.

Life would go on. He wished Lewis all the best out in the big city, but he had to give himself the same chance.

He flicked on the radio and poured a glass of orange juice. Now he was on his own, he knew he could drink from the carton all he liked. But still, it didn't feel right. Rather than focus on that, he enjoyed the tang of the juice and wiped the back of his hand over his lips. He sang along to whatever song it was playing and told himself that he deserved a fresh start. He'd done everything possible to save the relationship, so now it was time to heal and move on.

There would be days down the road that would be darker

and harder. But all he had to do was get through each one. Before he'd know it, he'd be through a week, then two. He'd be okay.

With optimism firmly in his heart, he ordered a pizza via his phone, then began the difficult task of taking down his and Lewis's photos. Five years accumulated a lot of memories, and Gabe knew he would still cherish them in years to come. But he didn't need to see them right now.

He also rooted through to find anything of Lewis's that had been left behind. He was adamant that he'd taken everything he wanted. So Gabe made himself be strong and either put anything he didn't need in the trash, or in a box for Goodwill.

Max's stuff was harder. They had picked out the golden retriever together when he'd been a puppy; they'd raised him together. But Lewis had become utterly distraught at the idea of leaving him behind, so in the end, Gabe had let him take him. Sadness threatened to engulf him as he thought about hugging him goodbye that morning. But they had agreed that they could try sharing him.

Gabe didn't really think that would happen. It would be too confusing for Max for one thing, and too painful for him and Lewis to have to meet up every time they wanted to hand the dog over. But in case of emergency, if Lewis couldn't get him into kennels, Gabe would want him to feel at home here again.

So he scooped up any toys he found and the blanket from the couch and stored them carefully in a closet out of sight. He could get rid of them another day if he felt like it.

By the time his pizza arrived, he had a tidy house and a box full of books, teddy bears and glass ornaments that he hoped would find new life in someone else's home. He kept his sadness at bay by putting a game on the TV and trying to fill his stomach with comforting hot cheese, bread and meat.

He managed about a third of it before his throat clamped too much and his belly began to ache. With a sigh, he put the rest in the fridge for tomorrow.

He probably went to bed too early, but if he woke before his alarm, he could always go for a run. Come nine o'clock, he was done rallying himself and putting on a brave face, even if he was the only one looking. He turned off all the lights, the radio and the TV, rendering the house dark and quiet once again.

The sheets still smelled of Lewis. Gabe was ashamed at his actions, but nonetheless crawled onto Lewis's side of the bed and hugged his ex's pillow tightly. His brain *knew* that this was the right path for both of them. But his heart ached, wondering if Lewis was all right in his new apartment. If he was cold or feeling a bit lost all alone in a big city.

He missed his damn dog more than anything. Neither of them had fallen out of love with Max, but Gabe had tried to be fair, and now he was the one by himself.

It was okay. No one would know a tough guy like him had cried himself to sleep. Just for tonight, he told himself. Tonight it would be okay to cry.

Tomorrow would be better.

CHAPTER

Three

JOEY

JOEY ONLY HAD ONE BAG AS HE STEPPED OFF THE BUS INTO THE center of downtown Greenwich, Connecticut. He tightened his grip on the strap over his shoulder. But unlike he feared, the whole street did not stop and turn to stare at him. In fact, no one paid him any mind.

Other than the woman trying to get off the bus behind him. "Oh, move along, won't you?" she groused.

Joey hopped off the last step and onto the sidewalk. The bus let out a sigh as the doors closed and it trundled on its way again.

He had been traveling for a couple of days. The last of his money had gone to cover the rent he owed on his apartment. So he'd only had enough left for a Greyhound rather than a plane ticket, then the bus fare home from the depot. He was sore and stiff and probably smelled funky. He popped some gum in his mouth to substitute the good brush he wanted to give his teeth.

Jesus fucking Christ. This was not how he even imagined coming back here. He'd considered it briefly when Below Zero were on their way up, high on the success of their first album and the Grammy they'd just won. But then he and Blake had rented their apartment, and there didn't really seem to be any point coming back where he knew he wasn't wanted.

Fuck. He'd have to tell Blake where he was. With the other guys, he could probably hold off admitting he'd had to crawl back home for as long as he could. But Blake would get it out of him after ten minutes on the phone. He rubbed his temples and decided to deal with that when it came.

For now, he just had to get home.

He walked down the street past a couple of banks and the independent clothes stores. Joey felt a pang of nostalgia that just made him sad as he took in the quaint storefronts.

He'd spent a lot of time on these streets. Anything to stay out of the house. Unfortunately, there wasn't anything to keep him away now as he trudged down the familiar paths.

The trees were turning as fall set in. Joey hated seeing summer end. It felt like the walls were closing in.

He could smell Maggie's Muffins half a block away. If he had anything but pennies left in his pockets he would have totally swung inside and helped himself to an almond bear claw. Nowhere else in the world did one like Maggie's, and he'd looked. Instead, he inhaled deeply as he approached, swearing that as soon as he had any cash, he'd go treat himself.

Except…then he'd have to see Maggie.

It was probably inevitable people were going to ask why he was home. What happened to his popstar career. But Joey couldn't stomach to think about that on his first day. Not until he'd had some sleep and a shower. The humiliation was too much.

All his dreams, all his fame and wealth and success hadn't been able to save him from coming back. No matter how hard he'd tried. How much he'd wanted it. Knowing he'd have to tell his story over and over again just made the bitter pill even harder to swallow.

He'd already made up his mind he was going to tell anyone who asked that L.A. was too fake and he'd always intended to come back to work on Broadway anyway. It was half true, after all. Martha, his agent, had him a couple of auditions already set up. It was a little tricky to negotiate from L.A., but the thought of trying to get a new agent on top of everything else was unfathomable.

Although they hadn't had much success, Martha had felt like his only friend on the really bad days since the band split.

Of course Blake was his best buddy. But he was so loved up with his new boyfriend he wasn't always around when Joey wanted to talk.

He didn't begrudge him. In fact it was the opposite, he was thrilled for him. But it had been hard on Joey at times, bottling it all in.

At that moment though he let it all go and just breathed in the delicious scents from Maggie's heavenly bakery. He smiled – right at the second the hottest guy Greenwich had ever seen stepped out onto the sidewalk.

Joey was so taken aback he stopped walking, quickly dropping his smile. The guy was tall, over six foot, broad and a good body, if anything could be seen through the wool cardigan he wore. Joey normally found cardigans on guys dorky, but this dude owned it. Perhaps it was the scruffy beard and wire frame glasses that made it work. He was kind of geek-chic, if a geek were to suddenly decide that hitting the weight station at the gym was cooler than chai lattes and vinyl records.

Joey screwed his head back on and started walking, trying to pretend he hadn't just been caught ogling. The guy gave him a nod for some reason and walked past.

What was the nod for? Did he recognize him?

Joey sighed to himself and shook his head. He probably did, and Joey couldn't help that. From the number of tell-all articles that had sprung up over the years, it was apparent that everyone in town knew about Joey Sullivan running off to be in a boy band.

Still, it would be *really* nice if the hunky man-candy didn't think that he was an utter loser without even meeting him. Joey glanced back over his shoulder wistfully.

He hadn't noticed the guy holding anything before. But now it was obvious he had a big cardboard box perched on one hip and a brown paper bag from Maggie's in his free hand. As Joey watched, Mr. Geek-Chic stopped and handed the bag to a guy sitting on the street who was obviously homeless from his grimy condition.

Joey felt several emotions at once. First, that that was probably one of the kindest acts of selflessness he'd ever witnessed. The homeless guy broke into a big smile as he pulled out the bagel. Then raised his eyebrows at the hot drink Geek-Chic offered him. Then he gave the homeless guy a business card and pointed down the road.

Joey wasn't sure where he was giving him directions to, but by then Joey was already wrestling with a bunch of other feelings.

He felt guilty he'd not even *seen* the homeless guy. He'd honestly just walked right by him. But if he had seen him, there was no way he could pretend that he would have done something so thoughtful as to buy him some food. Even if he had any money.

How did the guy know what the homeless man would like? What if he was wheat intolerant, or vegetarian? And he'd just gone and got him a bacon and cheese bagel. Maybe he preferred chicken? Or tuna? And there were a million kinds of coffee you could get, let alone teas. What if the homeless guy didn't like what he gave him? Wouldn't Geek-Chic be embarrassed?

Then a tiny, awful part of Joey felt horribly jealous.

No one would do that for him. Well, the guys from the band would, but they didn't know how bad things really were. He couldn't believe a stranger would be that kind towards him, to save him when he was at his lowest.

Because right now, he was pretty sure he was as low as he could go.

There was no knight in shining armor to save him from his fate. So he turned back around and carried on walking.

Do-gooders only did things like that to make themselves feel better, Joey was sure. Why else would strangers go out of their way to do nice things? Joey would give anything to help Blake, Raiden, TJ, even Reyse. Although Reyse Hickson didn't really need anyone's help right now judging by his chart positions.

Those guys were his brothers, and he'd do whatever he could for them. But some random dude on the street? Joey shook his head. He had to help himself out before he could even think about anyone else.

He clenched his fists as the sidewalk led him away from town into a more residential area. Fuck, when had he become so bitter? He remembered feeding a stray kitten one winter when he was a kid. Giving his friend Jilly his lunch money at school because the bigger kids took hers. He wasn't heartless.

But he was sure as hell angry and resentful right then for being forced into a corner like an angry alley cat.

He also knew that his jealousy wasn't entirely without bias. If it had been some soccer mom acting with such kindness, he probably could have seen the generous act more clearly for what it was. As it stood though, Joey couldn't help but think about Mr. Gorgeous Geek-Chic being sweet to *him,* specifically, without a deep longing.

What would it be like to be cared for like that?

He gritted his teeth as he walked up the hill. He didn't need caring for; he looked after himself. He loved his friends and, when he'd been able to, he'd given liberally to charity.

Right now, he had nothing to give. It was easy to stick your face on a campaign when you were adored. As it stood, he suspected no one would want him at the moment, and it wouldn't do any good if they did. He was a nobody again. He just had to protect his own skin, his own heart, and try and get through this.

With that thought still in mind, he turned down his old street, steeling himself for what was to come. He'd played to crowds of eighty thousand people, yet stepping back onto Carter Drive was somehow far more intimidating.

He trotted up the front porch steps he'd known his whole life. His heart was in his throat as he stood at the door, his hands trembling. There were so many things he would give to avoid this moment he was facing.

But the sad truth was, he'd already given them. There was nothing left.

He sang to himself in nothing more than a whisper, an old tune he'd heard as a lullaby. Murmurs of sunshine and loneliness.

"Please," he asked the universe. "A little kindness. That's all I ask."

He pressed the bell.

CHAPTER
Four

GABE

GABE SHOULDERED HIS WAY INTO THE GOODWILL STORE, careful not to spill his green tea. "Hey, Lara," he called out.

Lara looked up from the battered paperback she was reading behind the counter and waved. "Oh hey, hun." She slotted in her bookmark, pushed her glasses up her nose and scurried around to take Gabe's box from him. "What have you got for us today?"

"Oh, um," he said. Despite his best effort, his stomach dropped. "Just some of Lew's things, you know?"

Lara froze with her hands on the box and looked up at him. "I'm so sorry," she said. "I didn't think."

He shook his head. "It's fine," he said, mostly meaning it. "It's for the best."

Lara nodded up at him. She was barely five foot five. "That's the spirit. My mom used to say when one door closes, another opens. You never know what's around the corner." She winked at him and took the box to place it out of sight behind the counter. "Like, did you hear Joey Sullivan has come back?"

Gabe stepped closer and raised his eyebrows. "Who?"

Lara chuckled. "Who?" she said, shaking her head. "You know, Martin and Teresa's youngest. The one that went off to be a popstar."

"Oh, right, yeah," said Gabe. He sort of remembered something about that, but it was years ago. "He visiting his folks?"

Lara sat back on her stool and wrapped her fingers around her chipped mug of instant coffee. "Flick said that Di told her that when the band broke up, he blew all his money trying to start a solo career. She said she saw it on TMZ."

Gabe took a second to sip his tea. "Poor guy, that sounds tough. Still, it must be nice to come home to his family."

Lara nodded. "I'm dreading my ones running off to college," she admitted with a laugh. "Teresa must be so happy to have him home. Nothing like Mom's cooking, hey?"

Gabe offered her a sympathetic smile. Lara had lost her mom the year before and taken it pretty badly. He'd helped her with the arrangements seeing as her husband had skipped town years ago. It had been a beautiful ceremony in the end though.

That's why Gabe liked Lara; she always looked for the rainbow in the storm. The inheritance money meant her kids could go to the schools they wanted. She insisted they take it all, and spent her days working in the store quite happily.

Gabe admired hard workers. It was all very well being a popstar, but that Joey boy would probably need to get a real job now. Give back to the town where he'd grown up. Gabe was happy for him, getting the chance to get back in touch with everyone. Though he doubted their paths would cross much.

"You working today?" Lara asked.

Gabe shook his head. "Not today." This was one of his rare free Sundays, but he did find it hard to keep track sometimes.

Technically, his actual job was with the library as an assistant. He mostly stacked the shelves and managed the classes and groups that they offered the community. But then he also worked part-time every other weekend with the fire department, as well as a couple of shifts a week at the new homeless shelter in town, and taught a rock climbing class at the leisure center.

It was rare for him to have a whole day off, let alone two in a row like he'd just had. But his friends understood about Lewis. They knew Gabe needed a moment to catch his breath. He was utterly exhausted. So for now, he was sticking to his plan of focusing on himself and his well-being after the breakup.

He bid farewell to Lara, glad to be rid of Lewis's last few things. He felt like a weight had been lifted from his shoulders. As sad as it was, it was a new beginning, and those should always be celebrated.

He got back in his old car. It had been his dad's and was in pretty good shape, but there was no denying it was on its last legs. If it could just get him through this winter, Gabe thought, maybe he'd have enough saved up to get a new one.

He pulled away from the curb and checked the map on his phone for the directions towards the animal shelter. He'd given it serious thought, and a cat seemed just the remedy for his broken heart. It wouldn't depend on him being around all the time, but hopefully, they might be able to offer each other some love.

On his way, he passed the same guy he'd seen when he'd walked out of the bakery. He'd not spotted him around town before, and it made Gabe think. Could this be the famous Joey Sullivan?

He was a smallish guy. Petite was probably the word, although he had a tough look about him. From the way his jeans clung to his thighs as he walked, it was obvious he had good muscle definition. His golden curls caught the midmorning sunlight, and as Gabe drove by, he thought he caught a glimpse of a tattoo on his wrist by his sleeve.

Joey – if that was indeed Joey Sullivan – had his gaze focused on the sidewalk. His hand was wrapped around the bag strap over his shoulder, and his face was preoccupied with a frown. Gabe only really had a chance to look for a second or two before he had to focus back on the road, but he thought Joey maybe seemed sad.

He was probably bummed about not being a big-shot singer anymore. But at least he was going home to his family. Gabe wondered if he should have offered him a lift. He wasn't sure what part of town the Sullivans lived in, but Joey had to be tired after all his traveling.

The moment passed though. Gabe was already through the lights and down the road. So he contented himself with a glance in the rearview mirror at Joey's diminishing form.

Maybe he'd see him around again? Gabe wasn't sure why, but he felt the urge to talk to Joey quite strongly, despite never having interacted before. But he couldn't help but feel that Joey looked as lost as Gabe felt.

He shook the gloomy thoughts away and refocused on the GPS taking him to the animal shelter. It wasn't far, but it also wasn't a route he was familiar with. He thought he knew all the roads in and out through town, but it turned out he could still be challenged from time to time.

The lot wasn't busy as he pulled in. The building itself was a fair size, with big glass windows at the front by the entrance doors. A silhouette of a cat and a dog had been painted on one of them, along with 'Greenwich Animal Shelter' underneath.

Gabe killed the ignition and sat in the car with the keys held in his lap. He felt a terrible pang for his dog Max, but he wasn't replacing him. Max could never be replaced. He was just moving on.

At that thought, the pang was replaced with a thrill of excitement. Hopefully, he'd get back in the car with a new furry friend.

The woman at reception beamed when she looked up and saw Gabe. He placed her immediately as the mom of one of the kids that came to his reading afternoons at the library, but he couldn't remember either of their names. He'd just have to smile and hope it came back to him.

"Well hello, sweetie," the woman said. As he approached, she took her hands away from the computer keyboard she'd been typing at. Thankfully, she was sporting a name tag that read 'Brooke.' Brooke had dull brown, graying hair but a bright smile. "We haven't seen you here before, Gabe," she said cheerfully, her curiosity clear. "How can I help?"

Gabe slipped his hands into his pockets and rocked on his feet. He didn't feel like talking about Lewis, so he hoped she wouldn't ask.

There weren't many other gay couples in town. Certainly not ones that were involved with the community as much as he and Lewis had been. So they'd become something of a novelty over the past few years. News of their breakup had spread like wildfire, but Gabe didn't quite feel ready to face their questions yet.

"I was thinking about adopting a cat," he said. "Your website said I didn't need to make an appointment?"

"No, no, that's fine," said Brooke, bustling to her feet and coming out from behind the reception desk. "We've got plenty. I'm sure we can find you a purr-fect pet!"

She chuckled at her own joke as she fished a big bunch of keys out from a drawer. Gabe smiled too at her buoyant attitude.

"Do you have any preferences in mind? Breed? Temperament?"

Gabe shrugged, following her through a door out into a warehouse. It was a maze of chicken wire pens, about five feet tall, all lined up next to one another. The cacophony hit him the second the door opened. All around him were barks and meows and whimpers and claws on metal and the concrete beneath. He felt overwhelmed.

"Will you find homes for all these animals?" he asked in wonder, turning and looking at those he could see. They were in a dog section, and he had to fight the urge to take every one that he saw home.

Brooke touched his arm lightly, getting his attention. "Most of them," she said optimistically.

But Gabe's thoughts immediately latched on to what that meant. "What happens to the ones you don't?"

Brooke bit her lip. "We do our best," she assured him. She was still maintaining her smile, but it didn't quite meet her eyes. "It's our mission to find every little buddy their forever home."

He looked around again. The dogs around him were gorgeous, and a few of the cages had litters of puppies in them. These were the pets that would go the quickest and easiest, he was sure.

"You're still set on a cat?" Brooke asked him. Gabe nodded. "Well, come on then. I've got a gorgeous litter of Siamese kitties, as well as a very handsome Persian."

She started walking off and Gabe followed her. "Have you got one that's been here a long time," he blurted out, not really thinking his words through. "One no one wants?"

Brooke gave him a look of concern over her shoulder. "Have you had a cat before, sweetie?"

Gabe shrugged. "No. My family always had dogs."

If he was sensible he'd go back and check out one of those

lovely-looking terriers, or the collie that had wagged her tail at him. But this was his new start. He wanted a cat. One that no one else was willing to take.

He wasn't the only one who deserved a fresh start today.

Brooke sighed. "Let's get you going with one of the more easy-to-manage breeds," she said in a firm but friendly manner. It was probably a tone she used with her kids a lot.

But Gabe shook his head. "I want to see whoever is at the bottom of the list."

Brooke paused, then nodded her head and switched directions down a different row of cages. Maybe she thought once he saw the dregs, he'd listen to her and go for a more agreeable cat.

Gabe did his best not to look at any of the cute faces peering up at him. He could only rescue one of them today, as much as he wished otherwise.

They entered an area of empty pens. That was, all but one. "She doesn't like the noise," Brooke said with a sigh. "We found it's best if we keep her away from cages with other animals."

They approached the pen in the corner. A striped tabby was crouched in the corner, watching them come closer with wide, blue eyes.

Gabe felt his heart melt right through his ribcage.

The cat had a chunk of her left ear missing as well as a few toes on her front left paw. Her fur was patchy in places, and one of her bottom teeth poked up over her lip making her look kind of derpy. She backed away as Brooke put one of the keys into the lock and opened the door.

"See what I mean?" she said as the cat managed to back up even further and hissed. Her big eyes darted back and forth.

Brooke moved aside as Gabe stepped into the cage. With his bulk, it was no easy feat. He more or less crawled in. The cat stared at him as he sat himself down and looked back at her.

He had no idea what to do with cats. But when his dogs were ever skittish, he knew it was important to get them to trust you. So he held out his hand, offering the kitty his fingers to sniff.

"How long has she been here?" he asked.

"Nine months," Brooke admitted. "Came off the street. She's pretty difficult to manage. Not like most of the other cats here." She looked back towards the other pens, maybe hoping to encourage him to go look.

But Gabe smiled and didn't get back up. He knew how it was not to be like 'most of the others.'

He continued to sit and hold his hand out. The cat blinked at him, narrowing her eyes. Brooke stood still and watched them.

A few minutes of relative quiet passed. Neither he nor Brooke moved, and the din of the animals seemed to fade away. The tabby flitted her eyes back and forth, but she kept coming back to Gabe. He never shifted his gaze, hardly even blinking.

"That's it, good kitty," he coaxed in a soothing voice. She regarded him some more.

Just as his arm was starting to feel the ache of being held out, she put a tentative paw forwards.

Brooke took in a sharp breath, but it was quiet and she didn't move. The tabby froze, but after another minute she edged forward again.

It probably took five minutes for her to reach Gabe's fingers. She sniffed them experimentally. Gabe foolishly moved to stroke her, and she shot straight back to her corner to cower. But he wasn't deterred. If he could make that much progress in just a few minutes, just think what he could achieve in a week, a month.

It was obvious she was scared and had been treated badly, but that didn't mean she deserved to stay unloved.

He turned to Brooke. He could feel the big grin on his face.

"I'll take her."

CHAPTER
Five

JOEY

JOEY STEPPED BACK AS THE FRONT DOOR OF HIS CHILDHOOD home swung inwards. His mom stopped at the sight of him, her mouth popping open.

She looked older, but that was only to be expected. He'd not seen her in five years. She was still just as skinny, but her mousy brown hair had more gray in it and the lines around her eyes had deepened.

"Joseph?"

She was the only one that ever called him that. Despite his apprehension, Joey smiled. "Hi, Mom," he said, his voice catching slightly.

"Oh, my baby boy," she whispered. She rushed down the couple of steps to the porch where he was standing and pulled him into her arms. "You've grown so much."

He guessed he had. He'd been sixteen when he left home, chasing his dreams with Below Zero. Now he was a man. A broken man, he feared, but a man nonetheless.

She bit her lip and looked him over, taking him in. He noticed her eyes lingering on the tattoo that reached beyond his left sleeve. She didn't say anything, but he made a mental note to keep himself covered up while he was there. She didn't need to worry about the extent of his body art.

She'd probably seen it all in countless tabloids, but she didn't need reminders in the flesh. Joey's body was his business, nobody else's. Still, it would hurt to see any more disappointment in her eyes than there already was.

"You look well," he said to her. It wasn't strictly true, but it was worth the white lie for the smile it brought to her face.

"We've missed you."

Now that was definitely not true. Joey allowed her to pretend it was though and followed her inside the house.

Nothing had changed. The same old faded wallpaper and carpets greeted him as he closed the door behind him. He wiped his shoes on the doormat and trailed after his mom down the hall. He gripped the bag strap over his shoulder tightly.

Voices were coming from the kitchen up ahead. Joey tried his best not to tremble and forced himself to hold his head up high.

"You should have seen his face, Dad," Patrick Sullivan boomed amidst the laughter. "He didn't know what hit him."

"He didn't, did he, Pat?" Cathy, Patrick's wife, was cackling as Joey came to stand beside his mom's shoulder. They hovered on the threshold of the gleaming kitchen.

"Look, Martin," said Joey's mom softly. "Look who's home."

The mirth died in an instant. Joey did his best not to squirm as three sets of eyes narrowed in his direction. His dad, other brother and sister-in-law all had cups of coffee in front of them, the steam still coming off the drinks. There was one of his mom's homemade carrot cakes sitting on the table between them with a quarter wedge missing. It looked so good; Joey had to fight from licking his lips.

"Hi," he said.

His dad leaned away in his chair, slinging his arm over the back. "L.A. not such a magical wonderland after all, then?" He smirked.

There was no way Joey could safely answer that. He did his best to smile and not fidget. "You look good," he said instead, like he had to his mom.

Martin Sullivan was as robust as ever, just like Patrick. Bulky meatheads with small eyes and cropped brown hair. There was no mistaking the relation. Joey, on the other hand, was short and willowy, like his mom. Even if he wasn't a dirty faggot, he probably would have never lived up to his dad's idea of a man anyway.

A little cry drew Joey's attention to the crib set up at the other end of the table. He gasped and instinctively moved forwards, but Cathy shot out of her seat and raced over to the baby.

"He probably needs feeding," she said to Patrick, cheerfully ignoring Joey entirely like she always used to do.

Joey's heart ached as she pulled the six-month-old infant up from the crib and perched him on her hip. Michael. Joey's nephew. He had golden curly locks, just like Joey, and he felt his throat clamp up.

"He's beautiful," he rasped. Cathy continued to ignore him as she took a bottle of milk from the refrigerator and began heating it up.

Joey glanced at his brother, but Patrick was studiously looking at his coffee, his thumb rubbing in agitation at the handle. Joey gritted his teeth. He knew he'd become an uncle from one of his mom's few phone calls earlier in the year. He'd been foolish enough to hope that he'd be allowed to at least hold Michael, but it was pretty obvious they didn't want him anywhere near their precious son.

The trouble was, he *was* precious. From his button nose to his tiny fingers to his chubby legs that kicked in excitement as his mom prepared his food. But he would grow up learning that people like Joey were an abomination. Filthy perverts. They would never be allowed the chance to get to know each other, so Joey should just forget any idea of trying now. It would save him heartache in the long run.

"Isn't he gorgeous?" said Joey's mom in response to his comment. She beamed with pure joy at her first and only grandchild. As bitter as the situation felt to Joey, he couldn't help but be happy for her.

"Pat and Cath are staying here while they save to buy their own place," said Joey's dad. He wasn't looking at Joey and picked up his cup to take a sip as he nodded at Patrick. "Working *real* hard, is our Pat."

"He's so good to his family," Cathy gushed, smiling at him.

It felt like although they were largely ignoring Joey's presence, they were still putting on a big show for him. Like he should be jealous he wasn't working in the meat-packing plant like his grandad had before his dad and brother.

"That's great," said Joey. How much longer were they going to make him go through this charade? "Well, I can see you're busy, so I'll just head to my room."

"Oh," said his mom, her hands fluttering at her chest. "About your room-"

"You weren't supposed to be coming back," his dad interrupted matter-of-factly. "So we got rid of it all. It's Michael's room now. You won't be staying long though, will you? So it doesn't matter."

He turned his flinty eyes and arched a brow in Joey's direction. Challenging him.

"Yeah, that's fine," said Joey.

He couldn't deny his heart sunk at hearing they'd just trashed all his childhood belongings, but it wasn't exactly a surprise. He was still stunned he'd been given permission to stay even one night. But his mom had told him on the phone that he could crash there at least for a little while.

Joey wasn't sure what she'd said to convince his dad of even that much, but he was extremely grateful. And lord knew he wanted to get out from under that roof as much as his dad wanted him gone.

"I've made you up the camp bed in the basement," his mom said. There were unshed tears in her eyes, but she was determinedly smiling through them. "You'll be nice and warm, I'm sure."

"Come on," said his dad, getting to his feet. "I'll show you down."

Joey immediately tensed. His dad was certainly not offering out of kindness.

What could his dad really do, though? Joey was an adult now. He was strong and fast and wasn't going to take his shit like he'd had to growing up. If he didn't show weakness, he'd be okay.

"Sure," he said. He spared a regretful glance towards baby Michael, happily guzzling on his bottle, and followed his dad. Not before his mom touched his arm and kissed his cheek.

"Welcome home, Joseph," she said quietly, wiping the back of her hand over her eyes.

He hugged her, breathing in her familiar scent he hadn't even realized he'd missed. Then he walked along the hall to the stairs that led down.

As basements went, theirs wasn't so bad. Like the rest of the house, his mom kept it very clean. It was just stuffed with boxes of holiday decorations and old baby clothes that he supposed Michael would inherit now. In the corner was a flimsy-looking single camp bed. He dared to smile when he realized his mom had given him his old outer space comforter.

"This is not your home."

Joey turned to look at his dad, the smile dying on his lips. He was standing between Joey and the stairs back up to the house. He crossed his arms over his broad chest and glowered.

"I know," said Joey, his chin up.

"You're only here because I love your mom, and I can't have you breaking her heart any more than you already have. Do you understand?"

"Yes, sir," Joey replied automatically.

"You're to pay your way and keep out of our business. If I get even a hint you're not doing everything you can to get your own place, you'll be out on your ass on the streets as encouragement to try harder. Do I make myself clear?"

Joey gritted his teeth. "Yes, sir," he ground out.

He was tempted to ask what the hell it was he'd done so wrong to deserve being treated like a criminal. But he already knew the answer.

"You won't even know I'm here."

His dad nodded and marched back up the stairs without a second glance.

Joey let out a long breath and dropped his bag to the floor. *That could have gone a lot worse*, he reasoned as he flopped on the bed.

Something dug into his back though, and he quickly sat up again. Confused, he pulled the covers back.

He had to stifle his gasp with a hand, then glanced behind him to make sure his dad had closed the door. Confident he was alone, Joey reached out with shaky fingers.

Scattered over the mattress were a couple of wrapped-up sandwiches, several candy bars, a resealable packet of dried mango strips, and a squashed slice of carrot cake, also wrapped up in cling film.

Most importantly, there was also a wad of cash secured in

a clip. He picked that up first, ashamed at how fast he counted the bills. Two hundred dollars.

He clamped his jaw shut, but he couldn't stop the tears that cascaded down his cheeks. It was a big risk for his mom to do this. She must have dipped into her own savings. Still, if his dad had found what was in the bed before Joey...

He hadn't. She'd gotten away with it. So Joey hastily shoved the money into his wallet and the food into his backpack. Once he knew it was hidden, he unwrapped one of the peanut butter and jelly sandwiches, moaning as he bit into it.

He'd done it. He'd made it through the front door without too much drama.

Now all he had to do was get himself back out of it again. For good.

CHAPTER

Six

GABE

Even though it was a little corny of him, Gabe felt like the library was the heart of Greenwich. It had done its best to keep up with the times. There were banks of public-use computers alongside the rows of books, and they offered all kinds of classes and community groups throughout the day and into the evening.

Whether it was grandmas coming to type with two fingers or students fueled by coffee searching for textbooks, mother-and-toddler dance lessons or Spanish for beginners, the big building was always full of people from all walks of life.

Gabe's job wasn't particularly challenging. Mostly, he was responsible for putting books back where they lived, keeping on top of their filing system, and liaising with the various teachers to make sure their tightly packed schedules ran like clockwork. While it may not have been particularly intellectually stimulating, it was certainly good for his soul.

There were several sessions that Gabe also helped out in, like the after-school kids' art program he was currently washing up from. That was his favorite. He loved the kids' never-ending enthusiasm for pasting glitter and bottle tops onto card, nor the proud looks on their folks' faces when they were presented with the creations. It was pure and innocent as well as a lot of fun.

He'd actually been enjoying his afternoon, but as he was scrubbing green paint out from underneath his fingernails, a pang of sadness snuck up on him. He wasn't even sure where it came from, but he suddenly remembered that Lewis wouldn't be coming home after work. That Max wouldn't be waiting on the other side of the front door for their return, ball in his mouth and tail wagging.

Gabe shook his head crossly and turned his attention back to the paint. Maybe not. But Duchess, his new cat, would be there for him. She would be hiding under the coffee table and might very well hiss at him. But she couldn't fool him. She'd eaten all the food he put out for her every day, even if it was when he wasn't looking, and she loved the scratching post and fluffy basket he'd bought her.

One day soon, she was going to creep out and let him stroke her. Until then, he could just be patient, content in the knowledge that he'd got her out of the noisy shelter and given her a warm, safe, loving home.

He went back to the activity room and stacked the chairs, picking any stray feathers he found and wiping up the splatters of Elmer's glue that were starting to dry on the laminated floor. He had an hour left for the day, and as it was a Wednesday, it was normally his evening off. But one of the other climbing instructors had called in sick, so of course he'd offered to cover for her. He felt weary though. All he really wanted to do was swing by the store for supplies, then go home and cook him and Duchess a nice dinner each.

There was no sense in complaining though. So he vowed to embrace the rest of the day and have fun. He'd still get home in good enough time. Besides, it wasn't like he had a boyfriend there waiting on him.

On his way back to the reception he passed through the hot desks. These were simply rows of empty tables where people came with laptops and notepads to work, often scattering their materials over an entire table.

There was only one, solitary figure sitting there that evening. Gabe recognized him right away and couldn't help but pause in his stride as he realized who it was.

Joey Sullivan. Or at least, the guy he'd assumed to be him. The one from outside the bakery. He was even more gorgeous now Gabe could see him up close. He was wearing a t-shirt, displaying nicely toned arms with several tattoos on each one. Beside him were stacked several library-branded CD cases, and he tapped his foot as he listened to the music through the earphones plugged into his laptop.

He was staring intently at his screen, but something must have alerted him to Gabe's presence. He looked over sharply and pulled one of the buds free from his ear.

He went to speak, but then his eyes went wide. Gabe wasn't sure why; he was too busy being embarrassed at getting caught staring. The poor guy probably got enough unwarranted attention as it was. But despite his heartache, Gabe couldn't quite suppress the flicker of desire seeing him evoked.

"Can I help you?" Joey asked once he'd regained his wits.

Gabe cleared his throat and smiled, hoping he didn't seem creepy. Most guys didn't like being looked at like that. He was normally way more careful than that.

"Just wondering if you found everything you needed today, sir?" he asked in a friendly tone.

Joey frowned. "You work here?"

"Uh, yeah?" Gabe replied, unsure why that should be such a surprise. "I think we actually passed each other a couple of days ago," he said to try and break the tension that seemed to be between them. "By Maggie's bakery. I'm Gabe Robinson." Joey looked at him warily. He seemed skittish. Hardly a big-time popstar. "You're Joey Sullivan, right?"

Joey winced and Gabe immediately felt bad. But then Joey smiled. Gabe wasn't sure if it was forced or not. "Yeah, that's me," Joey said as he closed his laptop and pulled out his earphones.

"Oh, sorry," said Gabe, feeling flustered. He was making a mess of this. "I didn't mean to disturb you. Please don't leave on my account."

Joey shook his head. "I have to get going anyway."

Gabe tried not to take it personally, but he'd obviously upset the guy. "Well, it was nice meeting you," he offered as Joey slung his bag over his shoulder and picked up the stack of CDs. "Hopefully we'll see you back here sometime?"

Joey's eyes flicked to the CDs. "Yeah, maybe," he said before hurrying off.

Gabe sighed and gave him a few minutes before walking the same way back towards the reception desk. He was being ridiculous. But he'd sort of hoped to exchange a few more words with him. At least Gabe knew who he definitely was now.

Gabe had naturally assumed Joey would be relieved to be home after all the fuss and stress that must come with a celebrity lifestyle. But he'd seemed withdrawn. Maybe the quiet was a bit of a shock to him and he was still adjusting?

"Penny for them?" Mitch said as he approached the desk, causing Gabe to look up.

He smiled at his boss. Mitch was in his sixties and prob-ably should have retired by now. But like Gabe, he loved the people too much to leave. He was a big bear of a dude, solid with a gray mustache and wire-rimmed bifocals. Gabe had several friends with serious crushes on him, but Mitch had been very happily married to his wife Mary-Lou for over four decades.

"I just met Joey Sullivan, that guy who used to be in a pop band."

Mitch scoffed. "I know who Below Zero are," he said, fussing with his Rolodex. "Were. They did that *Oh oh oohh* song. Jenny cried her eyes out when they broke up, but good old Gran and Gramps promised to buy her Reyse Hickson tickets when they go on sale." He chuckled. "He's her favorite, but she was still pretty excited to hear that Joey had moved back here." He winked at Gabe. "I think we'll be seeing a lot more of her in the future."

Gabe laughed. He knew Mitch and Mary-Lou would love to see more of their grandkids. They had about a dozen scattered across the country.

"He wasn't what I expected," Gabe admitted, leaning on the counter.

Mitch arched an eyebrow at him. "And what were you expecting?"

Gabe shrugged. "I don't know? Someone larger than life maybe?"

Mitch looked at him slyly. "He's gay, you know."

Gabe felt the tips of his ears heat up. "So?" he replied in a vain attempt to pretend like that information didn't interest him. "I'm not looking for anything, and he'd be too young for me anyway."

"Not that young," muttered Mitch with a devilish glint in his eye.

CHAPTER
Seven

JOEY

IT WAS SURPRISING HOW EASILY JOEY SLIPPED BACK INTO OLD habits. It wasn't that hard to find all manner of ways to keep himself out of the house. As long as he had his laptop charger with him, he could make a cup of coffee last all day with free refills at the diner downtown. The waitresses were mostly motherly sorts during the day. So far they hadn't grilled him too badly about his return home, and when he caved and ordered food, he noticed the portions tended to be generous ones.

The library offered him the chance to listen to new music for free, which he appreciated more than the coffee. It lifted his spirits and kept him going through the rejection emails, although he had managed to get a few auditions. They hadn't led to parts, but Joey wasn't giving up and neither was his agent, Martha. He just had to get a bit of luck his way.

The library had the added advantage of an excellent view. Joey wasn't sure what a gorgeous hunk like Gabe was doing working there, but it made being stuck in his hometown slightly more bearable, although he'd avoided talking to him again. Joey was embarrassed at what Gabe must think of him after his fall from grace. So it was better to admire from afar.

His mom's money meant he could afford to travel into New York City when he had to. When auditions called him there, he spent the whole day either in cheap pizzerias or cafes, dreaming of the day he could call the city home.

Where possible, he left his house early and came back late at night. He felt bad for his mom, but it wasn't worth the hostile silence he received from Patrick or Cathy when he ran into them, or the sneers his dad threw his way. The basement didn't have a lock, so he kept his possessions in his one bag, taking everything with him wherever he went. God only knew what he'd do if his jeans ripped or his shoes broke. He had to make his mom's money last as long as he could.

Worry ate away at him day and night. He was exhausted and on edge all the time, which probably came across in his auditions and job applications despite his best efforts. Desperation was an ugly thing.

So when he happened across some sort of town fair one Saturday, he couldn't help but be drawn to the colorful stalls as a welcome respite from his continuous cycle of agonizing over work and finances.

The weather was cold but sunny as he headed into the park. He recognized a lot of faces as he looked around at the homemade pies and game stations. But with his earphones firmly jammed in his ears, he found most people simply nodded his way and didn't try to talk to him. His novelty was thankfully waning, although there was generally one person a day who still wanted to stop him on the sidewalk and get his life's story.

He didn't know which was worse. The ones who looked at him with pity or the ones who seemed to hardly be able to contain their glee. Some talked about Blake and the others like they knew them, which irritated him. Especially those who thought because they watched Blake's shows that they were his best friend. Those were generally the kind to rub his success in Joey's face.

Joey didn't begrudge Blake or the others. It wasn't their fault he was the only one struggling after the band's demise. But it was hard not to feel jealous, especially in his darkest moments.

So that was precisely why he was going to allow himself to enjoy some spontaneous fun at the fair. He didn't have money to waste, but that didn't mean he couldn't enjoy looking at the handcrafted Halloween decorations for sale, or the delicious smells of pumpkin pie and mulled hard cider.

A girl about his age perked up when she saw him approaching. She was standing behind one of the game stalls. It looked like a simple task of throwing tennis balls through holes that had been cut into the plywood, each with numbers painted next to them to indicate scores. She caught Joey's eye and broke into a huge smile. He felt bad walking away after that, so he pulled his earphones out and smiled back.

"Hey," he said. No one else was at her stall, so he didn't mind going over.

"Hi, Joey," she said breathlessly. He was certain he didn't know her, so he assumed she was a fan. It had been a while since someone had been this excited to see him and he felt a rush of gratitude towards the girl. "You want to play?"

"Sure," he said warmly, despite the fact he was worried about wasting money. It was for local charity though, he'd noticed, so that made it better. "How much?"

"One dollar for a shot, or six shots for five dollars," she said like she'd been practicing the line for days. "All proceeds go to the homeless shelter that opened last month."

In his darkest moments, Joey had wondered if he'd end up on the street. That made him even more okay to hand over a five-dollar bill. He knew he was only one step away from needing help like that himself.

He drew a little crowd as he failed horribly to get the balls through the holes. The girl clapped and cheered in a very sweet way though, keeping him smiling, and even slipped him an extra free ball to try one last time. When he got it through the biggest hole, the half a dozen people around him gave a little cheer and clapped him on the back. There was a couple with little twin girls both dressed as Wonder Woman who insisted on hugging him once he was done. Also two women slightly older than him in geeky sweaters that simply congratulated him good-naturedly.

The girl behind the stall asked breathlessly for a selfie together before he left. All in all, Joey felt a bit better as he carried on walking between the novelties.

He was naturally drawn to the firefighters congregated around the firetruck parked on an opening on the grass. They were allowing excitable kids to sit in the cab and showing them the hose, and Joey smiled at the happy scene it made.

Shamefully, he hoped there would be one or two hot guys he might entertain himself looking at. Sure enough, he quickly spied a promising specimen, only to do a double take.

It was Gabe. From the library.

What the hell was he doing dressed up as a fireman? It made more sense, given his physique, but he'd said he worked at the library.

He realized he wasn't the only one staring. Three women just in front of him were looking Gabe's way as they sipped something from thermos flasks. Their lips were moving, so Joey subtly pulled his earbuds out of his ears again.

"-wear it more often," said the blonde one.

The other two, a brunette and another blonde sporting

fluffy earmuffs, nodded. "He should do a calendar," said Earmuffs, sliding her gaze up and down Gabe's form. There wasn't much to be seen in his bulky firefighter's gear, so they must have known what he looked like when he was wearing less.

Joey felt a bit uncomfortable seeing as Gabe was currently holding a little girl on his hip, showing her the lights at the front of the truck. He looked fatherly, not provocative, but the women were practically salivating over him.

Joey wondered how old Gabe was. Whether he had kids of his own. Was that, in fact, his daughter? Joey placed his age at mid to late twenties, so it was possible he was a dad. The thought that he was married made Joey slightly sad, which was ridiculous. It wasn't like he'd have a chance with someone like that whether he was single or not. Or gay.

"He should work for the department full-time," Brunette said. "He looks like a *real* firefighter. Not like old Bertie over there."

They sniggered at an older guy who had a paunch and red nose. Joey glared at the women for their unkindness, even though they couldn't see him. The guy Bertie was obviously fit enough to still be serving in a job that saved lives, for fuck's sake. Who were they to judge him because he wasn't attractive enough?

They had answered his query regarding Gabe's job though. It sounded like he just worked part-time with the fire department on top of his other job. What kind of guy did that sort of thing for fun?

Joey thought maybe he'd like to find out.

He was about to take his leave and put his music back on, but Earmuff's next comment stopped him.

"It would be more appropriate if he stuck with the fires," she said sagely. "Pompeii said he was teaching in her art club at the library. I just don't think that's suitable."

"Is he not qualified?" asked Brunette.

Earmuffs shrugged. "No idea. But people like him shouldn't be around children. It's just confusing for them. They're too young to have that thrust in their faces." She waved at the display going on. "I wouldn't let Pompeii go over there with him."

Blondie raised her eyebrows. "Because he's gay?"

Earmuffs nodded. "I think I'll have a word with the head librarian. If they don't do something about it, I'm pulling Pompeii from the club."

"Isn't that a bit extreme?" asked Brunette with a nervous giggle. "I mean, as long as he's not talking to the kids about – you know – it doesn't really harm anything, does it?"

Earmuffs turned enough so Joey could see her arch an eyebrow. "I know equal rights is all the rage," she said snootily. "They have marriage now, which I guess is okay, but they shouldn't just be allowed in jobs where they can influence our kids, Jenny. We have to protect our children."

From what? Joey wanted to demand. His blood was boiling with rage. How *dare* these women stand there drooling over Gabe one second, then in the next breath question his right to be around children?

Jenny, the brunette, looked uncomfortable. "I don't know," she said, giggling nervously again. "He mows my mom's lawn once a week, every week since her arthritis got bad, and old Mrs. Turnell's. And he helped with that homeless shelter. Not sure how, but Lara said he was there two evenings a week, come hail or shine."

"None of those activities involve *children* though, do they?" replied Earmuffs, an icy tone creeping into her words.

Blondie arched an eyebrow. "He drove the scout bus into NYC over the summer," she said. Her tone suggested that she agreed with Earmuffs, and sure enough, the other woman nodded.

"Exactly. Why is it suddenly okay to allow a queer to do all these things?" She scoffed and sipped her thermos, leaving a bright red lipstick mark behind. "I don't care what they do behind closed doors, just, keep it away from my kids. You know?"

The other two women nodded, before Brunette grinned, breaking the tension. "At least he's hot though."

"*So* hot," the other two moaned in unison.

Joey had had enough. He shoved his earbuds back in and stormed off.

He couldn't even be happy for ten minutes without some homophobic asshole ruining it.

CHAPTER
Eight
GABE

A day helping his buddies out at the fall festival in town was just what Gabe needed to lift his spirits and keep his mind distracted. He was obliged to do thirty hours a month with the fire department. But when he could count a whole afternoon having fun, it sort of felt like cheating.

He couldn't be a firefighter twenty-four-seven. The shifts were too unsociable, and the pay wasn't all that great. But he loved the job all the same. It was rare they got any serious blazes in his district, just the odd grill pan left unattended or vandals causing trouble at the schools. Every couple of months Gabe got called out to big traffic accidents though, giving him enough action to be glad he didn't see more trauma on a regular basis.

Mostly, he loved volunteering because it gave him a chance to really throw himself into the heart of the community and do some good.

The regular guys were the real heroes though. Gabe was honored they'd let him and the other couple of part-timers come and join in an event that was meant to celebrate their hard work. But they insisted.

So he posed for photos and showed kids and adults around the truck proudly. He understood that all kinds of people found what they did interesting and exciting. It was a joy to share it.

What was even more of a joy though was when he looked up and recognized Joey Sullivan walking towards them, a few dozen feet away. Joey had been distracted by one of the girls manning a game booth. She appeared to be explaining how to play the game to him, holding up several tennis balls.

Joey was smiling easily. For a second, it took Gabe's breath away. He'd looked so pensive when he'd seen him before. Laden with heavy burdens. To see him happy made Gabe finally connect him with the pictures of the popstar he'd found online.

He hadn't meant to cave in and search for information on Joey. But after Mitch had told him he was gay, his curiosity had just got too much.

Sure enough, Joey was openly out. Gabe was still getting used to the idea that celebrities could do that and not have it damage their careers. So it made him sort of proud of the younger guy. Especially when he saw him and his bandmate give a speech from a few months ago at some awards show. His friend had come out at the ceremony and given an inspiring speech.

As much as the Blake guy's words had moved Gabe, he had replayed the video clip a few times just to watch Joey watching his friend. It had been a very pure, beautiful moment, seeing the pride evident in his eyes. Gabe almost felt bad that it was so public. But then, that was the point. To reach out to other people that were LGBT.

So he didn't need any more convincing about the newcomer's sexuality. But until now, Gabe hadn't been able to reconcile Joey's public persona with the quiet one he had met himself.

Nothing would have made him happier than to stand and watch Joey being excitable. He had to admit to himself that, even if it was just to do with Gabe's rebound, he was starting to become attracted to Joey. It was probably just a stupid crush. But after all his heartache, Gabe was okay with entertaining one or two idle thoughts about a gorgeous guy.

He was soon distracted by a small girl with bright red pigtails who wanted to understand how the lights and sirens worked. So with her folks' permission, Gabe hoisted her up on his hip and talked her through the systems. She asked surprisingly technical questions for a six-year-old.

"First it was cars, then it was trains," her dad said with a chuckle when Gabe praised her knowledge. "Now everything is firefighters. And Frozen," he added with a weariness that spoke volumes.

Gabe was happy to help the little girl into the cab with one of his colleagues, who took over explaining what everything did. That meant Gabe turned around just in time to see Joey storming past the truck and away from the fair.

Gabe wasn't necessarily thinking clearly as he hopped down. "Joey!" he called out.

He didn't stop, but he looked like he had earbuds in, so Gabe jogged the few feet between them and touched his shoulder.

Joey wheeled around, a look of alarm on his face. But he did pull his earphone out from one ear.

"Whoa, sorry," said Gabe, throwing his hands up. Joey raised an eyebrow and eased the other earphone free. He didn't run away at least. "I didn't mean to startle you."

Joey shrugged. "That's okay." They looked at each other for a moment. "So," Joey carried on while Gabe struggled with what to say. "You're a firefighter?"

Gabe laughed and rubbed his hand through his hair.

"Yeah, sometimes. Looked like you were having fun earlier. It's, uh, nice to see you again."

Joey chewed on his lower lip. "You saw me."

It was Gabe's turn to shrug. He didn't want to make it seem like it was a big deal. "I just happened to look over. Look, I'm sorry if I chased you out of the library the other day. Next time you come in you can say hi. I'm not that scary."

"I'm not-" Joey began. Then stopped himself. "You didn't chase me out. I'm just busy."

"Oh," said Gabe. "Sure, of course you are." He nodded, hoping that didn't come across as sarcastic in any way.

"Does the library have shitty pay?"

Gabe blinked in confusion. "Uh, no, not really," he said.

Joey shifted on his feet and looked embarrassed. He was clinging to the backpack over his shoulder like a lifeline. "I just wondered why you didn't stick with putting out fires."

"Oh," said Gabe with a relieved laugh. "Oh, I do all kinds of things. I like being around people." Joey frowned like that was a strange idea. He probably missed the hustle and bustle of his life from before. Wherever he lived. Did popstars settle down? Have one place they came back to? "I could introduce you to some of the folks around if you're still finding your feet?" Gabe offered.

That was probably stupid. Joey didn't need help from some small-town hick like him to make friends.

Sure enough, Joey wrinkled up his nose. "I don't really think I've got a lot in common with the people around here," he said. Gabe thought that was pretty snobby. "But, thank you. I appreciate it." Well, at least he wasn't totally rude.

"Actually," said Gabe, not wanting to let Joey get away with insulting his town. Sure, Greenwich wasn't Paris or Tokyo, but it was his home, and he thought it was pretty great. "There's a small LGBT community if you'd be interested. Some of us got together and helped set up this home-less shelter over the summer. It was pretty awesome."

"You just do everything around here, don't you?" said Joey, shaking his head.

Gabe wasn't fazed though. "Like I said, I like people."

Joey didn't have much of a reaction to Gabe coming out. A lot of people generally had something to say about that. Maybe Joey already knew?

He shook his head again. "You don't owe these people anything, you know?"

Gabe frowned. "The homeless?" He was disappointed in Joey at that. "Someone has to help them. You know around fifty percent of kids on the street are LGBT?"

"No, not them," said Joey. "That's great. And I did know that. I mean the others. The well-to-do…" He trailed off as he waved his hand towards the throng of the fair. "They don't thank you for it."

Gabe allowed a smile to creep onto the corner of his mouth. "I don't do it for the thanks."

He didn't know why, because this conversation clearly wasn't going all that well. But he dug in the back pocket of his overalls and fished out one of the shelter's business cards that he knew would be lurking there. He dusted off the remains of one of Max's dog biscuits that had obviously found its way in there too a while back and pulled out a pen from a front pocket.

He needed to get back to the truck, but he didn't want to leave things with Joey when they were so off.

"If you'd like to hang out or meet some of the other guys like us, here's my cell."

He handed the card over once he'd finished scribbling his digits on the back. He supposed it could be seen as a come-on. But he simply didn't like the idea of Joey being alone, like he always seemed to be. He could do with some friends.

Joey eyed the scrap of card for a moment like it was a live grenade. Then he plucked it from Gabe's fingers and slipped it into his back pocket without looking at it.

"Thanks," he said. "You're a nice guy. Just uh…" His eyes flicked back towards the crowd. "Look after yourself some-time, too. Okay?"

Before Gabe could decipher what that might mean, Joey turned on his heel and was gone.

CHAPTER
Nine

JOEY

"Joey Sullivan?"

"Yep!" Joey cried.

He launched from his seat in the sparsely populated auditorium and waved his resume and headshots in the air. The casting director turned and raised an eyebrow at him. Joey meekly brought his arm back down.

"In your own time, Mr. Sullivan," he said dryly.

Joey trotted up to the stage, handing his papers over to the P.A. sitting at the same table facing the stage as the director and casting agent. He forced himself to inhale slowly as he took center stage, then as he exhaled he spread his fingers out, releasing all the pent-up energy.

The house lights were down. He felt spurred on by the warm spots shining above him, illuminating him on the raised wooden boards. The performance atmosphere made him feel calm. He knew this was where he belonged.

The play was some Chekhov knockoff by a late nineteenth-century writer that Joey had never heard of. There was no singing, and certainly no dancing. But it was a genuine Off-Broadway production that he would get *paid* for. Providing he got the part.

He could certainly suffer a few weeks of dreary modernism if it meant being able to bring in some actual money.

He had this. Here, under the lights with the taste of the theatre dust on the tip of his tongue. He was home; he was safe. All the moments of uncertainty from the past several months would be worth it if he could just get this part.

He closed his eyes, brought the first few words of the monologue to the front of his mind, and began.

———

There was no way to know how it had really gone. Joey was cautious of getting his hopes up, but he knew he'd smashed his performance.

Deep down he knew he was better at acting, but his first love was always singing. Still, he would take any performing over nothing, and he had to admit the rush of knowing he'd done well was making him feel giddy as he walked along the streets of Manhattan.

He'd had a brainwave as he'd passed a gay bar, distinguishable with its rainbow flag hanging outside. The sight of it had left Joey feeling as comforted as he had on stage. Enough so that he'd swung on in and pushed his way to the bar to ask if they were hiring. Pouring drinks was a million miles from his dream job, but the thought of steady money alongside any gigs he could get was too tempting to pass up. Especially when he got a glimpse of the cute bartender.

Unfortunately, they didn't have any openings at present, but Joey said he was hoping to move into the area soon. The cute guy winked and told him to apply again when he did, as they were always changing up their staff. Then he gave him a shot on the house and let him sit on one of the stools for a while, watching as the patrons came and went in the jostling crowd.

Joey enjoyed a bit of casual flirting with the bartender and several other guys. He didn't even mind when they recognized him and asked for photos. There was no pressure for anything more; he was just able to relax and actually enjoy a little company for once. He suspected one or two of the guys were hinting they'd like to take him home, but it was early enough in the night that they were all reasonably sober. No one pushed him, and once Joey finished the beer that he'd indulged himself in buying, he kissed a few of his new friends goodbye on the cheek and headed out in the cool evening air.

It was getting late, but for the first time in weeks he felt good enough to pull his phone out and hit call on one of his most-used numbers. He didn't even care if it went to voice-mail. He felt so good he just had to share it.

"Joey!" Blake cried on the third ring.

"Hey, man," Joey replied, grinning as he strolled down the street. Since the band had split, he had by far missed Blake and sharing their apartment together the most.

"Is that Joey?" a muffled voice came down the line. "Say hi for me!"

Blake chuckled, the sound filling Joey with even more warmth. "Elion says hi," he said good-naturedly. Joey told him to say hi back. "So how are you, man?"

Joey could hear the concern in his voice and he felt a little guilty. But he simply hadn't had the energy to call in recent weeks. Blake's life was soaring high, and Joey couldn't bear to drag it down with all his doom and gloom. But today, with his good news, he finally felt all right to talk.

"I moved back home," he said in a rush. "But, it's okay, I'm doing pretty good, and I actually just had an audition that I feel really great about."

There was a slight pause. "That's awesome buddy," Blake said with enthusiasm. "Is that in Connecticut, or…"

Joey couldn't help but laugh. "Hell no, I'm in NYC." As if to prove his point, some asshole body slammed into him rather that step a foot to the right. Joey rolled his eyes but didn't mention anything to Blake as he walked on.

Blake's relieved laugh said it all. "So have you moved there? We'll have to come visit."

"Getting there," said Joey optimistically. But he could hear Blake considering his words from down the line.

"You're back with your parents, aren't you?"

Joey shrugged, even though only the pedestrians on the sidewalk could see him. "It's not so bad." Blake's silence was telling. "Look, like I said, I had a great audition, I'm sure I got the part. Mom's helping me out, and I just basically got promised a bar job near the theatre to tide me over. It's all going to work out. I'll move soon."

"Joey," Blake said quietly. "I can wire you some money."

The sympathy in his words almost threatened to spoil Joey's great mood, but he shook it off. In fact, he allowed his best friend's generosity to add to his happiness.

"I'm okay, I swear to you. Things are looking up. Besides," he added cheerfully. "I need to come and visit *you*. Check out yours and Elion's new pad, have a proper housewarming."

"Hell yeah you do," Blake agreed sincerely.

They chatted some more about the apartment. Elion had started school again and Joey talked with him a bit about his classes. All too soon he came up to his station and had to close the call.

"We'll speak soon though, okay?" Blake asked.

Joey grinned. "You bet. Watching your shows is not the same thing as talking for real. Not by a long shot."

Blake laughed, still a little self-conscious at being the subject of reality TV. What Joey wouldn't give to be in a position where success doing what he loved was tedious at times. Irritating almost, like a regular job.

He kept the tone light though as he approached the barriers inside the station, saying goodbye so he could board the train home. It wasn't so late he was at the risk of missing the last train. But it was dark and New York wasn't always the safest place for someone like him. Someone who struggled to pass as straight even without his mild fame making it more likely people would know who he was.

He was keen to find a seat and lose himself in his music. That way he could hold on to his good mood, and not contemplate running into his family when he arrived home.

Except, when he reached inside his jacket pocket for his wallet, he found nothing there.

Panic swept through him, cold and sharp. He always kept it in the same place, but when he confirmed it definitely wasn't there, Joey frantically yanked his backpack off and began checking all the pockets.

All his money and his MetroCard were in that wallet. He'd thought about splitting some of the cash his mom had given him, but it just hadn't seemed safe. Better to keep it all close to his chest or in his jeans, never leaving his sight.

"No, no, *no*," he moaned as he checked every single pocket again. But it was no use. He was totally fucked.

His heart was racing and he couldn't seem to catch his breath. Tears blurred his eyes. He had restrained himself so severely to make his mom's money last, almost to the point of starvation. He would have struggled to buy another ticket even if he *had* hidden some of the cash he had elsewhere. But as it was, he had nothing. He was stranded.

He must have been pickpocketed. He thought of the faceless guy that had slammed into him on the sidewalk. Had he relieved him of his wallet then?

People did a good job of averting their eyes as they bustled past him to make their own way towards the platforms. Joey was glad. He didn't want anyone looking as he lost his shit. Giving up, he grabbed his bag and stormed back out on to the sidewalk. He took a moment to try and catch his breath as the world whirled by him.

He couldn't get home. What were his options? He thought pathetically of Blake, how he and Elion were determined to have him to stay. But they were all the way in Ohio and absolutely no good to him now.

He could go back to the bar? See if he could hook up with someone for the night?

The thought immediately made him sick. It was one thing to feel a connection with someone and head home for some fun. It was quite another to seek out anyone specifically for that purpose. He knew other people did it and that was fine. But that was a step too far for him.

He checked his pockets one more time, just in case of a miracle. He did not find his absent wallet. But he did find something in the back of his jeans that he'd missed on his first frantic search.

It was a business card. The one from the homeless shelter, with Gabe's number on the back. Joey choked out a bitter laugh. He felt pretty homeless right now.

He angrily wiped his eyes. What other choice did he have? He couldn't call his mom; she wouldn't be able to get out of the house, even if she was capable of driving out far enough to get him. Blake and Raiden and the other guys from the band were scattered across the country, and he didn't know any of his other friends well enough to ask a favor like this.

Gabe had told him to call him. He probably hadn't meant

like this, but the guy liked helping people so much. Maybe he would know what to do.

Swallowing his pride, Joey typed in Gabe's number fast so he couldn't change his mind. Then he closed his eyes and hit call.

CHAPTER

Ten

GABE

"COME ON, THAT'S IT," GABE COOED.

He wiggled the feathered stick under the sofa and shifted on his stomach to try and see better. Duchess narrowed her eyes at him and lowered her ears. The space was so small under his couch he was amazed she could get them any flatter, but she managed it.

"Good girl. Who's a pretty girl?"

Despite her scruffy appearance and the fact that she hissed at him, again, he really did think she was a pretty girl. She was just hurting and scared. He understood she needed to protect herself. But at the same time, he really would have liked a cuddle.

His phone ringtone startled him so much in the quiet of his house he jerked and banged the coffee table. He cursed and hoped he hadn't disturbed Duchess too badly. She seemed no more annoyed than before though.

The ringtone was a generic one, so he knew before he got the phone out of his pocket and looked at the screen it wasn't a close acquaintance. It was getting late. As he eased his bulk free and sat on the sofa, he wondered who the unidentified number could possibly be.

"Hello, Gabe speaking," he answered. He thought a professional tone was best in case it was something to do with the fire department or homeless shelter.

There was a beat of silence, although Gabe could hear the wind blowing over the receiver. Whoever it was, they were standing outside.

"Uh, Gabe?"

Gabe had answered with his name, but the uncertain tone of the voice stopped him from rolling his eyes. He'd given his number out to several people at the shelter in case of an emergency. It could be that one of them was in shock and needed his help.

Sure enough, he heard a pitiful sniff from down the line. "Yeah, this is Gabe," he said gently.

"I'm sorry, I didn't know who else to call. It's…it's Joey."

Gabe sat up straight, instantly on alert. That was the last person he expected to call him on a Friday night in distress. "Joey, what's wrong?" he demanded.

"All my friends are out of state," he said after a few seconds' pause. Then he laughed, but there was a harsh edge to it. "Fuck, *I'm* out of state," he mumbled.

Gabe checked his watch. "Joey, have you been drinking?" he asked calmly.

There was a scoff from the other end of the line. "I had one beer," Joey griped. "And maybe a shot. But I'm fine." The irritableness probably shouldn't have made Gabe crack a smile, but one threatened to creep on his lips anyway.

"Good, that's good," Gabe said genuinely. "Are you okay? What do you mean you're out of state?" It was approaching eleven at night.

There was no response. Gabe frowned.

"Joey?"

"I'm in Manhattan," Joey blurted out. "I got mugged. Well, pickpocketed, I didn't see it happen, so I guess…" There was a little sob and a noise of frustration. "I'm stranded, and I don't know what to do. Sorry. I know it's late. I didn't have anyone else left to call. I don't know, I thought, maybe, you might know a bus or something?"

Gabe was already on his feet. "Calm down, it's okay," he said as Joey's voice became more frantic. "Have you got your card details on your phone? You can use that to get a new train ticket."

Again, he had to wait for an answer.

"I don't have any money in my account," Joey's small, defeated voice rasped. "That cash was all I had to my name."

Gabe was already shoving his shoes on and sliding his arm through a jacket. Duchess had water and food put out for her, and the back door was already locked. Gabe snatched his car keys up from the bowl.

"Where are you?"

"Forty-Second Street," Joey said, sheepishly.

"Okay," said Gabe. "I don't know exactly how long the drive will take. So I'll put it in my GPS and text you a rough ETA, all right?"

Another silence. This one seemed stunned though. "You're…you can't come get me."

Gabe didn't pause as he bent down to make one last check on Duchess before striding towards the front door of his house. "I can't leave you in the middle of the city," Gabe countered as he locked up. "Just stay put and text me if anything changes. Wait," he said, getting into his car. "Find a diner or something. Go somewhere warm and well lit. Don't hang around on the fucking street, all right? Joey?" he demanded when he didn't get an answer.

Joey chuckled. It was a lovely sound, and despite the circumstances, Gabe was ashamed to say it stirred something in him.

"I promise," Joey mumbled. "I'll find a place nearby and text you."

"Good," said Gabe, turning the ignition. "I'll see you soon."

"Gabe?" Joey said, making him pause.

"Yeah?" he replied.

"Thank you," Joey whispered before he cut the call.

Gabe hit the gas and was on the Connecticut Turnpike before he really considered what he was doing. GPS told him he had a little over an hour to get to where Joey was waiting. Plenty of time to consider how insane this was.

He'd barely met the guy. He wasn't even sure if Joey liked him. They didn't really know each other well enough to form any kind of opinions. And yet here Gabe was, driving out of state in the middle of the night to make sure Joey wasn't stranded.

It was *dangerous* in the big city at night though. Especially for someone as gentle as Joey. He had spirit, Gabe had no doubt. But he wouldn't last long in a fight.

What if someone recognized him and gave him trouble? What if they sensed he was gay and hurt him? Gabe was surprised by the knot that formed in his guts. Sure, his mom had always taught him to do the right thing, be a Good Samaritan. But Gabe couldn't deny he felt real fear at the idea of Joey coming to any harm.

So, he had to admit that maybe he cared for the younger guy, more than he would a stranger off the street. A really cute stranger with a great body and real talent. Gabe shook his head and switched lanes. That was irrelevant. The point was, he didn't know Joey very well, but what he did know of him, he quite liked.

If this crazy stunt was worth nothing else, at least they

would get an opportunity to get to know one another a bit better.

Gabe flitted between radio stations as he followed the coast down towards the city. He felt nervous, not just worrying over Joey's safety. He was stupidly feeling a little anxious about spending the ride back home together. What if it was awkward and they had nothing to say? If it got bad, Joey always had the option to fall asleep, or at least pretend to. But Gabe would prefer they at least made an attempt at conversation.

Joey had texted not long after Gabe had set off to say he'd found an all-night diner near Grand Central Station. Gabe was content that he was warm and protected until he could arrive. But then Joey texted again saying a waitress had taken pity on him and given him a cup of coffee to nurse, which was even better.

Being near the station meant there was actually some parking. So when he arrived, Gabe found a spot, then messaged Joey to let him know where he was and to come find him.

He drummed his hands on the wheel and turned the music down. It was fair enough he was nervous. Joey was a legitimate celebrity, and Gabe was just some small-town hick. They didn't really have anything in common.

There were probably teenagers all over the globe that had fantasized about a situation just like this. Rescuing Joey Sullivan when he was in trouble. Being the one he called when he needed help most.

Gabe felt honored and unworthy at the same time.

He was also getting ahead of himself. It was just a ride; it wasn't a date. And Joey had already admitted he'd only called because he didn't have any other options. Still, that didn't mean Gabe couldn't try and make the most of it.

Any chance to spend more time together was worth

taking as far as he was concerned.

CHAPTER
Eleven

GABE

WITHIN A COUPLE OF MINUTES, A FAMILIAR FIGURE ROUNDED the corner of the street. Gabe gave his lights a single flash so Joey could locate him quicker.

Joey opened the door and hurriedly slipped into the passenger seat. His cheeks were rosy from the cold night air and Gabe felt a tug in his heart. Joey was every bit as gorgeous as he remembered. Now he was safe too.

"Hey," Joey said timidly. He ran his fingers through his curly blond hair. "Thank you so much, I owe you, *big* time."

Gabe shook his head and pulled the car back onto the road. They had a long drive ahead, and it was best to get moving. "I'm glad you called," he said genuinely. He flicked his gaze towards Joey and smiled. "I'd hate to think of you stuck here. It's my pleasure."

Joey bit his lip and managed a small smile. "Well, there's not a lot of people who'd stick their neck out for me, so I appreciate it."

Gabe scoffed. He kept his eyes on the road, because it made it seem safer to talk like that. Also, the last thing they needed now was to crash. But really, all he wanted to do was drink Joey in. He could smell him in the warmth of the car's interior. Just the natural musk after being out for a day, but it was uniquely Joey in a way that made Gabe want to bottle it up.

He was being stupid. He was in Manhattan, for Christ's sake. Lewis's new apartment was probably within five blocks of them, and he was pining after this near stranger. But the way Joey hugged his backpack to him and stared out of the window with those big green eyes moved Gabe in a way he couldn't deny.

"I'm sure you have people all over the world who'd move heaven and earth for you," Gabe said with a laugh. "Being a big popstar and all."

Joey didn't say anything. He just continued to look out the window.

"So," Gabe continued, searching for something to say. "Were you here visiting friends?"

Joey perked up at that and looked his way. "I had an audition, for a play," he said, his eyes sparkling.

"Really?" Gabe asked, genuinely interested. "That's pretty cool. You get the part?"

"Don't know yet," said Joey brightly. He allowed the bag to slip between his knees and rest on the floor. It felt like he was letting down his shield. "But I've got a great feeling. It's only Off-Broadway, but it's a two-week run with a great director."

"Is this Off-Broadway?" Gabe asked, indicating the neighborhood they were passing through.

Joey laughed. It sent shivers down Gabe's spine. Fuck, he needed to get a hold of himself.

"That just means you can't fit more than two hundred people in the theater," Joey explained. There was a kindness to his voice though. He didn't mind that Gabe was unaware. "But there is a location aspect to it I guess. Obviously bigger theaters take up more room. Smaller theaters are more tucked away."

"But still," said Gabe. "Two hundred is quite a lot."

Joey nodded enthusiastically. "I'm hoping I'll get the part. I want to move here as soon as possible."

Gabe frowned. "You'd want to live in New York?" he asked as he merged onto the interstate.

Joey scoffed. "Hell yeah," he muttered. "As soon as I'm getting steady enough work. I just need enough money to pay a deposit on an apartment, even just a *room* somewhere." He smiled and looked over at Gabe. "Then I'll be able to walk home when some asshole lifts my wallet."

It was ridiculous, but the idea of Joey up and moving to NYC made Gabe sad. "Wouldn't you miss your family?" he asked. After all, Joey had only just come home after years away touring, or so Gabe had heard on the grapevine. Surely he wasn't thinking of leaving them again when he could commute to the city and live rent free?

Joey wrapped his arms around himself and looked out the window again. "They wouldn't miss me," he said simply.

Gabe frowned. Joey's posture was obviously defensive. "I'm sure they would," said Gabe.

Joey sighed, heavily. "No, believe me," he bit out. There was acid to his words. "Most of them would be happy if I died in a ditch. Why do you think I had to resort to calling you?"

Gabe blinked a few times. Ouch. That stung.

From the corner of his eye, Joey unfurled his arms, relaxing his posture. "Sorry," he said softly. "I didn't mean to sound ungrateful. Truth is," he added, like he was debating if he wanted to continue talking. "Truth is this is one of the kindest things anyone's ever done for me. A million times nicer than my family would be. That was my point."

There was a compliment buried in there. It was enough to

make Gabe smile again. "No sweat," he said, throwing Joey a smile.

Driving was easy now they were out of the city and traffic was light. It meant he could risk looking over at Joey more. It was good to see him letting his guard down.

"I have friends," Joey said abruptly. "The guys from the band. Blake especially. And guys we toured with, like crew and backup dancers. It's just...well none of them live around here."

"Joey," said Gabe. "It's fine, you don't have to justify yourself. You got in a shitty situation, and I'm kind of flattered I could help."

Joey played with the zip on his jacket. "You like helping people," he commented. "Don't you?"

Gabe shrugged. "Yeah. I feel like...you are what you put into the world. If that makes sense?"

Joey nodded. "That's how I feel about the arts," he said. His energy picked up again. It was as if it filled the car, like the scent of aftershave. "I have to leave my mark, give something to the world that will stay after I'm gone. Otherwise, what's the point?"

That sounded like a more pessimistic version of his outlook on life, but Gabe was pleased Joey understood what he meant at least.

"I like caring for people," said Gabe. "I didn't have the brains to go into medicine, so I do this and that instead."

Joey hummed. "I have a friend who's a nurse," he mused. There was a hint of pride there. "It is amazing, isn't it?"

Gabe nodded. "Firefighter is as close as I get."

"And librarian," said Joey. He seemed pensive when Gabe glanced over. "Do you think people appreciate you for it?"

That made Gabe frown. It sounded similar to what he'd said at the fair last weekend. "I don't do it so that people will like me," he said, choosing his words carefully. "I do it because seeing other people happy, makes me happy. Maybe it's selfish, or narcissistic or whatever. But knowing I made someone else's life that little bit better is more satisfying than, I don't know, money or whatever."

There was a silence after he finished talking. He wondered if he'd upset his guest, but when he was able to glance over at Joey, he saw he was looking at him strangely. Gabe wondered if he was seeing respect in his eyes.

"Yeah," said Joey. "That what my music does, or at least I hope so. It reaches out and leaves people with a tiny speck of joy they didn't have before."

That made Gabe think of pixie dust. That Joey and his band had been sprinkling happiness wherever they went. It was charming.

"The money must have been good too though, right?" he asked. Because he had to. On the drive down he'd questioned several times how a famous singer couldn't have any funds in their bank account. He'd decided that Joey just mustn't have had any cash in the specific account linked to his phone.

But Joey's expression told him he'd made a mistake. "Artists are the last to get paid," he said with a hint of bitterness. "I'm broke. Otherwise, I would never have moved home."

Gabe didn't say anything for a moment. For one thing, he was stunned that Joey could really be poor after all his success, after all that hard work. That was fucked up if that was really true.

The way he spoke about his family was more disturbing though. "Do you really not get along with them?" Gabe asked, wondering how bad it could be.

Joey fiddled with the air vent in front of him for a few moments rather than answer Gabe. But Gabe waited patiently.

"My dad has very strong ideas about what a man should be," Joey said eventually.

"Let me guess," Gabe said, immediately incensed. "Tough and drinking beer and marrying his high school prom queen sweetheart."

Joey's hollow laugh said it all. "You'd think he'd be happy my older brother ticked all those boxes already. But it turns out, having a flaming queer with a career in the arts is apparently the worst sin out there."

Gabe gripped the steering wheel tightly. No wonder Joey didn't like living at home. "So, all your family have a problem with you being gay?"

Joey shrugged. "Not my mom. But she doesn't get much of a say in things. She's been sneaking me food when she can. That cash was from her." Joey took in a shuddery breath of air. "Fuck, I really have nothing right now."

You have me, Gabe wanted to say. But that was ridiculous. He didn't want to put any pressure on Joey by suggesting there was more between them than there was. But the truth was, Gabe wanted to get to know Joey better before this. Maybe even become friends. Now he was totally committed to showing Joey there was someone else who actually gave a damn about him.

"Look," he said. "It's pretty late now. You wouldn't want to disturb them by coming home after midnight anyway, right?" His throat was dry, but he did his best to swallow. "So why don't you crash with me?"

The offer hung between them for several tense moments.

"I-I couldn't," Joey said eventually. "You've already been so kind. I couldn't impose on you like that."

"It wouldn't be an imposition at all," Gabe insisted truthfully. "I've only got a couch to offer, and last I checked it had a pretty angry cat underneath, but I've got a ton of blankets. It'd be no trouble at all."

He told himself he was desperate for Joey to say yes purely so he could at least give him one night's break from his awful family. Hell, part of him was tempted to suggest he move in with Gabe there and then. But he knew that was a kind of madness and kept his mouth shut. Joey was skittish. He didn't need to be scared off by offering too much, too fast.

"If it's really no trouble," said Joey slowly. "Then, um, that would be amazing."

The relief in his voice was all Gabe needed to know he'd done the right thing.

CHAPTER

Twelve

JOEY

JOEY WASN'T SURE IF HE WAS MAKING A BIG MISTAKE. BUT Gabe didn't seem like a serial killer.

His brain helpfully reminded him that most didn't.

His gut told him not to be so stupid though. That Gabe was someone he could trust. Besides, he'd made *zero* hints about wanting anything sordid in return for a place to sleep for the night. In fact, Joey was mildly disappointed as he watched Gabe rummaging through his cupboard for spare linen.

Sharing a bed with such a gorgeous guy might not have been such a hardship.

But Gabe fussed over sheets and blankets and squishy pillows as he made up the sofa in such a luxurious way it made Joey's flimsy camp bed in the basement look like a dumpster. He sighed, trying not to let his giddy relief show too badly.

"It's going to be so nice just to sleep," he said with a nervous laugh. "My nephew's teething and he wakes up at five every morning, without fail, screaming his head off."

Gabe laughed. "Bless him. I hope he's at least cute when he's not crying?"

Joey shrugged. Sure he was. But Joey wasn't allowed anywhere near him. It was like they were scared the kid was going to catch fucking AIDS or something. It hurt, a lot, so he said nothing.

Instead, he looked around at Gabe's place. It was nice, grown up. Lots of personal knick-knacks around that made it look like it had been lived in for a long time. Photos and ornaments and furniture that match. Again, he wondered how old Gabe was to have been able to accumulate something like this.

"Nice house." he said. He was aware he was still clutching his backpack strap over his shoulder, like holding on to that might protect him. At least he'd kicked his shoes off by the door.

"It's my parents' place," Gabe said fondly. "I inherited it."

"Oh," said Joey softly. "I'm sorry." The way Gabe had spoken so passionately about family, Joey assumed he had been close with his folks.

But Gabe's eyebrows raised in alarm. "Oh no," he spluttered with a laugh. "They're not *dead*. They just retired to Florida."

Relief flooded Joey. He was doubly glad that Gabe's parents were still with them, and also that he hadn't put his foot in it. "That's cool," he said. Florida wasn't his favorite place in the world, but he could understand the appeal of that much sunshine.

"I was a surprise baby," Gabe continued cheerfully as he put the finishing touches on Joey's bed. "So they are kind of old. Although you wouldn't really know it." He rolled his eyes affectionately. "My mom's *obsessed* with Disney. Florida was the ideal place for her to settle down, and my dad basically does anything to make her happy."

"They sound sweet," Joey said. He managed to keep the tinge of jealousy out of his voice. If his dad found out his mom liked anything, he always mocked the shit out of it. His mom always laughed it off as a joke, but Joey could see how much it hurt her when his dad ridiculed her TV shows or attempts she made to draw.

"They are," said Gabe. He sounded wistful.

"You miss them," Joey observed.

Gabe smiled. "Yeah, but we talk all the time on the phone. And I gave my new cat a Disney name that I knew Mom would approve of. It makes it feel like she's around." He shook his head. "It's dumb, I know."

It wasn't dumb, but Joey was too busy looking around to say so. "You have a cat?" he asked, incredulous.

Gabe scoffed. "I know, right?" He surprised Joey by suddenly dropping to his belly. "Here, Duchess," he cooed. "Come out and meet our guest!"

When nothing happened, Joey tentatively let his bag rest on the carpet, then crouched beside Gabe. He still couldn't see under the sofa where Gabe was looking, so he mimicked him and laid down.

There, in the dark, cramped space, was indeed a cat. She looked at them with wide eyes, her pupils so large Joey couldn't see the color of her irises. She had a couple of toes missing as well as a chunk from one of her ears, and her fur was all patchy. "That's Duchess?" he said. That was adorable. He'd never seen a less regal-looking cat in his life.

Gabe chuckled and sat back up again. Joey followed. "Well, I don't think she's coming out. She shouldn't disturb you overnight though."

"I don't mind," Joey said. He really didn't. He hadn't felt this relaxed in a long, long time. He wasn't worried sick about making rent or terrified his dad was going to come storming down in a filthy temper. He felt safe.

Which was strange, considering how he didn't know Gabe, and he didn't have a cent to his name. But for now, he was all right. He could sleep.

"Hey, are you hungry?" Gabe asked, already getting to his feet and heading towards the kitchen. "I have leftover lasagna and potato chips and carrot sticks and other stuff."

Wordlessly, Joey rose to his feet and followed. Gabe looked so happy as he rummaged through his refrigerator. "I'm okay," he lied.

"Are you sure?" asked Gabe. "I'm starving, think I'm gonna nuke some lasagna. I made too much, so you'd be helping me out."

Joey felt like maybe he was just saying that, but it was enough to give him an out. "Well, if it'd be doing you a favor?" He grinned, watching Gabe stick a couple of Tupperware bowls into his microwave and set the timer.

"Beer?"

Joey agreed with just a nod. There was a lump in his throat. All this kindness was overwhelming. Gabe must surely want something in return? But even as he thought it to himself, he discounted it. He knew enough by now to trust that Gabe was just a nice guy.

Joey leaned back against the wood dining table and looked around the kitchen. It really was a nice place.

"So how long have you lived here?"

Gabe took a swig of his beer. "All my life," he said. "I'm so lucky. My folks just let me rent it for just enough to cover their place in Florida."

"You like it here then?" Joey asked, sipping his own drink.

He couldn't imagine voluntarily staying in the same place for his whole life, let alone an area like this. Maybe it was Joey's own, personal experience of Greenwich – it was a big town after all. But mostly his life had been confined to downtown, which felt too small to him. Claustrophobic.

Gabe smiled warmly though. "Yeah," he said. "Home is where your heart is and all that."

Joey looked at him. He had beautiful brown eyes. "I always took that to mean home could be anywhere your heart was happy," he admitted.

Gabe picked at the corner of his bottle label. "And for you, that's New York?"

"It's anywhere but here," Joey said with a bit too much scorn. "Sorry, I guess…I've never felt welcomed like you do. L.A., New York, London. Places like that have always been more accepting of people like me."

Gabe frowned. "Yeah, I get that. I guess," he said. But he sounded sad. Hurt maybe.

Joey didn't know what to say though. He wasn't going to take it back and say he liked being home. Gabe thought this place was his community, that it loved him for giving it so much. But Joey had heard firsthand how people were willing to spit that back in his face.

Luckily, the microwave pinged and saved them from the awkward silence that was brewing. If Gabe had been slipping into a funk, he shook it off as he dished up their cheesy, meaty pasta.

"That smells amazing," Joey said. He was being truthful, but he also wanted to offer an olive branch too. Despite not understanding his attachment to such a crappy, limited town, Joey did really like Gabe. He was glad they were getting to know each other better.

"It's my mom's recipe," Gabe admitted. "I don't do it justice, but I try."

Joey had to disagree as they sat at the kitchen table and tucked in. He supposed he'd been deprived of home cooking for a long time, so that might be why he thought it tasted so divine. But it really was very good. He had to slow himself down from eating it too fast, otherwise he'd get indigestion.

"So," Gabe said. Joey looked up, aware his mouth was uncomfortably full. He tried to chew quickly but discretely. "I guess you must miss being in the band a lot. That would make it hard to come back here. It must be boring."

Joey swallowed and licked his lips. Gabe's words were cheerful, but Joey wasn't an idiot. He was upset that Joey hated his hometown so much.

"It's not boring," said Joey with a small smile. He placed his fork down. "It's…lonely. I don't have anything in common with anyone. I'm not trying to be a dick saying that. It's just…people love to settle down here and be close with their families and work in places where they already know half the people there. My family hates me, and…" There was no way to explain himself without coming across extremely arrogant. But he wanted to try and make Gabe see. "There's this *whole world* out there. It's filled with people in every color, who lead so many different lives. They have different traditions and cultures and the more you see of it, the more your own mind expands. But here, people don't like being challenged. So when there's something outside their narrow view on how life should be, they reject it." He looked back down at his half-eaten food. "They reject me. That's why I can't stay. Because I'm not wanted."

He could feel the tears stinging the backs of his eyes, but he managed to blink them away before he looked up again.

Gabe looked at him with pity. That just made things worse. Joey would have preferred it if he'd pissed him off.

"I guess we see the town kind of differently," Gabe said. Laying his own cutlery down. "I'm really sorry you've been made to feel that way. New York sounds like it'll be great for you."

Joey opened his mouth to reply, but he couldn't find the words. He wanted to say he was sorry. Sorry he'd been bullied through school and terrorized by his dad and had 'faggot' scribbled over his possessions more times than he could count.

He didn't understand how Gabe could be out and not have had the same treatment. But then, Gabe was the acceptable kind of gay. He was handsome and straight-seeming and didn't rock the boat. Not like Joey, always causing trouble just by showing up places.

"I didn't mean to insult you," said Joey.

But Gabe shook his head. "You didn't. Although that food has hit my system and I'm suddenly shattered. Do you mind if I head up to bed?"

Away from you.

Joey managed a smile. "Not at all."

Gabe regarded him fondly. "Help yourself to anything you want," he said. "I think I have a spare toothbrush too. I'll leave it in the bathroom. Do you need anything else?" Joey shook his head, so Gabe nodded back. "I'll see you in the morning then."

Joey watched him leave, hating himself. He didn't know how else he could have responded without lying, but his words had put a wedge between him and the first friend he'd made in years. Probably his only friend in Greenwich right now.

He forced himself to eat more of the lasagna, purely because he couldn't afford to let good food go to waste. Who knew when he'd be able to get something this good again, let alone for free?

But it felt like stones in his belly. When he couldn't stomach any more, he scraped the leftovers in the trash and washed the dishes, drying them then searching the cupboards to put them and the cutlery away in the right place.

He crept upstairs and brushed his teeth with the new toothbrush Gabe had left out for him. Who had spares of things like that, for crying out loud? But Joey was grateful. It meant he had one more task to occupy him before bed. But with his mouth scrubbed fresh and minty, all he really had left to do was sleep.

He traipsed downstairs, wincing at the squeaky steps that he inadvertently trod on. But Gabe didn't seem to stir from his room.

Joey looked under the sofa. Sure enough, Duchess was still crouched there. He would have said she'd been asleep, but as soon as he looked at her she cracked an eyelid open a millimeter to stare at him.

"Night, night, kitty," he whispered.

Gabe had done a nice job of making up his bed. Despite Joey's crappy mood, he was looking forward to snuggling up and getting some shut-eye. So he pulled off all his clothes apart from his boxers and turned off all the lights.

He sighed shakily and wrapped the comforter tightly around him.

Knowing he'd upset Gabe was eating away at him. He tried to close his eyes against the darkness and switch off. But he kept picturing the look of Gabe's disappointment in him.

Fuck, maybe the problem wasn't this town. Maybe it was Joey. Just ruining everything he touched. Maybe it had nothing at all to do with the fact he was gay, but simply that he was a selfish asshole.

He wished in a way that he hadn't called Gabe. He could have taken his chances in New York. It was likely he could have found a way to get through the night, then that way he wouldn't have fucked things up.

He was restless in the makeshift bed, tossing and turning as his thoughts darkened. It would probably be best if he left early in the morning. Crept out before Gabe woke up and had to deal with him again.

The idea made him feel sick though. Gabe needed an apology. He had dragged his ass out in the middle of the night because Joey was too dumb to keep a hold of his own fucking wallet. He hadn't complained once or made Joey feel bad or guilty. Then he'd fed him and offered him a bed for free.

Joey was a terrible person if he repaid that by shitting all over the life he led. The life he seemed very happy in. Who was Joey to judge that, really?

Apologizing in the morning didn't seem good enough. As if possessed by something demented, Joey yanked the covers back and marched back upstairs before his courage could desert him. Gabe's door was open a crack, and Joey approached it with his heart in his mouth.

"Gabe?" he whispered as he knocked softly.

There was a rustling of covers. "Joey?" He didn't sound sleepy. At least Joey hadn't woken him.

"Can I come in, just for a second?"

"Sure."

Joey crept in, not turning on a light. There was just enough moonlight that he could make out Gabe's bulk in the bed. Joey wrapped his arms around his skinny frame. He knew he'd lost weight and muscle mass since returning home. He wished he'd thought to stop and put some jeans on at least instead of racing up here in his damn underwear.

"I'm sorry," he blurted, still whispering. It didn't seem right to talk at a normal level. "You've been so kind to me and I was a complete jackass. I shouldn't have said those things about the people who live here." He took a deep breath. "About you. It's just my issues. Not you."

"Joey," Gabe said with a sigh. "You don't have to apologize. But...thank you. I get it."

Joey nodded, then felt stupid, because they were in the dark. He hugged himself tighter, unable to stop the tears that finally spilled onto his cheeks. "Tonight was the longest I've talked with anyone in months. The longest I've hung out with anyone. I…I had a nice time, despite ruining it at the end."

He could just see Gabe's form as he sat up in the bed and looked at him. He didn't like the thought that Gabe could see him back, even just a little. He was exposed; his skinny body and his multiple, personal tattoos.

"I had a nice evening too," Gabe said. He sounded sincere.

Fuck. Joey didn't want to leave. He couldn't stand being on his own another minute. Gabe was beautiful and hot as sin, but he was also kind and generous. Joey felt like he was severely lacking people like that in his life.

"If I stayed, could we just sleep," he managed to stammer out. He rubbed his face, trying to wipe away the tears, and took an unsteady breath. "I know you've done so much already, but I just…I don't want to be alone." Another breath in. "If that's way out of line, I can go back downstairs."

"Come here," said Gabe gently. He flipped the cover back and patted the mattress.

Joey walked slowly over. Despite being the one to ask, now he was nervous. It had been so long since he'd felt the comfort of sleeping next to somebody though, and Gabe made him feel so painfully safe. "I won't try anything," he said with a nervous laugh.

"I trust you," Gabe replied.

Joey sat on the mattress and groaned. The sofa had been a step up from the rickety camp bed, but this just felt like heaven. He quickly curled up, facing Gabe and hauled the thick comforter over him.

Gabe eased himself back down so he was laying down again. Looking at each other was too much, so Joey hastily turned. "Thank you," he rasped, squeezing his eyes shut.

"No problem," Gabe murmured behind him.

Joey was tense for a few minutes, but Gabe didn't move an inch. In fact, after a while, Joey heard heavy breathing that suggested he'd fallen asleep.

Joey allowed himself to relax again. To find that comfort and tranquility that he'd first felt when Gabe had insisted he stay the night. His bed was unbelievably soft, cradling him and reminding his back that this was how it should be supported.

It was pathetic, but Joey generally slept better when he was around other people. Even on the tour bus in those cramped bunks, he was always lulled to sleep by TJ's snuffles or Raiden and Reyse's whispered conversations. Knowing that Gabe was next to him and respected his wish not to do anything more than sleep was deeply soothing.

Shortly after, Joey could feel his own mind gradually switching off, allowing unconsciousness to creep over him.

It had been a long day. He was ready for it to be over.

Joey couldn't remember the last time he slept so well. But as he slowly surfaced, he couldn't understand where he was. The bed was all wrong, and there was far too much sunshine for the basement.

The most obvious difference though was that there was a firm, warm body by his side. Closer than that, even. Joey had his arm thrown across the broad chest and his head was nestled in the dip between the body's shoulder and pec. His leg was resting against a much bigger one, and worst of all, his morning wood was pressed into the other guy's hip.

After a moment of terrified panic, the events of the previous evening came flooding back to him. Gabe had rescued him from the city, and Joey had felt so wretched he'd asked to sleep in his bed.

He'd also promised nothing would happen.

Just as he was assessing the situation, trying to work out how to untangle his limbs from Gabe's stunning body, Gabe's eyes fluttered open. Of course they did. Because the universe couldn't cut Joey a break for a second.

"Sorry," he said, his voice coming out as little more than a croak. He was frozen, looking into Gabe's lovely eyes as he stopped blinking and focused. Then they widened when he realized what was going on. "I was asleep," Joey said by way of an explanation.

Gabe just looked at him, his plump lips parting as his gaze swept over Joey. He wasn't exactly pushing Joey away.

But that was crazy. Gabe couldn't possibly be interested in him in that way. He was a scrawny, pathetic, washed-up loser who couldn't stand all the things Gabe loved. And yet there they were, eyes locked together, soft breaths intermingling. Gabe's warm skin was exquisite pressed up against Joey's, and if he was not mistaken, it felt like Joey wasn't the only one suffering from a sleepy erection.

What the hell was he doing? He needed to get a hold of himself and leave. Gabe had already been so kind. Joey shouldn't put him in an awkward position.

Except in that moment, Gabe brought his arm over and slid it around Joey's waist.

Joey gasped and shut his eyes, cuddling closer and rubbing his nose against Gabe's neck. There was no going back now. Not when Gabe's fingers gently squeezed Joey's hip. It felt like an invitation.

He cautiously kissed his lips to Gabe's throat. The moan he felt from him in response was intoxicating, and in one natural move, they both turned their faces, mouths finding each other in a sweet kiss.

Joey's heart was going like a racehorse. Was this a huge mistake? Was he fucking up a friendship before it even had a chance to begin?

The pull was too strong though. He wanted Gabe so badly there was no resisting now he had him. He'd been drawn to Gabe the instant he'd laid eyes on him. He could worry about the future later. If this year had taught him anything, it was that he had to seize the moment before it passed him by. Before it was taken away.

Gabe had both his arms around his back now, cradling Joey as close as he could against him as they kissed. Joey wasn't sure how it was possible, but it was undeniable that Gabe felt some attraction towards him too. Maybe he liked to make himself feel better by fucking losers.

Joey screwed up his eyes and chased the nasty thought away. Even if Joey didn't think much of himself, Gabe didn't seem the type to use someone, let alone when they were vulnerable.

As if to reassure him against his negativity, Gabe moved one of his large hands to cup Joey's face. There was obvious power in his grasp, but he held Joey like a precious and delicate treasure.

Joey suddenly realized he wasn't being manhandled. Gabe wasn't crushing him or throwing him about. Oh fuck, it felt so nice to be treated with tenderness. Joey wasn't sure his heart could take it.

Gabe slid his hand gently down Joey's throat, over his collarbones and down his chest until he was holding him by the ribs. The splay of his hand was almost large enough to reach from hip to nipple. Joey felt like he could do a lot of damage with all his strength. The fact he was being so careful made Joey whimper.

Joey wanted to feel Gabe all over. To know he was safe as well as so turned on he felt dizzy. So he wriggled his body, slipping underneath Gabe's huge form. Their kisses were becoming more urgent, and the hot, rigid length of Gabe's cock pressed wonderfully into Joey's thigh.

"I want you," Gabe murmured into Joey's mouth. "I need you."

Joey shivered at those words. He couldn't have dreamed

Gabe would really desire him. Even if they had nothing in common, even if this was only once, Joey needed it like air.

Gabe moved his body so both their cocks were perfectly lined up and rubbing through their underwear. The way he rolled his body over Joey's made him moan wantonly.

This was too much. He didn't deserve this. He'd crawled into Gabe's bed because he felt awful for being rude. He'd only wanted some company; he never expected to tumble into his arms. But he wasn't strong enough to give it up now it was happening. In fact, he realized he was clinging on to Gabe's back with such intensity he knew it made him seem desperate. Maybe he was?

"It's okay," Gabe said. He ran his fingers through Joey's hair and kissed his cheek. "I've got you."

Joey believed him.

He kissed Gabe's collarbone, drinking the scent from his skin. He smelled warm, like baked goods, but spicy too, like cinnamon. Also musky from the day and night since he'd presumably had a shower. It was very masculine and Joey loved it. He didn't like guys who were ultraclean and drenched in aftershave.

"Yes, yes," he murmured as they undulated together, their bodies fitting neatly alongside each other. He wanted more, more, more. His skin was on fire and his breaths couldn't seem to quite get enough oxygen into his lungs.

Gabe captured his mouth again, their kisses frantic but still somehow gentle. Gabe didn't bite him or thrust his tongue in his mouth. He coaxed the kisses from Joey, unapologetically. Gabe lapped him up, making promises with his lips over and over again.

Joey wanted him to make good on some of those promises. "I want you, please," he begged. He couldn't quite bring himself to look at Gabe as he asked. It had been so long since he'd had sex in a bed, not a hallway or bathroom stall.

It had been forever since he'd done anything with someone he gave half a damn about. Someone whose full name he knew.

"You want-?" Gabe questioned.

"You," said Joey against his cheek. "Inside me. Oh god, Gabe."

Gabe nudged him with his nose so he could maneuver him for more kisses. For a moment, Joey was worried he might say no. "I want you so badly," Gabe said, allaying his fears. "But only if you're sure?"

Knowing what he did about Gabe, he probably wanted to take things slow. Ask Joey out to dinner, buy him flowers and all that stuff. But Joey had to be realistic. They were not compatible. This was purely physical attraction, and he wanted to take it as far as they could go, now.

"Please say you have supplies," Joey panted rather than directly answer his question.

Gabe laughed into his mouth. "I take that as a yes?"

Joey rolled his eyes. Of course Gabe was a stickler for consent. Joey sort of wanted him to just pin him down and take him. But that wasn't Gabe's style.

"I want you to fuck me," he said, grabbing Gabe's dark hair and looking directly into his eyes. "Take me away, please, Gabe."

Saying his name seemed to have an immediate effect on Gabe. He groaned and kissed Joey again, passionately. Then he reached over to his bedside drawer and snatched up a half-full tube of lubricant and fresh pack of condoms.

Joey's breath hitched as Gabe dropped them by the pillows and hooked his fingers into Joey's waistband, stripping him in one swift move that Joey was only too happy to raise his hips to help with. Then Gabe pushed down his own underwear, leaving them naked under the comforter. Joey whined and groped at Gabe's shoulders as he squeezed some of the lube onto his fingers and found Joey's hole, stroking it while their bare cocks brushed together.

He felt like he might burst in anticipation, shivering as Gabe caressed his sensitive flesh. Joey kept kissing him, whatever parts of his satiny, salty skin he could reach.

"Yes, please, oh my god," he stuttered.

He dug his fingers into Gabe's back. There was a chance at this rate he might leave bruises; Joey hoped Gabe wouldn't mind.

Because he knew this would probably be a onetime deal, the thought of leaving Gabe with some kind of mark, proof that they had been together, was extremely comforting. He wanted Gabe to miss him after he was gone.

All coherent thought evaporated from his brain as soon as Gabe pushed a firm finger inside, breaching into his most intimate area. Joey couldn't help but cry out and cling on harder.

"Sorry," Gabe said, immediately stopping. "I should have warned you."

But Joey shook his head and laughed. "Keep going. I want you to take me. I'm yours. I won't break."

Gabe kissed him some more as he pushed his finger in up to the knuckle, pulsing back and forth. Joey moaned into his mouth, running his fingers up and down his broad back, feeling the muscles working.

Luckily, Gabe listened to him and quickly added a second finger. Joey didn't want this to hurt, but he didn't want to spend half an hour prepping either. If they hung around, he might talk himself out of it. Right now he was just high on endorphins and chasing his release.

"How do you want it?" Gabe asked. He looked down at Joey with such intensity it made him gulp.

"Like this," Joey said. On his back. He didn't explain that was because he wanted to keep kissing Gabe. Wanted to keep looking at his beautiful face. Gabe didn't ask why though, he just shifted so he was hovering above Joey between his legs.

Joey automatically drew his knees up to his chest, exposing himself. Trusting his body to this man he hardly knew. He was scared, but he knew Gabe would take care of him.

Gabe wiped his slippery fingers on the bedsheets and snatched up the pack of condoms, making short work of rolling one down his hard, red cock. He wasn't so big that it gave Joey any alarm, but he would certainly know he was there.

"You're so beautiful," Gabe murmured, kissing him again as he angled himself, pushing his dick against Joey's eagerly throbbing hole.

Joey wanted to tell him how gorgeous he was too. How he'd craved him from the moment he'd laid eyes on him. But he didn't have the words. So he just continued kissing him hungrily, pushing his ass against Gabe's cock, feeling the tip push through his threshold.

He took deep breaths, forcing himself to relax. Gabe inched in, keeping the burn manageable.

"Yes, yes," Joey uttered, not capable of much else. That was ideal though. No thought, just action. Just touch and taste and the pleasure building from his toes to his belly.

Gabe bottomed out and gasped. His eyes were blown with lust and his skin covered with a layer of perspiration. He was perfection, a work of art. Joey held the side of his face, urging him down for another kiss, trying to explain how amazing he was making Joey feel.

After that, Gabe braced his elbows on either side of Joey's head, caging him with his big arms, and began to slowly piston in and out of Joey. Within a few strokes he found Joey's prostate, brushing against that electric bundle of nerves and causing Joey to cry out in pleasure.

Joey really hoped Gabe's house had thick walls. After so many illicit encounters where he had to stifle his cries, Joey didn't want to hold back at all. He wanted everything.

He grunted with every thrust, throwing his legs around Gabe's waist for a better grip and a deeper angle of penetration. He wasn't going to last long.

Neither was Gabe, though, judging by the look on his face. He was biting his lip and shaking. He moved to scoop Gabe up around his back with one hand and slid his fingers through Joey's hair with the other. Joey held him tighter in response, kissing him between gasps for air.

"Going to…" Joey uttered.

Gabe nodded, encouraging him. He reached down between them. Joey's cock had been rubbing quite nicely between their stomachs, but Gabe's fingers wrapping tightly around it was heaven. Joey wailed and dropped his head back, his orgasm rushing upon him like a wave crashing down on the shore.

His vision blacked out as he spilled his release between them. Gabe only thrust a couple more times before he joined him, arching his back as he came in the condom deep inside Joey's body.

Joey's vision came back to him slowly as he blinked up at the bedroom ceiling. Gabe was holding him like he never wanted to let him go.

In his post-coital bliss, Joey never wanted to let Gabe go, either.

CHAPTER
Fourteen

GABE

GABE REALLY DIDN'T WANT TO MOVE. HE WANTED TO CLING on to the moment. But his cock was softening and the mess between them was cooling and becoming uncomfortable. So he slid out of Joey as carefully as he could, kissing his cheek then hastily disposing of the condom and grabbing them both some tissues.

Once drier, he pulled the comforter up over them, lying beside a sleepy Joey as their post-orgasm-high faded. Gabe was inordinately pleased when Joey cuddled up to him, tucking his head down on Gabe's chest.

His first coherent thought was that he'd just had sex with someone that wasn't Lewis. It was strange how okay that felt. He and Lew had been sharing this bed up until a month ago. They'd not been intimate since the start of the year though, when things between them seemed to pass the point of no return.

Lewis was a lot like him physically; big and confident in bed. They'd switched positions a lot, their lovemaking often more like a tousle than anything gentle.

Joey had been so different. Not meek, but the way he'd

begged Gabe to take him, the way he'd surrendered himself to Gabe, had been deeply touching. The level of trust he'd shown Gabe when they didn't know each other all that well, was very moving.

Plus Joey was just hot. He was slim and lean but still muscled, with a beautiful face, stunning smile and sparkling eyes. His curly hair was soft as Gabe gently ran his fingers through it.

His tattoos were interesting as well, and plentiful. Even in the gloom last night Gabe had been able to see there were many of them, but in the morning sunshine he was able to appreciate that they were dotted all over his body.

Most of his skin was hidden under the comforter, and when they'd been fucking Gabe had been slightly distracted. But now he was able to see the edges of quotes in elaborate calligraphy, the tips of wings, a series of rings, rays of sunlight. Each image must have had a story behind it. Gabe would have loved to ask more.

In that moment though it was enough to simply lie there together. The fact Joey hadn't immediately run off was better than Gabe had expected. Not that he'd expected anything. This was the last thing he thought he'd wake up to when he'd gone to bed the night before.

Joey stirred up a powerful protective urge in Gabe. He wanted to ask him to stay the day, stay until he was on his feet again. Gabe wanted to keep him away from his damaging family, let him have a chance to breathe in a place where he wasn't on edge all the time. Where he'd have a proper bed.

But he had a feeling after their conversation the previous night that offering kindness and stability might have the opposite effect on Joey and make him bolt. He seemed so dead set on managing on his own, letting himself get swallowed up by a big city so he wouldn't have to rely on his neighbors.

Gabe couldn't really wrap his head around that. His natural instinct was always to help, to bond, to become part of the bigger whole that his community offered. But the way Joey had talked about his experiences growing up, it was clear he didn't feel the same way.

He'd sounded lonely. Gabe hated that.

"Are you all right?" he murmured.

As much as he'd rather leave it, he had to pop their little bubble and ask. He also had to consider if *he* was all right. He never tumbled into bed with anyone. Especially not so soon after the longest relationship of his life.

What he and Joey had just experienced together had obviously been tangled up in a lot of emotions. Maybe Gabe was just rebounding, and that wasn't fair on Joey. Maybe Joey was taking his anger and frustrations out in bed. Or, perhaps he'd just taken the first bit of kindness and comfort that had been offered his way.

Either way, it probably wasn't the healthiest of motivations. But Gabe cared about Joey, that much he knew. It could be that they'd regret what they'd done in the heat of the moment. At least they'd used protection.

What Gabe could do now though was continue to look after Joey. Not because he was obliged to, but because he wanted to. Even if this was his heart just trying to move on from the void Lewis had left, he'd very much enjoyed making love with Joey. That didn't stop after the orgasm.

"Do you want breakfast?" he prompted when Joey chewed on his lip.

When he raised his green eyes to look at Gabe, there was apprehension there. Gabe might have even gone so far as to say fear. He rubbed his hand up and down Joey's arm.

"Um," Gabe said awkwardly. "I feel like you're expecting

me to propose or something, and you're working out how fast you can scale the drainpipe."

Joey snorted, the laughter apparently startling him. Good, that was good.

"This was great. Lovely, actually," Gabe said truthfully. "But we don't really know each other. It doesn't have to be anything more if we don't feel it, but I'd still like to make you some eggs."

He was surprised how his own words disappointed him. He'd have been pretty keen if Joey had turned around in his arms and said he'd like to spend more time together. For a fleeting second Gabe pictured taking him out on a date later. It was Saturday after all.

But Joey gave him a small, relieved smile. "Thanks," he said. He laid his head back on Gabe's chest, not looking him in the eye. "Breakfast would be nice," he said slowly. "And, um, yeah. That was nice too. Really nice."

Gabe waited to see if there would be anything else, but it appeared that was all Joey was able to say for now. Gabe didn't mind. It didn't take a genius to see that Joey had a whole lot churning around in his head. So Gabe would take 'nice' for the compliment it was.

He kissed the top of Joey's curls, enjoying the cuddle for another few moments. But then Joey excused himself to use the bathroom, sheepishly scooping up his underwear as he went, and Gabe thought it best to give him some space.

He donned his robe and trotted down to the kitchen. There was no sign of Duchess, but her food bowl was empty. Gabe chuckled to himself and filled it up again before getting started on his and Joey's breakfast. At least he knew his cat wasn't starving, even if she was too scared to come out when he was there.

Some minutes later he had bacon frying in a pan, along with eggs and tomatoes, bread in the toaster and coffee in the pot. This was nice, in that mildly terrifying but also exciting way when you were taking baby steps to get to know someone. Gabe caught himself smiling as he flipped the rashers.

"I got the part."

He turned around. Joey was dressed and staring at his phone. The look of disbelief on his face matched the incredulous tone of his voice.

"What?" Gabe asked. He'd heard Joey just fine, but he wanted to make sure. Excitement already bubbled in him, which was kind of silly. But he couldn't help but feel happy. Joey needed some good news, and Gabe felt irrationally proud that he was getting to share this moment with him.

"I got that part in the play," Joey said. His face split into a wide grin and when he looked up his eyes were filled with unshed tears. "Oh my god."

Gabe let out a cry and punched the air with his spatula. "Yes, dude! Well done."

Joey didn't seem to know what to do. Gabe followed his instinct though and crossed the few steps between them to pull him into a quick hug. He didn't want to smother Joey; he wasn't his boyfriend. But in that moment Gabe could certainly picture what it might be like if they were dating.

Instead, he gave those pretty curls another swift kiss and let him go on the pretext of tending to the frying pan. "When do you start rehearsals?"

Joey shook himself and scrolled through the email or text he'd received. "Monday," he said. He bit his lip, and Gabe could guess what was worrying him.

"In New York?" he asked. That would mean train tickets. Joey had said that the cash that had been stolen from him was all he had. Gabe wasn't exactly rich, but he couldn't imagine not having a cent to his name.

Joey nodded. Gabe knew he was about to overstep his

boundaries and probably wreck what little trust he had built up between them. But there was no way he couldn't offer.

"If you need something to help you," he said. "Until you next get a paycheck, I can give you a loan. Just a small one."

Joey looked up at him. First his eyes were wide, then they narrowed with wariness. "Why?"

He shouldn't, but Gabe smirked. He tried to cover it up by fussing over the food he was plating up. But that was exactly the kind of response he'd come to expect from Joey now. Like the concept of simply being kind, or having kindness offered to him, what was entirely alien.

It wasn't funny though; it was deeply sad. "Because we're friends, or at least I'd hope we are?" He raised an eyebrow at Joey. Joey shrugged, but a small smile tugged at the corner of his mouth. Gabe took that as a yes. "And after the trouble you had last night, I'd hate to see that stand in the way of an opportunity."

Joey watched him as he put the two plates on the table. "That's really nice of you," he said slowly.

Gabe didn't want him to think he was pitying him though. "When would you get paid?" he asked as he indicated for Joey to sit. "You could pay me back in a couple of install-ments, if you wanted?"

Joey's face darkened at that, and Gabe could have kicked himself. But there wasn't much getting around the fact that Joey was in financial trouble. Gabe wasn't saying this to humiliate him. Sometimes, everyone needed a little helping hand.

Joey still hadn't sat and Gabe was starting to feel he'd really fucked things up. But then Joey's expression totally changed. "Hang on," he said. He dropped into the seat by Gabe and began flicking through his phone. "It's the twenti-eth, right?" Gabe nodded, confirming the date. "Then that means..."

Gabe waited while he scrawled through whatever he was looking at. The food was getting cold, but it seemed rude to interrupt. Especially if it was going to douse that spark of excitement in Joey's eyes.

"Yes!" he cried in delight. He looked up at Gabe, smiling, and Gabe couldn't help but reciprocate. "Normally my royalty payments are peanuts these days. But one of our songs was featured on a commercial a couple of months ago. We got a decent check for that, and a bump in sales." The relief in his voice was clear. "That should be in my account any day now."

"That's wonderful," said Gabe genuinely.

Joey nodded. "If I can ask for an advance on the first couple of days from the play, that'll tide me over until the royalty money's in my account. I won't have to borrow from anyone."

Gabe wanted to insist that it wouldn't have been any trouble to give him a loan. But this was obviously the better solution. Selfishly though, he knew a loan would mean that he and Joey would have had something tethering them together for longer than it took for the eggs he'd made to go rubbery.

Joey only seemed to just notice that he'd been given food. "Oh," he said apprehensively. "And you made breakfast."

"I said I would," Gabe told him kindly. But it was obvious to see that Joey was tallying up all the things Gabe was doing for him.

It was frustrating. Gabe wasn't doing anything here for a reward. But the way Joey had spoken of his involvement in the community, it was clear to see that he might not feel the same way.

"I should go," said Joey, as if to prove his point. His gaze was lingering on the bacon though, and he licked his pretty lips. "I've bothered you enough."

"Joey," said Gabe, mustering the last of his patience. "You've not bothered me at all. I've enjoyed your company and the food will only go in the trash if you don't eat it. Please don't rush off." He wanted to say 'don't run away,' but he feared that might have been too blunt.

Joey appeared to respond better to the straight talking though. He nodded and took a grateful bite of eggs. "I just hate not having anything to give back," he muttered once he swallowed.

Gabe softened a bit and squeezed his hand, just briefly. "I hate eating alone," Gabe said truthfully. "So consider me repaid."

Joey gave him another tight smile, then devoured the rest of his breakfast.

Gabe could only keep him there a matter of time though, that much was obvious. Joey kept checking his phone and bouncing his knee. Gabe didn't try and engage him in conversation as he flitted back and forth between his emails, bank app and a calculator.

"Do you need me to drive you anywhere?" he asked when Joey crossed his knife and fork. The question seemed to surprise him.

"Oh, no," Joey said guiltily. "I'll stay and do the dishes though. It's only fair."

Gabe smiled warmly at him. "I can tell you've got things to do," he said, careful to keep the regret out of his voice. This was for the best. Gabe couldn't go jumping in headfirst for heaven's sake. They needed a bit of space after rushing into bed like they had.

"I-" said Joey. Then he smiled and his relief was clear. Gabe refused to let it hurt. At least, he tried. "Thanks, but I can walk."

It was all Gabe could do to escort him to the door. If something more was going to happen between them, he couldn't press it. Shouldn't. He had to protect his own heart as well. Joey obviously wasn't looking to settle down here after all, and Gabe was still finding the occasional thing of Lewis's lying around the house.

"Drop me a text if you need anything," Gabe said. *Or even if you don't,* he added mentally.

Joey at least smiled and allowed himself to be hugged. "I will. Thank you for…everything."

And with that, he was gone.

CHAPTER
Fifteen

JOEY

"Joey?"

His blood ran cold. Usually, he did his best to creep in and out of the house and his family respected that by pretending he didn't exist. The play in New York had kept him out during most of the day for the past few weeks, but even though that was over now, he'd still maintained his routine of rising early and coming back late. It meant things were better for everyone.

But of course the one time he came home a bit earlier, his dad had heard him come through the door and now he was being summoned. Dread filled Joey's insides, and he debated stashing his Chinese food on the stairs so they didn't see it. It wasn't like they were feeding him, but he also didn't think it would go down well to flaunt that he was 'wasting' money on takeout either.

But then he ran the risk of his brother stealing it from him out of spite if he came across it. It was better to keep a hold of it and try his best not to draw attention to the bag.

He stepped into the den without a word. His dad didn't need ammunition and Joey had learned it was generally preferable to wait until he knew what the conversation was going to be about before he spoke.

"I hear you got yourself a job," his dad said.

His mocking tone set Joey's teeth on edge, even after all these years. He wanted to scream that he'd been an international popstar, for fuck's sake. But obviously that would only lead to his dad giving him even more grief about getting 'fired' as he saw it.

"Yes," was all he said. Luckily his mom wasn't there to draw his eye. He'd told her about the Off-Broadway play to try and reassure her that things weren't so bad, that they were picking up for him. It didn't surprise him that his dad had managed to wheedle it out of her. He sensed when she was trying to keep something from him and hounded her until she cracked. Joey didn't blame her.

He was still pissed though. It wasn't any of his dad's business how he made his money, only that he saved up and got himself the fuck out of here.

Joey had been looking at bedrooms for rent on the outskirts of the city. He'd have a commute for any work, which would cost more, but the rent was less and there were lots of opportunities. If he could just get a few more gigs, bulk up his savings, he'd go and get a bar job to top up the rest like he planned.

"Bet you're rolling in it again, huh?" said his dad with a smirk. "Big-time superstar."

His eyes were on the football game playing on the TV and he sipped a beer. Patrick mimicked him by his side on the couch while Cathy bounced baby Michael on her knee, as if there wasn't a conversation going on at all. He was sick, grousing with fever and tiredness.

"I'm close to getting a deposit together," Joey said, fudging the truth a little. But he wasn't giving his dad the satisfaction of knowing how close he'd been to destitution.

If it wasn't for Gabe, Joey wasn't sure what might have happened.

The thought of Gabe gave him that now-familiar pang, but he stored it for after he'd escaped from his family and could eat in peace. It hadn't passed him by that this little ambush had occurred while his mom was at the store.

"That's great," said his dad in that same jaunty voice. Like he was placating a toddler. His eyes flicked towards the Chinese takeout in Joey's hands. "But don't forget to pay us the rent you owe, either."

Ice shot down Joey's spine. That wasn't their deal. He kept out of their way, fed himself, took his clothes down the laundromat. He asked them for nothing but a roof over his head. He never even charged his phone or laptop here, for fear that his dad would call him out for stealing electricity.

"Rent?" he asked, trying to keep his voice even.

He didn't miss the filthy look his sister-in-law threw him as she cooed annoyingly loudly at her son. "Who's a good boy?" she simpered. "My perfect little man." Michael wailed, screwing up his ruddy face.

"Well, yeah," said Joey's dad over the din, like Joey was being deliberately obtuse. "No one gets a free ride. Right, Patrick?"

"Right, Dad," said Joey's brother sagely.

Joey could have screamed. Everyone knew full well the only reason Patrick had already made assistant manager at the plant was because their dad had picked him over several other far better-qualified candidates.

"I thought," Joey said carefully, "the plan was for me to save up and leave as soon as possible."

He could have sworn he heard Cathy hiss *Freeloader* under her breath. It was hard to tell with the baby crying.

Joey's dad arched an eyebrow and glowered at him. Joey resisted the urge to take a step away. He had his backpack on as per usual with all his things. If his dad made to go for him, he could bolt out the door faster than his dad could catch him. He hoped.

"You're here so your mom stops *sniveling*," his dad growled. "You've broken her heart and embarrassed this family enough. I've had the good grace to allow you to stay while you try and get yourself a respectable job. Then you go fairying around trying to pass off saying some pretty words in front of some other fags like it's actual work." He took a swig of his beer and sloshed it in Joey's direction. How many had he had? "I might feel different about letting you keep a dignified wage. But if you want to insist on singing and dancing like a fucking monkey, you can pay me a hundred dollars a week."

He laughed to himself as Joey's heart dropped like a stone. "How…" he stammered. "How am I supposed to save enough to move out if I do that?"

"Get a real *fucking job*," his dad bellowed, leaping to his feet. Joey jerked back, but his dad didn't lunge for him. However, Michael did intensify his howling at the sudden shouting.

"Look what you did!" Cathy snarled at Joey.

"I don't care how you do it," his dad continued over the bawling. "But by Friday, you will hand me a hundred dollars in cash, or I'll drag you out into the street myself. Am I understood?" Joey was too stunned to respond, which was a mistake. "I said am I *understood*, you little *queer?*"

"Perfectly," Joey spat out. Before he could suffer anything more, he stormed back out into the street. He couldn't linger in that house, not now. He'd just have to eat his Chinese cold, once he found a bench to perch on.

This was so un-fucking-*fair.* How was he supposed to get ahead if his dad was going to rig the system? He didn't know whether to cry or scream. If his dad was going to insist on bleeding rent from him, he'd be lucky to keep up payments, let alone save enough to get him the fuck out.

Joey felt so sick he didn't want to eat. But he'd learned he couldn't afford to waste food, so he turned into the first small park he came across and stubbornly sat in the dark fishing chow mien out with disposable chopsticks, mechanically swallowing down the noodles.

Maybe he should cut his losses and move out now, into the first dive he could afford. Freedom would be better than this surely, even if it came with near poverty and constant insecurity.

Irrationally, he pulled out his phone to contemplate texting Gabe. He'd stared at the other man's number more times than he could count since he rescued him after his pickpocketing.

After they'd had sex.

And fuck, was it good sex.

But Gabe wanted to mold Joey into something he wasn't. His intentions were good; Joey had no doubt. But Gabe saw him as a charity project, like the LGBT kids he apparently worked with at the homeless shelter. Joey had heard that from the head librarian the last time he had dared to go in. He'd been unashamedly avoiding the place so he didn't have to deal with seeing Gabe. But the other day he'd seen him out with a fire crew, so Joey had swung in to job hunt in a change of scenery.

He wasn't sure why the old librarian had dropped that fact about Gabe into their brief conversation, but Joey didn't doubt it. It was his way. Like taking in that mangled cat that Joey absolutely did not think was adorable.

But being Gabe's pet project would mean he'd try and domesticate Joey just like that cat. Joey didn't want to get comfy in fucking Greenwich, Connecticut. He'd suffocate here, as his father had just reminded him.

In his darkest moments though, like sitting on a park bench in the dark with cold Chinese takeout, Joey did allow himself to fantasize about Gabe taking him home again, just once more.

This time Joey would keep his mouth shut and not insult the man. They'd just talk about movies or something dumb and eat another one of Gabe's delicious home-cooked meals. Then Joey would allow him to take him up to bed, his intentions clear from the start this time, and they'd fuck until Joey could barely remember his own name.

Christ alive, it had been good. Great. *Exceptional.* Joey wasn't sure he'd ever had sex like that in his whole life. Not in all the countries he'd been to or the guys he'd picked up along the way. The way Gabe had held him…it wasn't that he'd dominated Joey exactly. But he'd been in charge at the same time as treating him with such tenderness it still made Joey's head spin to think about it.

He couldn't have that though. He'd been lucky to experience it once. Joey wouldn't lead Gabe on; he was too nice for that. So Joey would just have to cherish the memory and hope it kept him warm when everything else seemed so cold.

He still checked his cellphone though, with the intention of allowing himself just one quick peek at Gabe's name to cheer himself up. But on the main screen it flashed up that he had a text and a couple of missed calls. From Raiden.

That was odd. Blake was the only one from the band that ever called. The rest of the time, the guys just used text and group chats. By now they all knew Joey was back home. Even Reyse, who was busy promoting his new album. But they didn't know quite how bad it was.

The text message just asked Joey to call Raiden, which worried him. Had something happened?

Without thinking, he hit the redial icon.

"Jo-ey!" Raiden answered in his usual sing-song fashion. "Hey, man, what's up?"

Joey blinked in the darkness, taking stock. From that, he could gather that none of the guys had been in a car crash or anything. "Hey, Raiden," he said, keeping his voice even. There was probably nothing to be worried over at all. "Sorry I missed your calls. I know it's getting late, but I felt I should call back."

"Nah," said Raiden. Joey could hear him typing as he spoke. Multitasking, as usual. "It's not late. I just wanted to touch base. Blake said you were in a play and the reviews were sweet!"

Joey smiled, relaxing back against the bench. "Yeah," he admitted. "It was good."

He'd actually enjoyed the experience more than he'd hoped. The play was tolerable and the cast and crew top notch. But it had only run for ten days after a week's rehearsal. Joey had only just started really getting into it all when it had come to an end.

But Raiden was right. The reviews had been great, and that could be all he needed to get noticed by another director or casting agent. Hopefully.

"So how are you?" he asked his former bandmate.

He missed him in that moment with a pang that was almost physical. They'd never been as close as Joey and Blake were, but Joey would still count him as one of his best friends in the entire world.

"Actually, I had kind of a major breakthrough today," said Raiden down the line. "One of my songs got picked up."

Raiden had been dabbling with songwriting ever since the band first stepped into the recording studio together five years ago. He'd even got to work on a few of their album tracks, uncredited of course. But Joey wasn't surprised that was the direction he was taking his career in now.

"Man," he said, shaking his head to himself and grinning. "I'm so happy for you, that's incredible. Who snatched it up?" Joey mentally crossed his fingers that it was a respectable artist.

He could practically hear Raiden's glee down the phone. "Storm Sailor."

Joey sat up so fast he almost tumbled off the bench. Storm Sailor had always been a favorite producer of the two of them. They'd had several nights where they'd just stayed up late in hotel rooms getting drunk and geeking out over all the songs the Swede had worked on over the past several years.

"Shut up! No!" Joey cried, all his previous woes forgotten in the light of such great news for his friend. "Storm Sailor? Fuck, that's the dream, right there, dude! There'll be no stopping you now!"

Raiden chuckled. "I don't know about that, but it's a fantastic break. Thank you."

"You got any idea who he's going to have sing it?" Joey asked. He'd have to hear the demo, but immediately he was already cataloging all the obvious artists that could do one of Raiden's creations justice. His first commercial song, actually, so it better be somebody worthy.

Raiden laughed again, but softly this time. "I sold it to him on a few conditions," he said conspiratorially. "One of which was that I wrote it with the singer in mind, and he can't produce it if he doesn't go with the artist I want."

Joey snorted. "That's bold," he said. He was impressed though. Raiden was generally a very laid-back guy when it came to diva-like demands. But he always did know when to put his foot down when something really mattered. "Good for you. So tell me then, who is it?"

There was a pause.

"You."

Joey almost dropped the phone. "Me?" he squeaked.

"Yeah," said Raiden softly. "It's in your range; I can practically hear it already. Please say you will?"

Joey didn't understand. What was the catch? Storm Sailor was one of his idols. He knew he'd take any song of Raiden's and produce something phenomenal. And Raiden wanted – no – was insisting that Joey be the one to bring it to life?

"I don't-" Joey stammered. "Yes, I mean, fuck me, yes, dude. This is incredible!"

Raiden laughed down the phone, a throaty, genuine sound. "Amazing. I'll send you the details."

Joey looked up at the stars overhead, feeling the cold night breeze skimming around him. This was it. This was his turning point. If he could just nail this, it could mean international success.

He just had to hang on. Great things were only around the corner. He simply needed to keep working hard, and remember to have a little patience.

CHAPTER
Sixteen

GABE

Sometimes, Gabe didn't know if he was coming or going.

He worked at the library as Mitch's assistant every day from nine until three. On Mondays, he also sat in as an extra pair of hands for the mother-and-toddler group, then helped set up the chairs for the English as a second language class, then assisted with the women's flower-arranging club.

He just liked to be around in case the instructors needed supplies or someone to take a smaller group if they divided the classes up. Mostly though, he just liked to chat to the ladies and hear their news. Some of the young moms and older women were somewhat starved of adult company, and he knew because he was gay they saw him as being a sort of safe confidant.

The rest of the week was much the same. He didn't necessarily enjoy hanging around the accounting class or the ones on teaching people how to make spreadsheets on the computers. But if he wasn't there to help and lock up afterwards, who would? The rest of the staff had families to get home to. Besides, he made up for it with the activity sessions he loved, like kid's story time and puppy obedience classes at the community center.

Tuesdays and Fridays, he volunteered at the homeless shelter he and his buddies had put a lot of time into helping get off the ground earlier in the year. It was now the biggest in south-west Connecticut and had special provisions for LGBT needs.

Gabe worked in the kitchen to help get the evening meal ready. But more importantly, he'd had some training to be a guidance counselor so he could try and work with any of the queer kids that came their way. Out of everything he did, it was the most rewarding part of his week when he saw the look of hope on a teen's face that had obviously been absent for too long.

Wednesdays were his fun days. He loved the kids' art club because it was a release for all of them to just create and be expressive. Then he allowed himself to squeeze in some time for himself after that, going to the movies or seeing his buddies. Or sometimes, just getting an early night and sleeping.

Thursdays, he taught one of the beginners' classes on the climbing wall at the community center. It meant no matter how busy his week got with everything else, he could always get some time to climb himself.

Every other weekend he spent with the fire department, and on the Saturdays he wasn't riding with them he had a few houses around the neighborhood he visited to cut the lawn or do any odd jobs that needed heavy lifting or reaching up high.

All in all, Gabe lived a full and busy life, interacting with hundreds of people on a weekly basis. He considered himself very lucky, even if sometimes he felt drained from running around everywhere.

Especially because he knew that without being so distracted, he probably would have driven himself utterly and completely insane the past few weeks at hearing nothing at all from Joey after they had slept together.

He got that Joey was skittish and going through a lot. And the play was probably keeping him really busy. But for the love of god, would it have killed him to drop Gabe a line? He would have taken a wave emoji or even the smiley poop one.

Every time Gabe tried to tell himself that there was technically nothing stopping him from sending a text, he held back. He'd made his feelings pretty clear to Joey. He wanted to see him again. But he also had to be sensible. Joey was fragile, and not someone for Gabe to be messing around with during his rebound from Lewis.

Still, it didn't stop him from daydreaming forlornly, wishing Joey would take the decision out of his hands and make contact.

He was thinking something along those lines when he strolled into the library at nine that Wednesday morning. The library opened at seven, but he wasn't needed much before nine when the public generally started drifting in. He was surprised to see Mitch already looking stressed at the desk with a woman he vaguely recognized as one of the moms from art class.

As Gabe approached, Mitch glanced over at him. This caused the woman to look too, giving Gabe full view of her face. He realized she was Pompeii Slater's mom, Debbie. Pompeii was a sweet girl with an obsession with pandas and glitter.

While Pompeii always greeted him with a shriek and a hug, her mom gave him a brief scowl before quickly smoothing it out and turning back around to the desk.

"Thank you for your time, Mr. Curtis," Debbie said stiffly

to Mitch. She flipped her blond hair and pulled out some big, fluffy earmuffs as she marched past Gabe and out the front doors.

Gabe turned back to Mitch and gave him a raised eyebrow as he approached. "Everything okay?"

Mitch scoffed and shook his head. "Nothing you need to worry about," he said.

Gabe narrowed his eyes as he took his bag from his shoulder and placed it by the desk. Mitch's cheeks were red and he was scowling. Whatever Pompeii's mom had said had clearly shaken him. Mitch never got rattled unless his dog had chewed through another remote control or his wife was mad at him. Normally because the dog chewed up the remote. Nothing else seemed to ever faze him.

"Really?" Gabe asked, making his skepticism clear.

Mitch sighed and glanced towards the door where Debbie Slater had departed. "She was checking your credentials. Making sure you were fit to work with kids."

Gabe felt like he'd had a bucket of cold water dropped on his head. "What?" he stammered. "What did you tell her?"

Mitch huffed. "That you were fully qualified, of course. There's no way you could be involved with any of the classes if you weren't."

But that wasn't strictly true. While Gabe didn't have a criminal record, he'd never officially been vetted by the local police. Still, that shouldn't give anyone reason to be concerned.

"Why would she care about that?" Gabe asked. "Did something happen? Was there a complaint?" Mitch's expression confirmed his suspicions though. Gabe's heart sank. "It's because I'm gay. Isn't it?"

"I told her I wouldn't stand and listen to a bunch of claptrap," Mitch said gruffly as he fussed with his old Rolodex.

"Said you were perfectly capable and everyone loves you. Sent her on her way."

"Right," said Gabe.

He could hear his voice was flat though. God fucking damn it. It never failed to shock him just how shitty it felt when someone equated his being gay to being a pervert. Like who he was attracted to automatically made him a danger to children.

He swallowed bile in his throat. Mitch looked at him with pity, which only made things worse. "How about some tea?" Mitch asked. Gabe agreed, mostly so it would get his friend away and stop him looking at Gabe like that.

Gabe loved the art club. He didn't want to even think about giving it up. But he wasn't going to have anyone accusing him of something so disgusting as being a danger to their kids. That would be a serious risk to the library's reputation, and people relied on this place for so much.

He shook himself and tried to regain some composure before Mitch returned. Debbie hadn't officially demanded anything like his resignation, and even if she did, she was just a private citizen. She didn't have any power. Just a big mouth and a bad attitude.

When Mitch returned, Gabe took the green tea and sipped it while it was still a bit too hot. It meant he could put off discussing what had just happened. Mitch took the hint, and eventually he started chatting about the Halloween decorations he was putting up at home and what his grandkids were dressing up as for trick-or-treating. Good company and warm tea meant that Gabe's mood thawed, and he felt able to start some work for the day.

Really, what did it matter what one woman thought? It sucked that she'd taken time from her day to come to Gabe's job and cast aspersions, but hopefully this would be the end of it now. He couldn't really see her trying to pull the same stunt at the firehouse or the shelter. The library was by far the softest option if she was set on making complaints. So really, he had nothing to worry about. It didn't feel great to know someone was out there in town thinking ill of him. But that was her opinion, and Gabe guessed he had to respect that. Even if it did hurt.

He was lost in thought as he walked through the building and into the hot desk area. But then promptly stopped short.

Joey was sitting there with his laptop and another stack of CDs, his jaw clenched and his eyes red. He looked like he'd been crying.

Whatever had happened between them the past few weeks melted away as Gabe's heart swelled. He may have been confused about a lot of things, but he knew he hated seeing Joey in distress.

"Hey," he said softly.

He placed the books he'd been carrying down on one of the tables and approached. Joey looked up in surprise, yanking his earbuds out then immediately checking his watch in alarm.

Gabe stopped. Joey didn't say anything as he looked back up again, but it was hard not to assume what he meant by the guilty look on his face.

He'd intended to leave before Gabe started work.

On top of dealing with the complaint against him, Gabe wasn't able to school his reaction and hide how much that hurt. "Been avoiding me?" he asked, crossing his arms. He knew he sounded like a dick, especially when it was obvious Joey still had tears drying on his face. Oddly though that only angered Gabe further. Because god damn it. Joey didn't have to do everything by himself. He could ask for help.

He could ask Gabe to help him, and he would do it in a heartbeat.

Joey dropped his head and wrung his hands in his lap. "I'm sorry," he said.

The lack of excuses went some way to dissolving Gabe's flare of irritation. He sighed and pulled out the seat next to Joey. "You don't have to avoid me," he said tersely. "We're adults, we're friends. We had some fun. I'm not going to push you into anything you're not ready for, but I do like you. If there's anything I can help with, I will."

Joey gave him a rueful chuckle. "I know, I know," he said, shaking his head. "You're Mr. Helpful. I just want to try and manage something by myself for a fucking change."

Gabe rolled his eyes and squeezed Joey's knee. It was hard to stay mad at him. "You're doing amazing," he said. "You're so young and you've achieved so much."

"I'm not that young," Joey grumbled. But the twitch at the corner of his mouth suggested he'd taken the compliment.

"So how's the play going?" Gabe asked, giving him an out. "I bet that's been keeping you busy."

"It did," said Joey quickly. "And I'm sorry, I should have texted. I..." he huffed and flicked his eyes over at Gabe. "I don't want you to think I don't like you too."

Gabe snorted. "I get it, you're a Broadway star now, no biggie."

But Joey bit his lip and blinked rapidly, leaving Gabe with the impression he'd put his foot in it.

"The play was great, but it's over now," said Joey tightly.

Gabe wasn't sure how to respond to that. "I'm glad it went well," he said tentatively. "Hopefully that might lead to other roles?"

Joey looked at him. His green eyes were glassy, and he bounced his knee as he appeared to think something over. "I have another job," he blurted out. "It's an incredible opportunity. But I don't think I can take it."

"Why?" said Gabe, seizing on the fact that Joey was opening up to him.

Joey scrubbed his face. While his eyes were briefly closed, Gabe inched just a little closer, hoping it wouldn't spook him. But he wanted to be near him, even if he felt he should be careful how much he touched.

"You know Raiden, from the band?"

Gabe recognized the name, but probably couldn't pick him out of the five members. He nodded anyway, sensing that wasn't the most important part of the story.

"Well, he's starting to get ahead in songwriting, and Storm Sailor – the producer – picked up one of his tracks, and they want me to sing it. Which, is like, fucking incredible. It's basically guaranteed to be in the top forty, maybe even top ten."

"Joey," Gabe spluttered, glad there weren't other people around. "That's fantastic, congratulations!" But the look on his face suggested there was more to it than that. "So…what's the problem?"

"He's based in Sweden. He's only in the US for a week, and he's going to be in Chicago."

Gabe glanced at the computer screen. Joey was looking at hotels and bus options by the looks of the tabs. "Surely it'll be worth spending the money?" he asked. But even as he said it he did a quick estimation what travel and accommodation for a few days would cost. Joey was probably looking at a few hundred bucks at least. Considering what Gabe knew about his situation, that probably wouldn't be feasible.

"I keep telling myself the return is almost guaranteed," Joey said, flicking between some of his tabs. "But it's not absolutely certain. Even if it was, I still don't really have enough, and then there's money for food…"

He trailed off, looking forlornly at the screen. Gabe ached for him. It seemed like even though he kept telling himself not to get too involved or fall for Joey any more than he had, he couldn't help but care.

"How many days would you need to stay in the city?" he asked.

Something reckless was brewing in the back of his mind. He was probably making a big mistake, one that would get him hurt. But the more he thought about it, the more certain he became. He just needed to get all the facts before opening his mouth.

"Four?" Joey said. "It depends on how well the recording goes. It might only be two or three."

"And when would you be leaving?"

Joey narrowed his eyes at him. He was probably catching on to Gabe's intention, but Gabe kept his face straight for now. "Friday," Joey said slowly.

Gabe glanced at the bus fare on the screen again. Fuck it. He never took time off when he was with Lewis, always too concerned about letting other people down. But he wasn't working with the fire crew this weekend, and the library and shelter wouldn't miss him that badly for a day or two. Everyone else could just find cover for him. He covered for other people enough for heaven's sake.

"I could drive you," he said, turning his eyes hopefully to Joey's. "And we could split the cost of a hotel room."

Joey opened his mouth. Then he closed it again. He frowned at the screen and nibbled his lip.

"Just as friends," Gabe added gently, hoping Joey understood his meaning. He wasn't expecting anything in return from this. They could get a room with two beds and Gabe would behave like a perfect gentleman. "It'll be fun. What do you say?"

"You'd really do that?" Joey asked cautiously. "Just...up and go to Chicago, for me?"

The optimism in his voice made Gabe smile. "Yeah," he said. "It'll be an adventure."

Slowly, a smile spread over Joey's face too. "It will," he agreed.

Gabe clapped his hands together, a thrill of excitement bubbling through him.

"Let's do this."

Seventeen

JOEY

JOEY WAS PRETTY SURE THIS WAS A BAD IDEA. BUT AT THE SAME time, Gabe's offer had helped him out immeasurably. He just had to focus on the fact he was going to get to record with Storm Sailor, and ignore the hunk of a man currently sitting beside him in his old, banged-up car.

That was easier said than done though. Gabe was looking seriously hot in a rumpled hoodie and he had his glasses on for driving. Joey liked the way they framed his face and magnified his brown eyes to make him extra beautiful. Gabe had a soft spot for seventies and eighties rock music apparently, and was currently murmuring along to Bruce Springsteen.

He caught Joey looking over and smiled. Joey felt a rush of embarrassment, but he just looked out of the window as if nothing had happened.

He'd been a bag of nerves in the couple of days between making their plans on Wednesday and driving out on Friday. As much as Gabe had made it clear he didn't expect them to be intimate again on this trip, if they were going to share a room that left the possibility of a second go between the sheets dangling tantalizingly out in front of them.

Joey couldn't deny how the idea made his toes curl. Fuck, he wanted Gabe so badly. But their lives were so different, they had totally different goals and aspirations. And yet a voice kept whispering in the back of his head that they weren't talking about dating here. Maybe they could have a bit more fun before their lives veered off in different directions again.

Joey was also aware that part of his attraction to Gabe was that he'd been the only break from his family in town. Doing the play in New York had kept Joey out of the house and given him the opportunity to work with amazing people. But even though it was just the one night, Gabe had offered him the only respite to actually sleep in somewhere he felt safe. His home had felt like a sanctuary, and now here he was again, taking him away for a few days.

If he wasn't careful, Joey was going to end up with a complex. He needed to make sure his attraction to Gabe wasn't simply because he was turning into something of a white knight to him.

Except, Joey wasn't looking for a boyfriend or any kind of commitment. So would it really hurt to indulge in his little fantasy? He spent his whole life struggling to fend for himself, fighting for every inch. Was it so wrong to admit it felt pretty amazing to be cared for, just for a little while? It wasn't every day a gorgeous guy stuck his neck out for him, and Gabe had done that twice now.

"So, do you know what song it is you'll be singing?" Gabe asked, breaking into his thoughts.

Joey was glad for the question. It was a long drive ahead of them – thirteen hours according to the GPS, not counting gas and food breaks. It would probably be a good idea to spend some of that time in conversation, otherwise Joey was at risk of ogling Gabe too much and giving himself an awkward boner.

"Yeah," he replied. "Raiden sent me a demo. Storm Sailor will obviously put way more production into the real thing, but with Raiden singing over a basic version it was enough so I could learn it at least."

Gabe arched an eyebrow at him. "Why doesn't Raiden just sing it himself?" he asked. "Not to take it away from you, obviously."

Joey smiled at the fumbled amendment. "No sweat. Raiden has a great voice, but the key he's written this in suits my range better." He shrugged. "Plus, he's a decent guy. He knew how much I'd love this."

Gabe smiled even more. "That's great," he said. It was obvious he took pleasure from Joey's happiness. Joey had never met anyone quite so selfless before. It was charming.

"You ever been to Chicago before?" Joey asked.

He shook his head. "I haven't traveled a lot," Gabe admitted. "I never wanted to take time away from work."

Joey couldn't help but feel very honored by that. Gabe clearly felt he was worthy to step away from all his projects for, even if it was just a couple of days. "We'll have to make the most of it then," he said jovially.

He hadn't felt this good in months. He was on his way to an incredible opportunity, one that could turn his fortunes around, and he had a hot guy by his side. Gabe wasn't just hot though, he was kind and sweet and Joey wasn't really sure why he was interested in someone like Joey. Their values were so different. But here they were, so Joey wasn't going to question it too hard.

Time went by at an acceptable pace. Joey never liked traveling, he always got bored and fidgety. But Gabe helped keep him distracted with good conversation, music and snacks. Joey learned more about his elderly parents and heard a few stories from how they were getting on in their Florida retirement. Gabe undoubtedly missed them, but he was full of happiness at their contentment in their golden years.

Joey talked about the band. For the first time since the label dropped them, he didn't feel bitter reminiscing about their best experiences. He laughed as he recounted some of the crazy things they got up to on tour. Gabe appeared genuinely fascinated to hear about how records were made and what went into producing a music video. He was tickled pink as Joey told him how he had to hang upside down in front of a green screen so they could get the footage for the Hush Hush video, and how one time they'd been mobbed in Harrods in London so they'd taken the underground tube to try and escape.

"It only made it worse though," Joey cried as Gabe chuckled. "This little old cockney lady practically groped Reyse up and kept telling us how sexy we all were for 'young'uns.'"

"Man, it must have been some life," Gabe said, shaking his head. "Hopefully this song will be the start of all that again. *Way* more interesting than little old Greenwich."

Joey hummed but didn't respond. Yeah, of course he wanted to be performing again. The craziness just came hand in hand with that. But he didn't actually miss the shenanigans all that much.

For just a second he considered what it would be like to live like Gabe. To have a warm home to come back to, somewhere he felt safe and loved. But Joey couldn't do that. He couldn't settle down in suburbia, he'd suffocate. Still, it was a nice daydream to have, fleetingly. The idea of not continuously worrying what tomorrow might bring did have a certain appeal to it.

"How's your cat?" Joey asked, thinking of the time he spent in Gabe's house. "Did you ever get her out from under the sofa?"

Gabe snorted. "Poor Duchess," he lamented. "She's moved on to the crack between the dishwasher and the cabinet now. I don't even know how she gets in there. It's full of cobwebs, it can't be nice for her." He wrinkled his nose in distress.

Joey felt a pang for him. Gabe had so much concern for everyone around him. Even a mangy cat wasn't too much trouble for Gabe's big heart to worry about.

"I'm sure she'll get more confident soon," Joey said. He had little experience with cats, truth be told. But he wanted to make Gabe feel better. "Just smother her with love, she'll come around."

"Hmm," said Gabe. "That does seem to work with dogs, but I'm not sure about cats."

"You've had dogs before then?" Joey asked. Gabe did seem like the kind of person who needed things to care for. Joey wouldn't trust himself with a houseplant, let alone a pet.

Gabe took a moment to answer, his face pensive. "I had a dog. Max. But my ex took him when he moved out."

"Oh," said Joey.

Immediately, he had several thoughts fly through his brain. The first was how much seeing Gabe's distress hurt him. The second was that the way he spoke of his ex made it sound like a recent breakup. All kinds of questions about the other guy tormented him all at once. Mainly, Joey unfairly wondered how he compared to this ex. Did Gabe miss him? Was Joey just a bit of rebound entertainment?

Joey had to remind himself that he didn't want to be Gabe's boyfriend. So if he was just a rebound, that would be fine. It would probably make things easier in fact.

"I'm sorry," he said.

Gabe shrugged. "The breakup was as amicable as these things can be," he said. Joey noticed he was focusing awfully hard on the road as he spoke though. "I miss Max being there when I get home though. Max is the dog," he added, glancing

Joey's way with a shaky smile. "Not my ex. I have to admit, I don't really miss him."

A very bad and selfish part of Joey jumped for joy at hearing that.

"But you got a new cat, not a dog?" he asked instead.

Gabe nodded. "I didn't want to feel like I was replacing Max," he said. "So I thought an entirely different pet would be safest."

"Sometimes a change is good," Joey murmured.

They drove on for a while after that just listening to the radio and talking about music. Gabe was more into rock and country than Joey's preferred dance and pop, but they both agreed that good melodies were what made a track great, regardless of genre.

They stopped for gas and supplies a few hours after that. However, traffic was bad along one of the interstates, and Joey was starting to think they were going to have to stop for the night somewhere.

It was foolish to think they'd manage almost thirteen hours in one day, but a part of him had really hoped they'd make it to Chicago before they'd have to bunk down for the night. But pushing Gabe to drive for that long was unsafe and unfair.

And it seemed like the car agreed.

"Uh oh," said Gabe after a few more hours had passed. He pressed his hand on the dash and drew it back again.

"What?" asked Joey, confused. He knew nothing about cars himself, but when he mimicked Gabe and touched the plastic of the dashboard, he was pretty certain it shouldn't have been that hot.

"I think the radiator might be overheating," said Gabe, chewing his lip. "It does that sometimes, the water's probably low."

Joey frowned and tried not to be too alarmed. "Is that bad?"

Gabe shook his head. "It's not going to break down anytime soon," he said confidently. "Or, at least it really shouldn't. But the sooner we stop and let it rest, the better."

Joey swallowed, abruptly nervous. Which was stupid, because the whole plan had been to share a room from the start. But he was suddenly facing the prospect right now, and it felt like it had come out of nowhere, not giving him enough time to prepare.

"Should I look for a hotel then?" he asked.

Gabe nodded as Joey pulled his phone from his pocket. "Just whatever's closest," he said.

All right, Joey thought. *Here we go.* Of course, probably nothing would happen. Gabe had said as much a couple of times. They would just find somewhere to rest their heads and let the car cool off for the rest of the drive tomorrow. It was going to be fine.

Joey wasn't sure if he was relieved by this promise to himself, or disappointed.

CHAPTER

Eighteen

GABE

OF COURSE, THE CLOSEST PLACE JOEY COULD FIND WAS A seedy-looking motel that probably charged by the hour and had seen a dead body or two in its time. But there wasn't anything else for miles, and Gabe didn't want to risk pushing the car any further when steam was now creeping out from under the hood. It was a relief to pull into the dark parking lot, at least with regards to the car's wellbeing.

It was times like these, as they walked over to the lit reception, that Gabe became aware of his sexuality. He could more than likely pass for straight in most instances, but coupled with Joey it would make most people guess about them. That might lead them into trouble, if they were unlucky.

But Gabe held his head high as he pushed the glass door and led the way inside. He'd deal with that if it became an issue.

However, fortune was on their side. As they stepped into the light, they were greeted by a young woman who immediately perked up as they approached.

"Hi," she said, putting her phone down. "How can I – oh!"

She blushed and looked between Joey and Gabe. "Oh my god, you're that guy aren't you? From the band? With the *'Oh oh oohh'* song?" She blushed even more. "Sorry, apparently words aren't happening for me this evening."

Joey laughed and held out his hand to her. "I'm Joey," he said warmly, despite how tired he looked from traveling all day. "So nice to meet you."

The young woman giggled as she took his hand. "Joey, that's right. Me and my sister saw you guys a couple of years ago. We had a blast."

"I'm so glad to hear that," Joey told her. It was amazing how Gabe could see him come alive at times like this. He was made to be a star.

"So can I get you guys a room?" she asked, looking between them again, apparently unfazed that they were together. Gabe liked the idea that they might seem like a couple and that she wasn't bothered by it.

They weren't a couple though, he reminded himself before he could get too carried away. "Yes," he replied with a smile. "A double if possible?"

She bit her tongue between her teeth as she scrolled through the computer system. "We've only got kings available for tonight," she said. "I could book you two side by side if you like?"

Joey looked up at him with wide eyes. That would be double the cost, and while Gabe was keen to remain a gentleman, he was also on a budget, and Joey even more so. Silently, Gabe raised an eyebrow, asking if sharing would be okay with Joey.

When he nodded, Gabe was ashamed by the thrill of excitement that flew through him. *Nothing* was going to happen. Just because they'd had one night together didn't mean they wouldn't be able to keep their hands off each other now. Gabe was here to support Joey, to be his friend. If he pushed for anything sexual that would be horribly taking advantage.

But with Joey's nod of consent, that committed them to sharing a bed for the night. Gabe felt strange as he paid the girl with his card and gave her the few details she needed. Like he wasn't quite in his own body.

Silently, the two of them walked back outside to find their room on the second-floor balcony. The air was cold and Gabe hastily unlocked the door with the key and ushered them and their luggage inside.

"Well, it's not bad," said Joey as he flicked on the lights. Gabe had to agree. There weren't any obvious stains anywhere and the room itself didn't smell musky. It was simple, but it did the job.

"You want to watch some TV or something?" Gabe asked, locking the door behind him and resting his carryon case on the floor.

"I'm pretty beat," Joey admitted.

Gabe sighed with relief. "Me too," he said. "That's the longest I've driven in ages."

Awkwardly, they navigated taking turns in the bathroom. Gabe had specifically brought t-shirts with him to sleep in with his boxers, so he didn't feel quite so exposed as he lay in bed waiting for Joey to emerge.

He'd just left a lamp on so he could reach over and turn it off when they were ready to sleep. It meant Joey was illuminated as he stepped back into the room, clutching his toiletries to his chest as he switched off the bathroom light behind him. He was also wearing a t-shirt with his underwear, reassuring Gabe they were on the same page.

Joey scuttled over to his side of the bed and slipped between the covers. Gabe turned off the lamp and plunged them into darkness. "Night," he said, settling on his side, looking away from Joey.

"Night," came the reply. Then, after a few moments: "Thank you for today. I'm glad you're here."

Gabe grinned to himself in the darkness. It was probably a good thing Joey couldn't see how pleased that compliment made him. For Joey to admit he was happy to have his company seemed like a real achievement to Gabe.

"It's my pleasure," he murmured.

Gabe had been so tired during the last hour or so of the drive, he would have sworn he'd have fallen asleep as soon as his head had hit the pillow. But lying there now, he couldn't have felt more awake. His whole body was on alert, hyper-aware of the warmth coming from Joey beside him. He could hear Joey's breathing and felt the covers move when he shifted.

Had he rolled away from Gabe? Was he lying on his back...or maybe even facing him now? Gabe wanted to turn and find out. But he knew if he found himself face to face with Joey he wouldn't be able to resist leaning in for a kiss.

He squeezed his eyes shut and took a long, quiet breath in. He would absolutely not put Joey in that position. He needed a friend in Gabe, someone he could rely on. Not some horny, selfish dickhead on a rebound.

Except, in that moment, Joey moved again, and Gabe felt him press up against his back, his hand slipping over his chest.

"I'm sorry," Joey whispered against his neck. "Tell me to stop, and I'll stop."

Gabe's voice caught in his throat. He took Joey's hand in his own, intertwining their fingers. "What do you want?" he asked, his words barely a rasp.

Joey hesitated for just a second. "For you to hold me," he said.

Before he could question it, Gabe turned, pulling Joey against his chest and wrapping his arms around his slim body. Even through the t-shirt he could feel the heat from his skin. Gabe nuzzled his face against Joey's soft curls, inhaling his scent. God, he was beautiful.

Joey clung to him like a life raft. His top leg looped over Gabe's, connecting them further, and Gabe felt the shaky breath that escaped Joey's lungs as he snuggled closer. Their hardening cocks found each other, touching through the cotton barrier of their underwear. Gabe tried not to rub against him, but when Joey rolled his hips, Gabe moaned and responded in kind.

Joey looked up at him in the dark, seeking his mouth for a kiss. Gabe was in no position to refuse. He accepted Joey's lips hungrily, running his fingers through Joey's thick hair.

He wanted to pull their clothes off, to feel skin on skin again. But there was something deliciously comforting about feeling too hot under the comforter, wrapped in each other's arms. Joey was a little more impatient though, and while the t-shirts might have been too much effort to remove, he was obviously not happy with the boxers.

He reached down and tugged at Gabe's waistband. The demanding little action made Gabe smile, so he hurriedly yanked them off. Seeing as he'd had to briefly separate from Joey's body anyway, he took the opportunity to haul his shirt over his head as well, leaving him entirely naked.

Joey had done the same just as quickly. So when they moved back together, only seconds had passed, but Gabe's heartbeat had rocketed. He pulled Joey's gorgeous, naked body back against his own. This time there was nothing between their two cocks, and now they were hard as steel.

Joey moaned as they rubbed together. Gabe swallowed the noise with a kiss, their lips urgently coming together. Gabe licked into Joey's mouth with his tongue, lapping up the taste of him, not wanting this moment to end.

There was no room for thought, only touch. Gabe hadn't

brought any supplies with him as he'd refused to entertain the notion that something might happen. But that was okay, sometimes full fucking wasn't always the best. Right then, he wanted nothing more than to hold his and Joey's hot cocks together in his hand and thrust until he came. He needed release now, desperately, and he wouldn't have wanted to hang around taking the time to prep for anal.

Joey seemed just as happy to frot as he clung to Gabe and pushed into his hand. "Yes, yes," he whispered.

Gabe placed his hand on the mattress and rolled on top of him. Fuck, Joey's lithe body felt so perfect pinned under his own. He straddled Joey's legs, surrounding him. Keeping him safe. Making him Gabe's.

Joey kissed him with desperation, cupping his hand against Gabe's jaw and rutting his dick wantonly against Gabe's. He was uttering small, throaty squeaks with every thrust, and they were driving Gabe wild.

"Gonna," Gabe groaned, unable to give much more of a warning. Joey nodded against Gabe's cheek, his breathing fast and ragged.

"Yes, Gabe," he cried.

Gabe seized his mouth for a kiss as his orgasm tore through him. Joey went rigid, chasing his own climax as they both shot hot and wet between their bellies.

Several moments later, Gabe gave a last shudder before collapsing as carefully as he could over Joey. He didn't want to crush him, but he didn't want to let go of him yet either, despite the cooling mess between them. Joey held him just as tightly, which Gabe took to be a good sign.

This felt so right. Gabe knew he shouldn't be thinking anything along those lines, but the truth was their chemistry was so natural and explosive. Joey felt like he slotted in with Gabe like he was simply meant to be there.

That was probably just the endorphins from the orgasm

talking. He needed to get a grip on himself, starting with cleaning up so they could be comfy. Sleepily, he managed to put his hand on one of their pairs of boxers and mop up the worst of the cum. Joey immediately came back for a cuddle once Gabe had sorted the practicalities out.

"Sorry," he said again with a nervous laugh.

Gabe kissed his temple and stroked his back with light touches from his fingertips. "Nothing to be sorry for," he said, meaning it. "That was amazing. Again."

He felt Joey smile where his cheek was resting against Gabe's chest. "It was," Joey agreed.

It was pretty remarkable how something simple could feel so incredible. It probably depended on the people involved. Gabe was pretty sure anything with Joey would feel wonderful, because it was him.

Joey shifted though, looking at Gabe in the limited amount of street light filtering through the edge of the curtains.

"I don't..." he began. "I'm not sure..."

Gabe stroked his check. His skin was so soft. "Like I said before, this doesn't have to be anything and I won't ask you for more than you can give. But, I do like you Joey. If you want to try this again while we're away, it can just be a bit of fun. Or it can be a trial to see what might be."

Joey seemed to think that over. Gabe could feel his eyelids drooping, but he didn't pressure Joey for a response. "Okay," he said eventually, tucking his head into Gabe's chest. Gabe wasn't entirely sure what that meant, but he guessed he'd find out in the morning.

For now, he let himself fall asleep, content with the gentle soul he had cradled in his arms.

Nineteen

JOEY

THE LAST TIME JOEY HAD WOKEN UP NEXT TO GABE HAD BEEN with a hard-on too. But this time, Joey didn't feel so terrified of it. In fact, he was warm and content as he stirred into consciousness.

Gabe had been open with him last night. He'd said again that he was keen for something, that he liked Joey a lot. But the details of where they might take their relationship seemed to be in Joey's hands.

It was stupid to think about a 'relationship.' But maybe they could just enjoy their time together on this little trip. That would be safe enough, surely?

Speaking of which, Joey was feeling something he hadn't for a very long time: devilish. They were both still naked and Gabe's lovely big cock was half-hard against Joey's stomach. Gabe looked like he was still asleep, but Joey could fix that soon enough.

He began by kissing along Gabe's throat and the dip next to his collarbones. Gabe hummed and stirred, so he couldn't be too far from surfacing. "Morning," Joey whispered as he continued to kiss down his chest, finding a nipple to suck on.

He'd initially planned on just diving down to his dick and waking him up in style. But Gabe seemed like the kind of guy who would appreciate clear consent. Joey had to admit there was something very lovely in that. He'd always told himself he liked it when bigger guys just did what they pleased with him. But if he was honest, maybe Gabe's tender approach was better?

Gabe hummed again and ran his fingers through Joey's hair. He seemed to have a thing for it, which amused Joey. He'd always hated how cherub-like it made him look, but maybe there was an advantage to curls after all?

"Morning," Gabe mumbled as he gave a little gasp. Joey was teasing the hard nub of his nipple and running his hands over Gabe's glorious abs. "Oh yes, baby," he said.

That was a good enough go-signal for Joey. He kissed down Gabe's belly, licking at his happy trail and nuzzling the coarse hair between his legs. Gabe was trimmed but not overly groomed. Joey preferred it when guys didn't look like perfectly smooth Ken dolls.

Gabe was fully hard by the time Joey slipped his lips over his prick. He was too big to swallow whole, but Joey liked using his hands as well when he gave head anyway. He reveled in mouthing Gabe's succulent tip, stroking the shaft as he worked his tongue and lips.

Gabe was whimpering and gasping. Joey had pushed the comforter down when he'd moved, so Gabe was watching him fuck him with his mouth, his arm thrown over his head. He looked decadent, like he wasn't used to having his cock sucked and wasn't sure he was worthy of it.

Joey wondered what his nameless ex had been like in bed. Joey would bet money on Gabe being a generous lover, and some people might take advantage of that and not give their fair share back. Well, Joey wasn't like that, especially not after all Gabe had done for him.

He may be struggling to say how grateful he was with his words, but he could try and explain the way he felt with his body.

"Joey, I-" Gabe spluttered. Giving him a warning. "Oh my god, so good, gonna come…"

Joey sucked harder, working his tongue to pleasure him as best he could. Gabe convulsed, then Joey was swallowing down his warm, salty cum. He waited until Gabe relaxed and his cock began to soften before easing his mouth off and wiping his face. His jaw ached a little, but he didn't mind. It felt worth it for the goofy grin on Gabe's face.

"Come here," Gabe said, his voice hoarse. He pulled both Joey and the comforter up, snuggling them together. Joey was honestly okay to leave his own erection to wilt, as he was buzzing from giving Gabe his own orgasm. But of course, Gabe was too considerate for that.

He cuddled Joey to his chest and kissed him, tasting his own intimate flavor on Joey's lips. He reached down and wrapped his hand around Joey's cock and began to tug.

"Gentler," Joey blurted out before he could stop himself. But if he could trust anyone to ask for how he really liked to be jerked off, Gabe would be the one.

"Like this?" Gabe asked, immediately changing his technique. Joey had his eyes almost closed and his face pressed up to Gabe's neck, too afraid to look at Gabe while he asked for what he wanted. But he nodded, and Gabe tried again with the altered style.

"*Oh*," Joey groaned. It felt so good it was almost painful, and he tried not to writhe. He wasn't going to last long.

Gabe kissed down his face, along his jaw, encouraging Joey's lips to meet his own again. Joey obeyed. He felt safe, cradled up to Gabe's side, his kisses lavishing affection on him and his fingers gently teasing his throbbing, weeping cock.

"That's it, come for me," Gabe whispered.

Joey didn't need much more encouragement. It only took a few more strokes for his climax to build before he was shooting his load over Gabe's hand and their bellies.

He slumped against Gabe's side, panting. "Fuck," he said with a tentative laugh. Gabe chuckled too.

"Less clean up with a blow job," he commented as he fished up the same pair of boxers they'd also used as a rag last night. Joey snorted.

"Sorry."

Gabe dropped the underwear and pulled his face in for a kiss. "You apologizing after sex worries me slightly," he said, raising an eyebrow.

Joey gave him a sheepish smile. "Um…sorry?" he said. But his smile broadened, showing Gabe he was messing with him. Sort of. "I guess it's been a long time since I slept with anybody more than once."

"How long?" Gabe asked, brushing his hair back. Joey's initial reaction was not to respond, that it wasn't any of Gabe's business. But he realized he didn't mind discussing his past with Gabe. He trusted he wouldn't judge.

"Um, there was a dancer on tour a couple of years ago," Joey admitted. He was another twinky sort of guy. They'd had fun, but it had always only been drunken fucking, some-thing to entertain them both rather than anything emotional. The guy had been pretty, but dull as hell.

Then there was Derrick.

"There was this producer we worked with, on the first record." Joey didn't want to look at Gabe, so he focused on his fingers running over the chest hair that ran over his pecs and down his sternum.

"A producer?" Gabe repeated. Joey could hear the warning note in his voice already, so he continued before he chickened out.

"Yeah, you know the type. Or maybe you don't. Married, to a woman, kids. But I was young and star struck and he did kind of look after me. I mean, he didn't treat me badly. I just think, well, there was quite an age gap, and I was pretty clueless."

Gabe didn't say anything. He didn't berate Joey for being a fucking idiot. He wasn't disgusted that he'd engaged in an affair with a married man. He didn't even pity him. He just hugged him tighter and kissed his temple slowly.

"I'm sorry, I shouldn't have asked."

Joey shook his head and mustered the courage to look at him. "It's fine. It's not something I'm proud of, and yeah, maybe there are issues there I should probably deal with at some point. But it actually feels good to tell someone."

"Did no one else know?" Gabe asked. He was very gently running his fingers over Joey's cheek and neck. It was ticklish but not provocative. No one had touched Joey like that before.

He shook his head. "No, he told me it had to be a secret." He'd not even confided in Blake, which still made him feel terrible. He and Blake told each other everything.

Gabe mumbled something like 'mother fucker' and pulled Joey in for a hug so tight he risked leaving bruises on his skin. Joey loved it though. It felt like a huge relief to simply have someone agree that that had been a crappy thing to experience as a teenager, all alone.

"My ex's name is Lewis," said Gabe, without prompting. "We just drifted apart, but we were together for five years. He moved to New York City about six weeks ago with our dog and he's a lawyer."

He let Joey go enough so they could look at each other. "Okay," said Joey. He'd be lying if he hadn't secretly hoped that this Lewis was a cheating asshole, but that would have meant Gabe's heart would have been properly broken. So it was good if it was an okay breakup. "And it's definitely over?"

Gabe's face dropped in concern. "Oh, babe, yes. One hundred percent over."

"Um, good," said Joey. He played with the edge of the comforter. "Because, um, I like you. And I thought, maybe, we could try and see what happens if, uh, we keep seeing each other."

He could feel his cheeks burning, but when he peeked up, Gabe's expression was pure joy. "Like dating?" he asked.

Joey shrugged. "I mean, I'm broke, and my schedule is wildly unpredictable. You spend all your time rescuing kittens or whatever, but-"

Gabe interrupted him with a kiss. "Shut up," he said with a grin. "We can just try, take it one day at a time. And not try with anyone else. Sound doable?"

It sounded kind of terrifying. But at the same time, sort of wonderful. "Yeah," he agreed. "I mean, let's get through Chicago, then see where that takes us."

Gabe's eyes flitted over his face as he carded his fingers through Joey's hair. "Yeah," he said, leaning down for another kiss. "Let's do that."

Twenty

GABE

GABE HAD NEVER BEEN TO A RECORDING STUDIO BEFORE. HE guessed, in retrospect, he'd seen them in music videos over the years. The kind where they showed footage of the artist singing into a mic with big headphones over their ears. But when he and Joey walked into the big, glass-fronted building later that day, it felt more like they were entering a fancy hotel.

"Wow," said Gabe, looking up and around as they approached the gleaming desk. Joey grinned back over his shoulder at him.

"Good afternoon," said the pretty girl at the desk. "How may I help you today?"

Joey looked a little flustered as he cleared his throat. "Um, yes, Joey Sullivan. I'm here to see Raiden Jones and, uh, Storm Sailor." He practically whispered the producer's name, like he was afraid of being caught out.

But the receptionist smiled. "Of course. Please take a seat and we'll be with you in just a moment, Mr. Sullivan."

Joey gave Gabe a little shrug and they both wheeled their overnight bags to sit on the sofa as instructed. Joey's knee was bouncing and he kept glancing anxiously around. He had seemed fine on the rest of their drive this morning. Great actually. Gabe couldn't have been more thrilled with their conversation after spectacularly failing to not have sex, twice. But if they both felt the attraction, there was only so much he wanted to fight it.

Yes, it was soon after Lewis. But Gabe and Lewis were over for good, of that he had no doubt. Gabe had had a fair amount of time now to consider how he felt about Joey, and although he still remained cautious, he wanted to try and trust his heart again. Joey could be prickly, and he was going through a lot right now. But he was also sweet and fun and ambitious and cute in that mouth-wateringly sexy way Gabe couldn't resist.

If they made each other happy, they could work out the rest as they went along.

He placed his hand on Joey's knee, stopping it from bouncing. "Hey," he said with a smile. Joey looked at him. "This is going to be fantastic. You gotta just enjoy it, okay?"

The tension eased a little from Joey's shoulders. "Yeah, you're right," he said. He took Gabe's hand and gave it a quick squeeze. "I really am happy you're here with me."

Tingly warmth filled Gabe's insides. "Thank you for letting me tag along."

"Joey?" a voice called from across the lobby.

Joey leaped to his feet, his head snapping around. "Rai!" he yelled, breaking into a run.

A tall guy with broad shoulders and a slim waist laughed and threw his arms open to intercept Joey as he catapulted himself into him. This must be Raiden Jones, also formally of Below Zero. Gabe thought he had some Asian heritage in him with his dark, almond-shaped eyes and black hair that swept across his forehead and rested just above his shoulders.

From the satiny t-shirt he wore Gabe could see an impressive body despite his willowy figure. There was no doubt this guy worked out and probably looked gorgeous naked. But Gabe just smiled to himself. Those thoughts flitted through his mind without any kind of physical reaction. He could acknowledge Raiden was hot, but Gabe only had eyes for the excitable Joey as he hugged his friend tightly.

Gabe picked up both their bags and wandered over. He didn't want to intrude on the moment, but Joey looked back for him as soon as he let Raiden go. "Hey, Gabe," he said a little breathlessly. "This is Raiden. Raiden, this is my friend Gabe. He gave me a lift."

Raiden stuck his hand out and gave Gabe's a shake. "Nice to meet you," he said with a slight Southern drawl. His movements were careful and smooth, reminding Gabe of a cat. Not his cat, who hissed and hid from everyone. But a regular cat who wasn't scared of people.

"Nice to meet you too," Gabe said.

Raiden clapped his hands together, looking from Gabe to Joey, a smile spreading across his face. "So are you ready to do this?"

"Hell yeah," said Joey.

Gabe had worried that they should check into their little hotel first, but Joey had wanted to get to work right away. They had only driven for a few hours that morning, but still Gabe worried that Joey would be tired.

However, Raiden had texted saying the track was progressing well and they wanted to get the vocals down as soon as possible. Joey pointed out that if they messed around trying to find their hotel then trekked it into the city, that would only give them a couple of hours to work with. He explained that if they were lucky, they could get everything they needed from him today.

Gabe understood that time was money, and when Joey

had listed several of the songs that Storm Sailor had been responsible for producing over the past few years, Gabe realized they weren't fucking around in the minor leagues here. But at the same time, after the progress they'd made at the motel last night and that morning, Gabe really didn't want to rush this trip.

He knew he should be thinking that if they could travel early tomorrow morning, even if they had to stop again before reaching Connecticut, he could be back at work by Monday afternoon and not take so much of his annual leave. But on the other hand, he wanted to protect these first few days of him and Joey officially trying to be together. Like a fragile flower desperately doing its best to bloom.

Gabe followed on after Joey, who had taken his own suitcase back, and Raiden who strode confidently down the hall lined with frame after frame of gold records. It looked like a *lot* of famous artists had walked these halls before them.

As they reached a door labeled 'Studio One,' Raiden looked over his shoulder and winked at Joey. Then, without a word, he pushed into the room.

Gabe hung back a second, feeling a bit like an impostor. This was Joey's world, not his. He was just here to support him. But Joey looked back to make sure Gabe was there and waved him on over the threshold into the recording studio.

The room was atmospherically lit. Not dark, but kind of moody. There was a huge mixing desk in front of a glass window that stretched the length of the room. Beyond that was a brightly lit room with an enormous drum kit set up, several empty guitar stands, keyboards of varying sizes and a grand piano. In the corner was another small booth that, at a glance, looked to be padded with thick foam. A wide microphone hung down on wire from the ceiling.

A man in a chair by the desk spun around to face them. He might have been in his late thirties or early forties, but it was hard to tell from the tinted sunglasses he wore. He had long hair down his back, more of a beard than Gabe, and his ears were pierced several times. He was fit looking for his age.

"Joey Sullivan," he said in a throaty voice with only a hint of a Swedish accent. He offered out a large hand for Joey to shake. "Welcome."

"Thank you for having me here," said Joey a little breathlessly. "It's an honor."

The guy, who Gabe assumed had to be Storm Sailor, waved him off. "No, not at all. Raiden here has written you a great track. He saved me the hassle of negotiating with several different artists like I usually have to. Your agent, Martha, is lovely by the way."

"She's pretty awesome," Joey agreed with a nod.

He looked around like he wished he had more eyes, trying to take it all in. Like a kid in a candy store. Gabe's heart swelled a little with pride.

"So, are you ready to jump in or do you need a minute?" the producer asked.

Joey shook his head. "Ready whenever you are," he said, grabbing a bottle of water from his bag. "I'd like to do some warmups in the booth, if that's all right?"

"Sure," said Storm Sailor. "I'll keep the feed muted until you're ready, then just give us a wave."

Joey glanced nervously at Gabe, who wished he could give him a kiss or at the very least a hug for support. But he wasn't sure they were there yet and he didn't want to overstep his boundaries. So instead he just smiled and nodded.

It was amazing. As Gabe settled in one of the comfy spinning chairs he watched as Joey took himself through the two doors and opened his mouth, presumably to warm up his vocal chords. But Gabe couldn't hear a thing.

"So where are you boys staying?" Storm Sailor asked as he

fiddled with a number of sliders on the desk. Gabe realized he was the one being addressed when Raiden quirked an eyebrow at him.

"Oh, um, just this little place downtown," he said dismissively. "It was whatever we could find at the cheapest rate last minute."

He was suddenly gripped with the fear that maybe he should have inferred they had two separate rooms. But he didn't get the chance.

Storm Sailor frowned, already dialing a contact on his cell phone. "Well, that won't do. Sorry, man. I thought my people had that fixed for you." Gabe wasn't sure what he meant, but then the call connected. "Yeah, Oscar? Get Joey Sullivan a room at the Four Seasons for tonight. A double okay?" He looked at Gabe, who took a second to nod. "Yeah, a double. Make sure there's the usual welcoming pack too. We fucked up." He looked at Gabe again. "You boys need upgraded flights home too?"

Gabe was stunned. He'd met this man about three minutes ago. "Uh, no, we drove. But thank you."

Storm Sailor nodded and rubbed his beard. "Okay, we'll get you gas money. You okay with that, Oscar? Thanks." He closed the call and shook his head. "That's what happens when you book these things in a rush. We dropped the ball. I hope you don't mind."

"Oh, of course not," said Gabe. "That's incredibly kind of you. Thank you, Joey will be thrilled."

Storm Sailor nodded like it was no big deal, then slipped some headphones on and started talking to Joey about some notes he had regarding the song. Or something. Gabe wasn't really sure.

Joey acted like it was crazy the way Gabe spent his time volunteering and helping others. Yet, this guy had just thrown several hundred dollars at them without even pausing. Gabe was so touched, he couldn't wait to share the news with Joey. Hopefully, this might change his mind a little bit. He could understand someone who'd grown up the way Joey had feeling like they always had to rely on themselves, wary of trusting others. But this made Gabe feel like he'd been right all along.

He realized Raiden was looking at him. Raiden had his own laptop on his knees, his elbow propped up on the armrest as he rubbed his chin. Gabe smiled awkwardly at him.

"Hot damn," Raiden said. "You and Joey are together, aren't you?"

Gabe ran cold. Had he just put his foot in it? Raiden seemed only curious though, his eyes not leaving Gabe's despite the fact he was getting flustered. The seat he was in suddenly felt too small and he fidgeted.

"Uh, not officially," Gabe said, anxious he was doing the right thing. "It's new."

"Yeah, it sure is," said Raiden. "No offense, but usually he has real shitty taste in guys. You seem delightful."

Gabe rubbed the back of his neck. That seemed an odd word to use to describe another guy, but Raiden's tone didn't suggest sarcasm. His stare was a bit intense though.

"So, you're cool with him being, uh…" Gabe asked.

Raiden frowned then leaned back in his seat. "Oh! Gay?" He scoffed. "Knew from the second I met him. You know he's been out for years, right?"

Gabe fiddled with the cuff of his hoodie. He wished he'd worn something a bit more presentable, but he'd assumed he'd get time to change at the hotel. He remembered he should probably cancel the reservation at some point.

"Yeah. I guess this is a bit strange for me. We're pretty different."

Raiden rolled his eyes then clicked and typed a few things

on his computer. "My mom's a botany professor, my dad and his entire family are in the military. She always says it's opposites that attract."

"Oh," said Gabe nodding. He was starting to like Raiden, he thought. He was a little hard to read, but he seemed sincere in what he said. "Well, thanks. Like I said it's very new. But I like him."

Raiden nodded, narrowing his dark eyes. "Just be careful," he said.

"I don't want to hurt Joey," said Gabe quickly. "I think he's great."

Raiden considered him for a moment. "Not what I meant," he said. "*You* be careful. Joey…he doesn't always know what's good for him. Sometimes he'd rather be a fucking ass and do it all alone than let someone else in."

Gabe glanced uncomfortably at Joey singing in the booth. Storm Sailor had his headphones on still and was nodding along to the beat.

"I thought you and Joey were friends," he said slowly.

Raiden's eyebrows shot up. "Oh hell yeah, of course. Love him like a brother."

"Then why would you say that about him?" Gabe asked, hurt on his behalf. Joey would hate to know his friend was saying unkind things.

But Raiden closed his laptop and leaned on his knees, getting closer to Gabe. "Because I like you. And sometimes my little buddy in there needs saving from himself. You notice it's not TJ or Blake recording this track?"

"Joey said it was in his range," Gabe said quickly.

Raiden nodded. "Because I wrote it specifically for him. Because hell would freeze over before he took money from me or Blake. Fuck, Reyse could walk through those doors with a check for ten grand and that boy wouldn't take it. He has to earn his way. His dignity's the most important thing to him. You remember that, and let him do things for himself, you might just stand a chance."

Gabe looked over at Joey. He was taking a break and swigging some water. He waved happily when he caught Gabe's eye.

"I want to stand a chance," Gabe said, returning the wave.

Raiden slapped his knee, the sudden contact making Gabe startle then laugh. "If anyone does, buddy, I think maybe it's you. Good luck."

Gabe bit his lip. Storm Sailor was ready to begin recording, so he unmuted the channel and made communications two-way. Gabe didn't get another opportunity to talk to Raiden again as he and the producer began piecing the track together.

If one of Joey's closest friends reckoned he was in with a shot and had essentially given his blessings, Gabe wanted to go for this. No more doubts. It didn't matter if it was fast moving on from Lewis if it was right.

He just had to make sure this was really what Joey wanted too, and protect his own heart from getting broken again.

Twenty~One

JOEY

SEVERAL HOURS LATER, JOEY AND GABE FOUND THEMSELVES standing in one of the elevators at the Chicago Four Seasons, tiredly waiting for their floor to arrive. Joey may have been exhausted, but he was also buzzing with the adrenaline of the afternoon.

The recording session couldn't have gone better. Joey wasn't used to singing a whole song by himself, but it seemed like Storm Sailor had been impressed with his work. They'd done a couple takes of the whole thing, then three or four of each verse, chorus and the interlude. Some lines had been niggly and Joey had performed them individually, but Storm Sailor had insisted that he'd knocked it out of the park.

Joey had been anxious, wanting to do a few more takes just for safety. But Raiden had given him That Look and he knew he was just fussing over nothing.

The plan now was to finish producing all the effects tomorrow, when the guys would also work with some backing vocalists to enrich the sound. But as for Joey, he was done until they finalized the video shoot in a few weeks' time.

Which left him and Gabe to enjoy the rest of their night. He'd been blown away when he'd heard that their hotel had been upgraded to one of the nicest places in town. When he'd been in the band they'd got stuff like this all the time, so when Raiden didn't say it was being offered, he assumed he just had to make his own way. This was an excellent surprise, to say the least.

Gabe had hinted numerous times how nice it was and so generous of Storm Sailor and his people. He was so naive, bless him. This was just what the industry did. When you were on top, you had to enjoy it while it lasted. Because at any moment it could all be taken away from you.

But right now, yeah, Joey was thrilled that they had been given this gift. Especially after he'd taken the plunge that morning and promised to try at whatever this was between him and Gabe. He honestly didn't know what they could have in terms of a relationship, let alone anything like a future together. All he knew was that he really liked spending time with him, and he just wanted more.

It felt like taking that leap of faith had been rewarded. He'd expected to spend the night at an okay hotel, at least one better than the motel they'd stopped off at the previous night. But nothing fancy, and he certainly hadn't expected to go out for dinner or anything. That would have been throwing money away.

No, he'd had his hopes set on a Chinese takeout and maybe some more sex. He'd not missed the fact that Gabe had stepped into a drug store on their way to the hotel after the recording session was done.

The universe had done him a kindness though. They walked along the plush carpet on the thirty-fifth floor until they found their room, unlocking the door with a swipe of a key card. Gabe gasped as he led the way inside.

A beautiful king-sized bed covered with crisp white linen

greeted them. Windows on two of the four walls gave them a spectacular nighttime view of the Magnificent Mile and Lake Michigan. A large TV was mounted on the wall as well as framed paintings of impressionist flowers. But what caught Joey's attention was the sofa, and the countertop above the mini fridge and safe. Or, more specifically, what was on their surfaces.

There were several vases of colorful flower arrangements that left the room smelling sweetly. Gift baskets of food were wrapped in crinkly cellophane, containing fruit and cookies and teas and bottles of wine. A bottle of Champagne and two glasses were chilling in an ice bucket. There were also two identical-looking piles on the bed. At the bottom were impossibly soft robes and fat, fluffy slippers. Next, a brand-new tablet with wireless, noise-cancelling headphones, a gift card to a very fancy-looking restaurant called Alinea, another for the Skydeck at Sears Tower and, finally, a pair of gorgeous silver cufflinks from a store called Shane Co. A quick glance in the large bathroom to his left showed Joey another gift basket, this one filled with high-end toiletries.

"Wow," said Gabe, still clutching his case. "Oh my – I mean – fucking *wow*."

"Yeah," Joey agreed with a chuckle.

He knew it was hollow though as he crawled onto the ginormous bed, careful not to disturb any of their presents as he curled into a ball. Fuck. Two nights ago he'd been afraid of his drunk father storming down the stairs and shaking him awake on his pitiful little camp bed and demanding the rent he said he owed him. Tonight, he was in one of the best hotels Chicago had to offer, surrounded by expensive gifts with several large locks on the door to keep the world away.

This. This is why he never wanted to be poor again. He never wanted to be at other people's mercy. Because money gave you security, and security meant you didn't have to worry about where your next meal was coming from or if your shoes would get you through the winter or if you got sick what your health insurance would cover.

It was okay. If he just kept working, he could get a little slice of happiness, he was sure. Not luxury like this every day, but something slightly better than the miserable life he was living now.

"Hey?"

Gabe's hand slid over his shoulder and the bed dipped as he sat down behind Joey's back. He didn't realize he had balled his fist around the comforter and there were tears in his eyes.

"Sorry," Joey said, trying to laugh. "It's just been a long day. A long few months."

Gabe swung around and spooned himself against Joey, wrapping his arms around him and cuddling him close. "How about," he began, kissing the sweet spot just under Joey's earlobe. "We...run a bath, with bubbles. Have some strawberries and Champagne, order room service, and then snuggle in bed with a movie?"

Joey squeezed his eyes shut in an attempt to stop the tears. He wasn't entirely sure why he was so upset all of a sudden. He should be happy he had all these incredible things around him tonight, like a normal person.

"That sounds amazing," he said. He tried to wipe his eyes without Gabe catching on. He either got away with it, or Gabe pretended not to notice.

They followed Gabe's plan to the letter. The bathtub was humungous, so they were both able to fit in. Although they'd each had a lukewarm shower at the motel that morning, it felt like they were washing off several days' worth of travel as they slipped under the scorching hot water and suds.

Joey had it in mind they'd get up to some naughtiness. After his mini freak-out he was ready to shake it off with another orgasm. He'd almost forgotten how addictive they were from other people instead of his own hand.

Gabe sat at the back of the tub with Joey sitting in between his legs, facing away. But instead of the expected groping, Gabe proceeded to wash Joey's body with a loofah and some divine smelling bath cream. He followed it up with a shoulder massage that had Joey moaning sinfully.

By the time they got out of the tub he was all floppy and sleepy, and his fingers and toes looked like prunes. Gabe soon had him bundled up in his robe before depositing him on the bed with the promised Champagne and bowl of fresh strawberries. They made quite the domestic scene as they huddled over a takeout menu Gabe found on his phone for a good local Chinese, and soon they had a sizable amount of food on its way.

Joey let Gabe pick a movie; he didn't care so long as there was the noise of the TV. When they found an old Jaws rerun, they declared it a win and nestled down amidst the dozen or so pillows scattered over the bed.

Joey felt like he was in heaven. But he also felt a bit ashamed of his outburst earlier. What right did he have to be sad when he'd had one of the best days of his life? What was wrong with his brain?

Luckily, their food arrived before he could get too melancholy again. And quite frankly, it was very hard to feel sorry for yourself when you had Kung Pao chicken and cold Champagne to wash it down with.

Joey looked over at Gabe as they ate. His cheeks were slightly flushed and his hair a little mussed from the bath still. He'd used some of the hair oil from the gift basket on his neat beard so it was soft and shiny and smelled of roses. His eyes were glued to the screen as Jaws attacked the small town once again. He didn't know how to use chopsticks, so when the shark thrust out of the water, he froze with a plastic fork of chow mein halfway between the container and his mouth.

How could he be so hot yet so adorable at the same time?

Gabe flicked his eyes over and smirked. "Do I have plum sauce on my face?" he asked.

"Yes," Joey lied, as it was a good excuse to lean over and kiss his cheek.

They were living in a fantasy, but for one night it could all be real. For one night, Joey could forget the rest of the world and pretend that the two of them could make this work. That they could find a way to fit their lives together.

Slowly, they made their way through the boxes of food until Joey felt a bit sick, but in the best way. Jaws finished and some terrible B-movie from the seventies started that Joey had never heard of, but that was okay. He wasn't exactly paying attention to the TV anymore.

He plucked Gabe's almost-empty glass from his fingers and placed it on the nightstand by his own flute. They'd already discarded the takeout boxes, so there was nothing to stop Joey from slipping his leg over Gabe's and straddling his crotch. Gabe looked up at him, amused, as he rested his hands on Joey's hips.

"Hello," he said.

"Hi," said Joey impishly as he leaned down for a kiss.

Gabe tasted of food and wine and his own spicy musk. Truth be told, Joey had preferred him yesterday when he'd been more naturally sweaty after a day traveling. But he could soon get this pristine Gabe all hot and bothered again, he was sure.

Gabe's big fingers were surprisingly nimble as they undid the tie holding Joey's robe together. His cock was already coming to life and stretching to the ceiling as Gabe parted the fluffy cotton. Joey copied him, unfastening the other robe, eager to get to his chiseled body once again.

"What do you want?" he asked Gabe between kisses.

"You," said Gabe simply. He ran his hands up Joey's body and pushed the robe off his shoulders, leaving him naked.

"*How* do you want me?"

Gabe shuddered. "Fucking hell, like this," he said. "Ride me, you gorgeous thing you."

Joey moaned and squeezed Gabe's big shoulders. "You got supplies, didn't you?" he asked. If he hadn't, Joey was prepared to call the front desk and ask them for what they needed, god damn it.

Thankfully, Gabe nodded. "My bag, front pocket," he said. Although he was kissing Joey passionately and gripping onto the back of his head, so it made it a little difficult for him to move. Eventually, his need grew too much, and Joey pulled free.

"I'll be right back," he promised with a grin.

He could feel Gabe's eyes on him as he hurriedly fetched the condoms and lube from the pouch he'd indicated. When he returned, Gabe wrapped his arms around his back as Joey straddled his hips again, their cocks bumping together. "I love your body art," he said, kissing a trail up Joey's neck. "One day I'm going to ask you what every single tattoo means, and kiss them all."

It was Joey's turn to shudder. "They're mostly just nonsense," he admitted. Some days he couldn't stand to think of the crap he'd permanently put all over his damn body. Images that didn't mean anything no matter what Gabe thought.

But Gabe shook his head and smiled. "They're beautiful. You're beautiful."

Joey huffed, embarrassed. "No, I'm not," he mumbled. "I'm

like a reverse ugly duckling. Kind of cute as a kid, now just squishy looking."

Gabe stopped his ministrations and cupped Joey's face with both his wide palms. "You don't really believe that, do you?"

Joey shrugged and tried to look away. But Gabe put just enough pressure on his face with his hands to make it difficult. He could have, if he'd really wanted to. But Gabe didn't want him to. So he didn't.

"Yeah," he admitted instead. He knew that's why he was struggling for work now. If he was as adorable as he'd been at fifteen, he'd be raking it in.

Gabe scanned his face with troubled eyes. "I think you're so beautiful I can't bear it," he said. "I spotted you that first day, outside Maggie's bakery, and I couldn't stop thinking about you since." Joey bit his lip, feeling his cheeks burning. "I…I want you to say you're beautiful. For me."

Joey looked at him skeptically. "Even though I don't believe it?"

Gabe rubbed one of his thumbs over Joey's cheekbone. "You might start to?"

Joey huffed again. This was ridiculous. He knew he'd been losing his looks when Derrick had dumped him. Some people suited their puppy fat, and then just didn't make all that attractive adults. But Gabe was looking at him hopefully, and Joey was starting to realize he didn't want to refuse Gabe anything.

He took a slow, deep breath. "I'm…beautiful," he said, feeling like a complete dick.

But Gabe immediately leaned upwards and met his mouth for a searing kiss. "So beautiful, baby."

Joey had to admit there was something warm lodged in his chest. Maybe he didn't have to believe it. Just knowing Gabe believed it might just be enough.

"Can we please have sex now?" he grumbled. Luckily, that made Gabe laugh.

"Yes, you little brat, we can have sex." There was no rancor to his words in the slightest though. Joey excitedly reached for the condoms, pulling one out for Gabe and discarding the rest of the box. Then he drizzled lube on his fingers and reached around to stretch himself.

When Gabe had suited up, he ran his hands over Joey's body and kissed his lips, his throat, his clavicles. Joey moaned, forcing another finger in. He didn't have time to hang around, he needed Gabe inside him, now.

"Take your time," Gabe urged. "It's hot as fuck watching you do that."

Joey snorted. "Pervert," he said, but only because he couldn't take the way Gabe was looking at him so adoringly. "That'll do. I want you now, please."

Gabe kissed him, hard, before shimmying down the bed a little so Joey could angle himself better. His weight helped as he started to push down, but he really should have stretched a little longer. He was just going to have to let gravity do the work now.

Both he and Gabe gasped as he eased Gabe's thick cock past his threshold. "Oh, oh, oh," Joey whimpered. It burned, but he knew it was going to feel so good if he could just get past this moment.

"Fuck," Gabe whispered. "Oh fuck, babe, you feel so good. Just take your time – *ah.*"

Joey nodded, doing his best. He didn't want to hurt himself, but then something relaxed or gave way, and he slid down all the way making both him and Gabe moan. "Okay," Joey said, catching his breath. "Okay, that's good."

"That's amazing, oh fuck, let me know when you can move, please."

Joey looked down at him while he let the burn fade. His

stunning body was covered in a sheen of sweat, just like Joey had wanted. "This," he said sluggishly, tapping Gabe's firm pecs. "You shouldn't cover all this…with cardigans."

Gabe laughed and caught his hand in his own then kissed his fingertips. "You love my librarian cardigans," he said.

Joey bit his lip. "I think I do."

He tried rolling his hips and Gabe's tip stroked his prostate, making him cry out. There was no more talking after that. Just a steady build of gasps and snatched utterances as Joey picked up the pace, riding Gabe's hard cock.

He had both his hands gripping firmly onto Gabe's shoulders. Gabe was steadying him with one hand on his hip, and the other loosely wrapped around his bobbing cock. He remembered what Joey had said about not liking it too rough. That, even more than all the physical sensations he was experiencing, tore a sob from his chest.

"It's all right," Gabe rasped. He moved his hand from Joey's hip to his face and pulled him down for a kiss. "I've got you, baby. Just stay with me."

Joey nodded, finding a smile for him. "Okay," he said, getting his rhythm back.

Christ almighty did Gabe feel incredible inside him. Joey could feel his climax building, ebbing like waves over his too-hot skin. He was going to shatter into a thousand pieces.

"Getting close," he managed to stutter.

"Me too," Gabe said. He nodded encouragingly. "Keep going, just like that. So good, holy fuck."

Joey dropped his head, bearing down and riding Gabe with everything he had. The bed was shaking. Joey really hoped this fancy-ass hotel had thick walls. "Yes, yes, yes," he cried.

He wasn't sure who started coming first, but it seemed like suddenly they were both arching and convulsing as their orgasms took hold. Joey gnashed his teeth as he spilled himself over Gabe's chest. This was becoming his new habit, he thought absently.

That was before all energy left his body and he slumped on top of his lover. Gabe caught him in his arms and stroked his back. "Told you I had you," he said sleepily.

Joey laughed. He was starting to believe it.

SURPRISINGLY, THEY MANAGED TO FIT EVERYTHING IN THE BACK and trunk of Gabe's car. It had looked completely out of place sitting on the curb outside such a prestigious hotel. But the banged-up car hadn't been towed and the doormen had even managed not to look perturbed at its presence.

Joey hadn't wanted to leave before he'd heard from Raiden to assure him that they were definitely done with his part of the recording. "It'd be a pain to have to turn around and come back again," Joey joked. "Let alone expensive."

Gabe got the feeling though he didn't want to really leave his popstar bubble again. That he wanted to cling to this life until it was torn away from him again.

That made Gabe a little melancholy. To think that Joey was so reluctant to head back to Greenwich. But it wasn't entirely unexpected, especially after last night. Fucking hell; Gabe had never seen such luxury in all his twenty-seven years.

Joey had reacted strangely to it though. Gabe couldn't quite work out what had brought on his moment of sadness. Mostly, Gabe had been concerned with pulling him back out of it again, and he'd achieved that with great success, or so he'd like to think.

More than likely, there was always going to be a gulf between them. Joey was pulled by the validation he obviously got from performing. At least, Gabe hoped that was just it, rather than the celebrity status that came with it. He couldn't be sure though. There was such a gaping hole in Joey's heart that love from his family should have filled. Joey didn't seem so shallow that he'd crave adulation from strangers like that. But how well did Gabe really know him?

Gabe would just have to hope that it was the love of the craft that drove Joey. Judging from his exuberance in the recording booth yesterday, it wouldn't be too hard to imagine that was the case.

Even so, there wasn't much in the way of stardom to be had back in Greenwich, which probably explained Joey's quietness on the drive home. Gabe wasn't exactly feeling chatty himself, if he was honest. He'd also been hoping to extend their stay in the city, even if it was just at a regular hotel. That way they could avoid too many tricky questions about their future, for now anyway.

After several hours, Gabe asked Joey to look up somewhere for them to stay the night.

"Is the car overheating again?" Joey asked in alarm, reaching out to touch the dash.

Gabe smiled over at him. "No," he said truthfully. He'd topped up the coolant before they'd left the motel Saturday morning, and the car had been running fine since. "It's just we could push on, and maybe get home by the early hours. Or…"

He glanced at Joey. He was offering another night, just the two of them. Safe away from Joey's horrible family.

Joey's eyes sparkled, a small smile tugging at his lips. "I'll find us something reasonable."

Of course, Gabe could offer Joey to stay the night at his. A part of him ached to ask him to move in, even if it was just while he looked for a place in New York. But instinct told him not to. That that would be too much too fast for Joey.

Instead, he could offer one more night away from reality. It was the best he could do.

———

It was past midday when Gabe strode into the library on Monday. Mitch had given him the whole day off, but once Gabe had dropped Joey back at his family's place, he hadn't felt like being alone.

Joey had so obviously not wanted to go in, Gabe had cracked and asked Joey round to his home, just for the afternoon. But Joey had been determined, leaving the car after a quick kiss goodbye.

He'd also insisted Gabe take most of their gifts from Storm Sailor at the hotel. He'd joked that he had nowhere to put them, but Gabe had a suspicion that he was more worried about his dad stealing or wrecking them. Gabe agreed to take pretty much everything, on the understanding he was just holding Joey's share until he wanted it back.

After he had unpacked and located his skittish cat (under a blanket in the laundry basket) he hadn't fancied staying alone in his house with his thoughts. He missed Joey already, which was stupid, but he couldn't help it. They had left it that they'd text, but no firm details of meeting up again.

If Gabe didn't drop into work, he would just sit on his couch and get in a funk. This way, he could join in with the parent-toddler group and be distracted by hyperactive two-year-olds for an hour.

"Hey, Mitch," he said. He approached the desk with a wave. "Thanks for feeding Duchess while I was away. If you saw more than her tail disappearing, I'll be jealous though." He chuckled at his own little joke, but then he saw Mitch's grim expression and his mirth dispelled.

"Oh, hey, Gabe," Mitch said heavily. "I thought you weren't in until tomorrow."

Gabe stopped in front of the desk, resting his hands on it. "You know me," he said cautiously. "Like to keep busy. Is everything okay?"

Mitch clenched his jaw. "Why don't you step into my office for a moment."

Dread pooled in Gabe's stomach. What the hell had happened? Immediately, he thought of all the dreadful things that could have occurred in the few days he'd been absent. Jesus, had something happened to Mitch's wife, Mary-Lou? Or someone else in his family?

Worry was already eating him up as he sat down in Mitch's pristine office. Tidiness was ingrained in his boss after all his years in the Navy, and the small but immaculate space was a prime example of that. Gabe perched on the edge of the second chair, as he was a bit too large to sit all the way back.

He looked expectantly at Mitch, praying the news wasn't too bad.

"Do you remember Debbie Slater?" Mitch asked.

Gabe blinked. That was the last thing he'd expected him to say. "Pompeii's mom?" he said. "The one that..." Oh. Oh no.

"Made the complaint against you," Mitch growled. "Because she's a bigoted..." He stopped himself short. "Yeah, her. Well, turns out her husband works on the town council. Some little pencil pusher, I'm sure. But one that yaps loudly enough to get the attention of some important people."

Gabe ran cold. "Mitch," he said slowly. "What's going on?"

Mitch looked down as he rubbed his thumb along the

spiral binding of one of his notebooks. "There's been a formal complaint brought up against you with the council. They said you weren't fit to be around kids. That…that you'd been behaving inappropriately."

"What the hell does that mean?" Gabe cried. He tried not to let his temper flare, but he felt sick. "Are they saying I was inappropriate with one of the kids? With their kid?"

Mitch shook his head. "No, thank god. They're not that fucking stupid. Just that your lifestyle outside of work cast doubt on whether or not you were fit to assist in an educational program." He scrubbed his hand through his hair. "Look, son, it's none of my damn business. But are you seeing that Sullivan boy? The singer?"

"Joey?" Gabe clarified. "Yes. No. I mean, it's new. And complicated. What the hell does he have to do with anything?"

"There were pictures of you on the Twitter…thing. Apparently. Isn't he a little young?"

"He's twenty-one," Gabe shot back.

"Gabriel, don't get mad at me," Mitch said sternly. "I'm on your side. Good, I'm glad to hear that. Unfortunately, some people think fact-checking is optional, evidently. They were saying he was younger, and it made some folks uncomfortable."

"Lewis didn't make people uncomfortable," Gabe said, trying to keep his tone in check.

"Lewis was a respectable lawyer," Mitch said apologetically. "This Joey is a wild rock star. Or, so that's what I'm hearing. Anyway, you know how it only takes an excuse or two to get these folks riled up. They take one little thing they don't like and twist it and suddenly…"

"Mitch," said Gabe. His hands were trembling, so he clasped them together. "Do I need to go to the police station?"

"Maybe," Mitch replied, deeply troubled. "At the moment it's not gone that far. But there's pressure from the board that funds me and the library to 'protect' the institution." He used air quotes to show what he thought about their idea of protection.

"What kind of pressure?" Gabe asked. He felt numb. This couldn't be happening.

Mitch shook his head. "They've asked that you take some temporary leave from work. Paid, of course," he added quickly.

"Mitch!" Gabe cried, unable to hold it in any longer. He leaped to his feet and yanked at his hair. "This is *discrimination!* This can't be legal! What, a couple of people on the town council found a way to flex their homophobic muscles, and they get to fucking *fire* me?"

"Not fired," Mitch retorted firmly. "They don't have any grounds. But it was strongly hinted to me that if I wanted to keep the funding this place gets for all the community work we do, I should encourage you to take a vacation while this is all sorted out."

Gabe felt dizzy. "This is *blackmail*," he hissed. "And what do they mean 'sorted out'? I'm not going to magically turn straight. If they think a gay man can't work in a place with kids…they're going to find a way to take my job, aren't they?" This wasn't just about the art club anymore. They had children at the library all hours of the day.

"Over my dead body," Mitch snapped. "Look, Gabe, whatever this is, it's just temporary, I swear. Some folks don't like the fact that the world is changing, and every now and again they like to throw their toys out of the stroller and pretend they're still in charge. That's all this is."

"But meanwhile my reputation is in the middle of it," Gabe said, sinking back into his chair. "My job. Mitch, I have bills to pay." He was lucky he didn't have a mortgage, but he paid his parents rent. Their home in Florida would be at risk if he let them down.

"We just need to ride it out," Mitch said soothingly.

But Gabe couldn't feel so calm about it. The bottom line was, if he were straight, no one would be calling his decency into question. Had these people spoken to the shelter as well? He worked with teens there regularly. What about the firehouse?

Fuck, all it took was for one unsavory rumor to spread. That was the sort of damage that might never be undone.

"I…" said Gabe. He got to his feet and rubbed his temple. "I think I need to go make some phone calls."

"Go home," Mitch insisted. "I'll let you know the second anything changes. I promise it'll be okay."

He couldn't promise that though. No one could.

Twenty~Three

JOEY

"MOM?" JOEY CALLED WHEN HE WALKED THROUGH THE FRONT door of his parents' home. All the cars were gone from out front, but the door hadn't been double-locked. His mom didn't have her own car, so if anyone was going to be in, surely it'd be her.

"Joseph?" His mom's voice sounded unsure, so Joey dropped his bag in the hall and followed it to the kitchen.

She was rubbing her face as he walked in. But it wasn't enough to hide that she'd been crying.

"Oh, *Mom*," he said, rushing over to where she stood by the sink to give her a hug. "What happened?" Anger bubbled inside him. If his dad had laid a finger on her, he was going to fucking kill him.

"Nothing, nothing," she said thickly. Her hands fluttered over his back. "I'm just being silly."

He leaned back and scowled at her. He very much doubted that.

"Sit," he said firmly, escorting her to a chair. "When was the last time anyone made *you* coffee, hmm?"

His mom chuckled sadly and wiped her eyes with the back of her sleeve. "Honey, you don't have to."

He did though. God fucking damn it. There wasn't much more he hated in this world than seeing his mom cry.

"There," he said a few minutes later. He placed two cups down on the kitchen table, along with a packet of cookies he found in one of the cabinets.

She smiled weakly at him as she wrapped her hands around the cup. "Thank you. Did you have a good trip?"

He didn't really want to talk about himself, he wanted to talk about her. But, much like somebody else he knew, she was a caring soul who would rather be cheered by other people's good news than dwell on her own issues. The way to get her to open up might lay in sharing his news.

"I went to Chicago," he said. He'd only told his parents that he had work out of town for a few days, not the details. He didn't want his dad ruining everything. "I recorded a song with one of Europe's premier producers, and I think I might have a boyfriend."

That was overstating it quite a bit, but it was too complicated to try and unravel what he and Gabe really were there and then. Besides, it was worth it for the smile that blossomed on her tear-stained face.

"A boy, really?" she whispered, reaching out to clasp one of his hands with her own.

A smile twitched at his lips. "A man," he said. "A good man. I don't know if it'll work out, but-"

"Sweetheart," she said firmly. She squeezed his hand and frowned. "If he's good, the rest will take care of itself."

"I don't know, Mom," Joey said. He pulled his hand free and took a sip of sugary coffee. "We don't have much in common. I have to focus on work right now."

Her face fell. "That's true," she said. "Have you, um, got that rent money for your father?"

Joey scowled. "I won't get paid until the record is released. And I thought the deal was to let me have a chance to get my own place? How the hell can I do that if he's bleeding me dry?"

Her face crumpled and he immediately felt shitty. This obviously wasn't her fault. "I guess I let him think you'd only be here a few weeks," she said, tears welling in her eyes again. She studied her coffee and rubbed the handle with her thumb. "I'm sorry."

"Don't be sorry," Joey said with a sigh. "He's the asshole."

"Joseph!"

"He is!" he fired back. "Mom, you know he's always hated me. Nothing I ever do is good enough. I'm a living, breathing embarrassment, and now he's finally getting to punish me."

His mom bit her lip, then drank some coffee. "He means well," she said. He didn't think she believed her own words. After all these years though, making excuses for him was second nature.

It broke his heart. She was such a beautiful soul, and his dad had slowly crushed it. She had a degree in fine art, for fuck's sake. She could have been anyone. Instead, she was more or less a prisoner in this house.

Joey thought about Gabe. Yeah, he was his knight in shining armor now. But how many years would it take for him to become his keeper, clipping his wings?

The idea broke his heart. But Gabe was meant for a small life. He gave everything he had of himself away to others, his feet firmly on the ground. Yeah, the two of them were having fun now. But Joey wouldn't let anyone stop him reaching for the stars. Not like his dad had with his mom.

He didn't think he'd have the strength to break things off with Gabe while he was still living here. The pull was too strong. Joey had only said goodbye to him half an hour ago and already he felt a pang in his chest, wanting to be near him again.

But when he moved, that's what he'd have to do.

"Sometimes," his mom said softly. She was staring absently out the window into the backyard. "I forget what month it is. The days just…all seem the same." She blinked and looked back at him, taking his hand once again. "That's why it's so lovely having you here. It makes a nice change."

If Joey creeping out at dawn and in at dusk, banned from the dinner table, forbidden from even getting too close to his nephew was his mom's idea of a 'nice change,' things were maybe worse than he thought. He was pretty sure she had depression, but bringing that up in this family would be a stupid idea, let alone suggesting she might go get some help.

"I'm glad," he said to her. He didn't really know what else he could do.

"Mom?"

Cathy's voice rang through the house as the front door slammed. Joey and his mom instantly sprang apart. Initially, he felt guilty. But then he was angry at being made to feel guilty for just sitting and having coffee with his own mother.

So he didn't move from the table as his sister-in-law bustled in with the baby. He sat up straight and looked her in the eye as she entered, taking a small amount of pleasure as she startled at the sight of him.

"Joey," she said, rubbing Michael's back as he wriggled around to look at him and his mom. "What are you-" She paused and licked her lips. "You're not normally here during the day."

"I was just leaving," Joey said coolly. But first, he made a point of standing and pulling his mom into a hug. After all, she wasn't Cathy's mom. She didn't give a crap that she was standing here, alone in the kitchen, crying her eyes out in the middle of the day.

"It'll be okay," he whispered.

He didn't bother going down to the basement. Everything he owned was crammed into the backpack he'd left in the hall. So he tugged it on again and headed out into the cold, fall air.

The sad thing was, his first instinct was to go to Gabe. By now, he knew where he lived and the times he worked at the library, although he was pretty sure he had the rest of the day off after their trip.

But he couldn't rely on Gabe. The way he made Joey feel was addictive, like a drug. If he got used to it, he'd end up stuck in this shitty town, just like his mom. She had loved his dad once. Now she was a ghost of who she used to be.

Joey began the familiar trudge towards the center of town. He could spend the rest of the day looking for rooms for rent and maybe even applying for bar work. The longer he could avoid seeing his dad and having to cough up the rent he wanted, the better. If Joey gave him a hundred bucks now, he'd struggle to make it into New York for any work that came up.

He stopped abruptly on the street and balled his fists. Why was nothing ever fair, or simple? Being with Gabe made him feel so good. He was hot and kind and thought Joey was fucking beautiful. Why the hell couldn't he have more ambitions? That way they could try and escape this place together.

But no, as usual, Joey was on his own. Maybe it would be better if they didn't see each other anymore. What the fuck had he been thinking? He'd obviously got caught up in the moment, suggesting they try and date. It was only going to cause them both heartache in the long run. More heartache.

He rubbed his chest and choked back a sob as he started walking again. Like he said to his mom, it would be okay. He'd spend the evening at one of the diners and fill up on cheap coffee while he searched for something, anything to get him back into the city where he belonged.

He'd had an amazing time with Gabe these past few days. If that was all he got, well, he'd just have to count his blessings.

He didn't feel very blessed as he huddled against the wind though.

Twenty~Four

GABE

It had been a long week. Gabe had kept himself as busy as he could with his other commitments. But it seemed like everywhere he went, he found himself having to explain again and again what was going on.

Just as he'd feared, rumors of his supposedly unsavory behavior had traveled like wildfire through town. And while his friends were fiercely loyal and dismissed the slander for the lie it was, Gabe had definitely noticed people he didn't know, or didn't know so well, giving him the side eye.

He had stopped eating almost entirely and struggled to get more than an hour or two's sleep at a time. He was so consumed by worry and disgust it was making him grumpy and he knew he wasn't fun to be around. Which was probably why he'd not minded that he and Joey hadn't spoken much since their trip had ended.

There had been some communication, so Gabe wasn't too worried. But he was so conscious of being terrible company that he hadn't pushed to see Joey, and not reacted badly when Joey hadn't offered any plans to meet up either. But there had been the odd hello, light chat and heart emojis.

Gabe still got a thrill every time Joey's name flashed up on his phone.

Gabe had decided not to tell Joey about the allegations and the legal trouble he would most likely be facing. The truth was, Debbie Slater might not have felt emboldened to make her claims if someone hadn't snapped photos of Gabe and Joey in Chicago then plastered it all over Twitter. Even though Gabe absolutely did *not* blame Joey for his current predicament, Joey probably would naturally shoulder some of the guilt anyway. That was the last thing Gabe wanted.

Besides, Mitch was right. Hopefully this mess would all just blow over, and Gabe could tell Joey everything when he was in the clear.

In his more positive moments Gabe idly daydreamed of the best dates he could put together for Joey to really spoil him. He wanted to have him over for dinner again, but this time he would cook from scratch and properly wine and dine him. He thought they could go rock climbing; Joey would probably be great at it. Then there were lots of places they could drive out to that were picturesque or interesting.

That's what Gabe kept coming back to when his thoughts got really dark. These people could be as salty as they wanted. However, Gabe had found someone he craved spending time with. Someone who liked him back, even if he was scared to admit it.

What it all came down to in the end was that Gabe had done *nothing wrong,* and that was the truth. He'd not acted even remotely inappropriately with anyone's kids, and he and Joey had merely been seen in each other's company. They weren't even holding hands in any of the photos that had been put online. If people hadn't already known they were gay, he doubted anyone would have guessed they could be dating at all.

So he had made it through the week. Saturday morning

came in the form of a shift with the fire department. Gabe was grateful to be kept busy with several calls, none of which were too dangerous, but nobody had much time to ask him about his woes either.

He had reason to be cheerful though, a light at the end of the tunnel. Once his shift was over and he'd been able to head home to shower and change, he found himself strolling over the park near the baseball field to his favorite bench. This was where he'd come for years to sit and think whenever something was on his mind.

That was most likely why Lewis had suggested it as a good place to meet.

Gabe's ex-boyfriend stood as Gabe approached, giving him a small wave. Gabe returned it, but he was soon distracted by the enormous golden streak that was charging his way.

"Max!" Gabe yelled. He dropped to his knees to greet the golden retriever, not caring if his jeans got muddy on the slightly damp grass. "Oh who's a good boy? I missed you, yes I did."

Max did his best to lick every inch of Gabe's face as he laughed and ruffled his fur. His heart felt like it was going to burst with happiness. Irrationally, he also felt a pang that Joey wasn't there to meet Gabe's beloved dog as well. But that probably wouldn't have gone down well considering Gabe was specifically there to talk with Lewis for the first time since their breakup.

Speaking of which, he realized it was probably time to stand and face Lewis. Gabe felt slightly nervous, but it wasn't nearly as painful as he'd imagined it would be as Lewis approached and pulled him into a hug.

"Hi," Gabe said into his jacket.

"Hi," Lewis said back.

He was handsome as ever, with dark blond hair, chiseled

jaw and sparkling blue eyes. He was just as well built as Gabe remembered from all the years he'd spent touching his body. But now…now his physical presence did nothing for Gabe. It was almost a relief. If he had needed any encouragement that their split was the right decision, this was it.

He was definitely not in love with Lewis anymore. And he still wished stupidly that Joey was there by his side.

Lewis caught him smiling as they pulled apart and perhaps misunderstood. "It's *really* good to see you," he said. He reached out and touched Gabe's cheek with the back of his fingers. It was something he always used to do. The familiarity of the gesture meant Gabe didn't react or step away before it was over. But the intimacy made him a little uncomfortable.

"Thank you for coming," he said, hoping to keep things formal. He motioned to the bench and they both took a seat side by side. Gabe was careful to steer Max between their knees so there was space between their thighs. He knew Lewis was just acting on old habits, but Joey was at the forefront of Gabe's thoughts.

This wasn't a social call.

"Did my message make sense?"

Lewis nodded, rubbing his hands together. "Some lady has decided she doesn't want a gay man near her precious angel, and has decided to make some noise about getting you fired."

Gabe sighed. "Yes, that's about it I think."

"Haven't these people got anything better to do?"

Gabe chuckled. "I know, right? Anyway, my boss thinks I might need to go to the police to tackle this head-on. But his son's in the force, and he thought it might be even better to send her a lawsuit for defamation of character. Scare her off before anything really gets going."

Lewis smiled. It was still as dazzling as Gabe remembered, but it struck him now how it was also a little showy. It probably did Lewis very well in court, but to Gabe, it almost seemed a bit put-on.

"I think that's a fantastic idea," Lewis agreed.

Gabe pulled his gloves on, much to Max's dismay as he had to stop stroking him for a moment. But as the daylight was fading, the temperature was dropping drastically, and despite his layers Gabe was already starting to shiver. Luckily, he had his hat, otherwise he'd be freezing by the time he walked back home again.

"The trouble is," Gabe admitted. "I can't afford a lawyer. Not when I don't know how long this might stretch out for. I was really hoping you could give me a little bit of advice, then point me in the direction of anyone who might be willing to do pro bono around here."

Gabe absolutely hated the idea of asking someone to work for free. But Mitch, and his police officer son Ollie, had insisted that because he was the blameless victim he should at least ask. Gabe was also being truthful about his finances. A lengthy lawsuit would destroy him unless he could get a pro-bono lawyer. So if there wasn't anyone he could find, he'd have to just trust the police could make Debbie and her followers go away.

Because that was the worrying thing now. In the past week, she had got a petition of over fifty signatures demanding that Gabe's suitability to work with kids be investigated thoroughly. There were fifty people out there who Gabe didn't know had a problem with him, simply because he was gay.

The idea tore him up inside. He loved just like anyone else. He'd never cheated on a boyfriend, he was responsible, and he undoubtedly didn't flaunt anything in anyone's faces. Yet they still had joined in with the hate when someone else had found the guts to stand up first and protest. Part of his worst moments this week had been when he'd lost hours obsessing over who these people were.

Did he know any of them? Did he think of any of them as friends?

This was why he needed to make all these allegations go away as soon as he could. Otherwise, he would drive himself insane.

"I looked into local firms," Lewis said in response to his question. "But they're all too small to be able to afford to do pro bono. But," he said before Gabe could react with disappointment. "*My* new firm insists we do a certain number of hours per year pro bono. So, how would you feel about me helping you out?"

Gabe's mouth dropped open. "You'd do that?" he said, fighting back tears. The relief was palpable. "For me?"

Lewis gave him a smile. "Well," he said. "I thought I could move back in for a few days. See how it goes."

He slid his hand up Gabe's thigh.

Gabe jumped so violently he almost dislodged himself from the bench. Max barked. "What the hell are you doing?" he demanded before he could think.

Lewis looked stunned. "Jesus, Gabe, calm down."

Gabe's heart was racing and he instinctively looked around to check if anyone was watching. "I, why…Lewis, we're over."

Lewis looked at him sadly. "I know. But, haven't you thought about us at all? Maybe that we made a mistake?"

Gabe licked his lips. He didn't want to hurt Lewis's feelings, but the truth was he hadn't missed him, not really. He'd definitely missed being a part of a couple in the early days. But he knew with absolute certainty that he and Lewis weren't meant to be together. They never had that spark.

Not like he had with Joey.

The realization hit Gabe like a sledgehammer. He'd only

known Joey for several weeks. And there was a logical part of Gabe's brain that warned him he was probably just in the throes of honeymoon lust. But he couldn't deny that Joey fit with him in a perfect way that Lewis never had. Even with all the friction they had – *especially* with the friction they had. He and Lewis had ticked along, a perfect, easy couple.

Love wasn't easy. It was damn hard. Gabe thought maybe he knew that now.

"I'm sorry, Lewis," he said carefully. He held his gaze and tried to make him understand. "I know it's difficult, but I think our breakup was for the best. For both of us."

Lewis leaned back and frowned. "You can't know that," he said. "You don't know how I'm feeling."

Gabe bit his lip and looked at his hands in his lap. "I know how I'm feeling."

Lewis scoffed. "Fuck, Gabe," he said, his voice catching. Gabe felt awful, but it would be crueler to string Lewis along when there was no hope. "It wasn't that long ago we talked about getting married."

"But we never got engaged, did we?" Gabe pointed out as kindly as he could.

Lewis ran his hand through his thick hair. Then he looked sharply back at Gabe. "Is there somebody else?"

He always had been astute. No wonder he went into practicing law.

Gabe rubbed his thumb against his chin. "It's very new," he said by way of confirmation.

Lewis jumped to his feet and Max scrambled backwards, startled. "Fucking *hell*," he cried, throwing out his hands. "Did the sheets even get cold, Gabe?"

"Lewis, chill the fuck out," Gabe snapped. "I wasn't looking for anything, all right. It just happened."

Lewis scoffed. "Oh, it 'just happened.' Do you expect me

to believe that?" His eyes narrowed and he stepped back towards Gabe, finger pointing at him. "How long?"

"How long?" Gabe repeated, confused.

"How long were you guys fucking behind my back?"

Gabe spluttered he was so shocked. Heat rose into his cheeks despite the bitter wind. "No," he shouted. "No, Lewis, absolutely nothing happened while we were still together. I didn't even *meet* him until after you'd moved out! You're being paranoid."

Lewis looked absolutely disgusted at him. "You expect me to believe that in the few weeks I've been gone, you met someone so great you won't even *consider* giving us another shot?"

Gabe slumped. This was awful. He didn't want to hurt Lewis, but he couldn't lie either. "We had our shot, Lewis. If we couldn't make it work in five years, it's not going to. I really like this guy. I'm so sorry."

Lewis snarled and turned away from him, his ears pink. "Fine, forget it," he said over his shoulder. "Good luck with keeping your job."

Now it was Gabe's turn to stand, horror welling up in him. "You're not going to help me with my lawsuit? Just because I won't date you again?"

Lewis half-turned, his eyes glassy. "I'm not going to hang around and watch you make doe-eyes at someone else. I've got too much dignity for that."

"But," said Gabe. "You said none of the law firms around here can help me either. Is there someone else at your firm-?"

Lewis gave a hollow laugh. "That would come out to the sticks for a little case like this?" He shook his head. "No. I'm sure you'll find someone in Connecticut though, if you look a bit further afield. Like I said," he added through a clenched jaw. "Good luck."

Gabe watched aghast as Lewis stormed off over the damp

grass back towards the lot where he'd parked his car. Dusk was setting fast and Gabe wouldn't be able to see him for much longer. But he didn't call after him. What could he say? Lewis was being monumentally unfair, but if he wanted to try again, Gabe absolutely couldn't offer that.

So he just stood there. Max stayed by his side until Lewis whistled for him from the shadows. Poor Max looked between Gabe and Lewis's vanished form several times before the whistle came again, sharper this time. Being the good boy that he was, Max gave Gabe one last forlorn look then bolted after Lewis, leaving Gabe all alone.

What the fuck? He'd had a brief moment of relief and happiness before it had been torn away again, leaving him feeling even worse than before.

He scrubbed his cold face. What the hell was he going to do now? Look for another lawyer, he supposed. Or just deal with the police and hope this all got solved in a civil manner.

Either way, that felt like something he could muster the energy for tomorrow, before his shift. It was dark and cold and he felt wretched. The only thing he wanted now was to see Joey. To hold him in his arms.

Maybe he would tell him his troubles. Wasn't that what you did with the person you loved, after all?

He smiled despite the shit show of meeting up with Lewis. He loved Joey. He was almost certain of it.

Everything else could wait. He needed to talk to Joey, face to face, as soon as he possibly could.

CHAPTER
Twenty~Five

JOEY

J OEY'S COLD HANDS FUMBLED FOR THE PHONE AS HE TRIED TO yank it from his pocket before it stopped ringing. The blasted thing never rang, so whoever it was, it was probably important.

Sure enough, his agent's name was glowing on the screen. "Hey, Martha!" he cried, picking up the call just before it went to voicemail.

"Joey," she said. She had a well-educated accent that he'd always loved. "I wasn't sure if I'd catch you, I know it's getting late there."

They were only three hours ahead of L.A., but the implication that he could be busy was much appreciated. That was one of the reasons Joey really liked Martha. She always did her best to make him feel better.

"I'm just heading home, actually," he said.

He'd had enough of the town's diners and cafés for one day. With any luck, he hoped he could slip into his parents' house unnoticed and chill out in the basement for a while. It was Friday night, so there was bound to be some sport on and his dad and brother would probably already be through a few beers.

"I'll be quick then," she said. Joey imagined her smoothing down her well-tailored blazer and pencil skirt as she looked out her window over L.A. "Are you free a week from today for an audition in the city? I've got you in for a new Netflix show, I think it'll be just your sort of thing."

Joey stopped walking in the shadows between street-lights. "What?" he stammered. Netflix? That was incredible!

"You know how the eighties are all the rage right now?" she explained. "This show – Beat It – it's set in a recording studio in 1986. It's a drama, but part of that will be recording original songs as well as covers. So, one of those shows with a soundtrack."

Joey felt dizzy. "That…that sounds perfect."

"I know," she said. He could hear the smile in her voice. "It's not a main part, per se. But a side character that has an arc with one of the stars. You'd be going for Donny Shaw, a troubled up-and-coming singer. One of those juicy parts with lots of guts that you love."

"I do," he said, rubbing his chest. "Martha, that sounds like a dream. Thank you."

"Don't thank me yet," she warned. "You still have to get the part."

Joey nodded in the darkness. "Send me everything. I'll be ready."

They closed the call and he began slowly walking again. Was this really happening? His mind was already whirring at what this could mean for him.

A steady paycheck. Quality content, or at least he assumed, coming from Netflix. He'd be based in New York, just like he'd hoped.

However, now…now another idea crept into his head.

If he was going to be fixed in New York City, he could get

a place more in the suburbs. That would mean he wasn't that far away from Gabe.

Could it really work? Maybe he didn't *have* to stop seeing Gabe.

He wasn't an idiot. There was still every chance that Gabe wanted to change him too much and Joey would have to break away from him. But if he got a job in L.A. or anywhere else far away, they didn't stand a chance. If Joey was in New York City though, it seemed okay to think about giving them just a bit more time to figure things out.

Every time he got too giddy, he tried to rein it in. Nothing was certain, *nothing*. But for once…it didn't seem so terrible to hope.

Plus, he'd also heard from Storm Sailor's people. The date was set for the video shoot in a couple of weeks and Joey loved the concept. They'd also sent him the finished track, and quite frankly, it was fucking awesome. If he could time the song's release with hype about him getting the part in the show, if he got it, that might just be what he needed for a comeback.

He unlocked his phone again as he took the shortcut through the park. He and Gabe hadn't spoken much that week besides silly little niceties. Joey had been trying to keep his distance, in order to protect his heart in the face of what he felt was an inevitable parting of ways. But now he just wanted to talk to Gabe and share his good news. It felt amazing, to have someone nestled in your chest, their presence always thrumming like a hummingbird. It made Joey feel like he wasn't so alone, knowing Gabe was out there, just on the other end of the phone if he needed.

Expect when he looked up, Gabe wasn't on the end of the phone at all.

He was about thirty feet in front of him.

It was dark in the twilight, but Joey could make out his

broad form easily as he marched across the park. Joey went to cry out and wave, but then he realized Gabe was walking towards someone else and a dog was lunging itself at Gabe, its tail wagging furiously.

Joey smiled. Gabe was so well loved, even dogs threw themselves at him. It would be rude to shout out to try and grab his attention from the other person. Joey would just walk over and say hi. He was sure he'd be welcome.

He felt like he was being buoyed along by a balloon as he climbed the slight incline to reach Gabe and his friend. But before he could get any closer, he stopped in his tracks. The other man – and Joey was sure it was a man – flung his arms around Gabe and tucked his head into his neck. That seemed like an awfully intimate embrace for a friend.

Joey stood still and watched the other man brush his fingers against Gabe's cheek and his blood ran even colder than it was already in the freezing air.

Suddenly, an idea popped into his head. Joey looked between the mystery guy and the dog. Gabe said his ex had left with their dog only a matter of weeks ago, and Joey knew from photos he'd seen in his house that it was a golden retriever. The dog by the two men ahead was definitely big enough to fit that breed.

Was this Gabe's ex? Lewis?

Joey watched with a sick sensation in his gut as the two of them sat on the bench, the dog wagging its tail happily between them.

Joey knew he'd been distant this week, but he hoped his behavior couldn't be seen as giving Gabe the cold shoulder after their weekend away. Even though Joey *had* been considering breaking things off, he had a chance now. He might not have to do that.

It would be unbelievably cruel if Gabe had been pissed at

his lukewarm texts and reached out to Lewis in the meantime.

Joey felt like his heart was in his mouth as he watched the two men talk, unnoticed.

And then the guy ran his hand up Gabe's thigh.

Joey's adrenaline kicked in in the blink of an eye, and before he knew what was happening, he'd already spun around and was marching away from the scene.

Jesus H. *fucking* Christ. What had he been thinking? That someone as gorgeous and kindhearted as Gabe was just going to sit around waiting for Joey's salty ass to mellow enough that they could make a go of it?

He scrubbed angrily at his eyes as he took the nearest exit out of the park and began walking a longer route home.

Home. Ha. It wasn't home. It was his parents' place that his dad was deigning to let him sleep in, for now, only because Joey had given in and coughed up a hundred dollars. When it came down to it, it was still cheaper than a hotel, and Joey was still doing his best to spend as many hours of the day out in town and away from his family.

This is what he got for daring to stop job hunting a little early. He felt so good he was confident he could sneak in and just lay on his bed for a while. He'd been going nonstop for so long, after his good news he'd just wanted to have an evening off.

But no, he'd had to run into Gabe and his gorgeous ex, who were obviously not quite as broken up as Gabe had made them out to be.

For fuck's sake. Had Joey really considered letting himself be tied to this crappy town with that guy? What a joke. The sense he'd been played was eating him up.

So he was Gabe's rebound fuck. Okay, he'd been worse. He could get through this. He just needed to forget about his heart now and think with his head. If he nailed this audition, there was every hope his luck could change.

His phone ringtone made him startle. He fished it from his pocket, optimistic it was someone about the TV show again. But for the first time in weeks, when he saw Gabe's name flash up he felt a sinking sense of dread instead of joy.

He sent the call to voicemail, then placed his phone on silent. He didn't even want it to vibrate. Let Gabe call himself silly; Joey had seen everything he needed to.

———

No one seemed to notice as Joey slipped down the front door and into the basement. It only seemed fair, as the universe owed him a bit of good fortune. He'd picked up some pasta on the journey back, but he only managed a few bites before his stomach rebelled and threatened to send it all back up again.

It was too early to sleep and he was too wired in any case. So he put his earphones in and placed his music on shuffle. His phone was set up so that even if he got calls or texts, it wouldn't interrupt the playback. Normally, the function irritated the hell out of Joey. He'd missed many a call thanks to that. But for now, it was perfect.

He was alone. He'd always been alone, so it shouldn't take that long to shake off the hope he'd built up that Gabe might stick around. It had felt nice to be a part of a couple, however briefly. But Joey was tough. He'd survived the band's destruction, so he could survive a broken heart too.

He stared at the dank ceiling and let the music wash over him. He purposefully picked thumping rock and dance tracks so the beat could pound into his head and keep him distracted.

It obviously worked, as he had no idea he had company until his mom suddenly appeared in his line of sight.

He bellowed out a curse and yanked the earphones free. "Sorry, Mom," he spluttered, trying to slow his heart rate down. "You scared the life out of me."

He laughed and she managed a small smile, but she looked troubled. "I tried calling down, but I didn't want to be too loud in case I disturbed the others." She meant his dad and brother no doubt.

"No, no, that's fine," he said. He held the earphones up. "It was my fault, I couldn't hear."

She shifted on her feet and looked down at him sitting on the camp bed. "There's, huh, someone here to see you. A man. He's, um, very handsome."

The sparkle of tentative excitement in her eyes made the ache in Joey's chest worse. If Gabe had shown up on his door, today of all days, Joey wasn't sure how he was going to react. The betrayal felt like a gaping wound.

He closed the music app he'd been using on his phone. Waiting for him were several missed calls and text messages, all from Gabe. His heart sank.

"Oh, right," said Joey, mustering up a smile. "Thank you, Mom."

He pocketed his phone and followed her up the stairs. As they went through the door, the sound of the crowd cheering at the game blaring from the living room was clear. At least it meant that they most likely wouldn't have heard the doorbell ring or his mom calling down to him.

Joey really didn't want an audience for this.

His mom gave him an encouraging smile and headed back towards the kitchen, throwing a hopeful look over her shoulder. She was excited for him. If only she knew the truth.

Taking a deep breath, Joey unbolted the door and greeted the person on the other side.

Gabe looked up immediately, a smile lighting up his face. Joey felt like his heart physically cracked. Gabe was bundled up against the snow that had started to fall, the soft, white flakes glinting in the night.

"Hey," he said. "I'm sorry, I tried calling."

"I know," said Joey flatly.

The look of hurt was fleeting, but Gabe quickly smiled again. "Can I come in? It's freezing."

Joey looked over his shoulder. Even if he wasn't cut to the bone by Gabe's actions, he wouldn't want to risk inviting him into his house, not with his dad just in the other room. "Let's step outside," he said.

He grabbed his coat and jammed his feet into his shoes, bracing himself both for the cold and the conversation ahead. He had to be strong. The most important thing was to protect himself.

"So," said Gabe warily as the door closed behind them. Fuck, the wind was bitter. Joey hugged himself. "You…saw my calls?" Joey shrugged.

"Sorry, I've been busy."

"Right," said Gabe, frowning. "I guess, well, I've had a hell of a week too."

Joey stared at him. He was pissed at *Joey?* That was rich, considering he'd just seen him cavorting with his ex. "Yeah, I know," he said with a scoff.

Gabe looked hurt again. "You…know?"

"I'm not an idiot," Joey snapped. "So I'd appreciate it if you didn't treat me like one."

"I don't think you're an idiot," Gabe replied, his frown deepening. "But I'd really appreciate it if you heard my side of things before you jumped to any conclusions."

Joey let out a hollow laugh. At least Gabe wasn't going to deny it. If he'd tried to get Joey to go along being his thing on the side, that would have hurt even more. Fuck, had his ex ever actually been his *ex?* Or had they been carrying on this whole time?

Joey didn't want to know. Ignorance was better than being tormented by the ugly truth.

"I think I've seen enough," said Joey, stepping back towards the house. "Look, this was never going to work anyway, was it? All you want is this pathetic little life and I'm made for bigger things. That's just it." He knew he was being spiteful, trying to hide the desperate hurt that was over-flowing from his battered heart. But he couldn't seem to stop himself. "I'm out of your league."

He turned to let himself back in, but realized with a horrible spike of humiliation that he didn't have his keys. He jabbed the doorbell anyway, praying his mom heard him.

"What the *fuck?*" Gabe shouted. Joey flinched and looked back to see Gabe advancing up the porch steps, tears in his eyes. "Joey, you can't possibly believe what you heard? You know me!"

"I didn't hear, I *saw*," he shot back. "With my own eyes. So let's just both forget about it, okay? It was a mistake."

He stabbed the doorbell again. Fuck, he needed to get away from this situation *now*.

"You know what?" Gabe shouted. The tears were spilling down his cheeks behind his glasses. Joey told himself he didn't care. Gabe had brought this on himself by being a lying, cheating bastard. "You're a selfish fucking *brat*, Joey Sullivan."

The door finally opened. But it wasn't Joey's mom on the other side.

"What the *hell* do you think you're doing?" his dad hissed in a menacing tone. Joey's blood ran cold.

He glanced back at Gabe, who threw his hands up, stepping away. "Nothing, man," he said, thickly. "I was just leaving. Have a nice life, Joey."

His rancor was completely unfair. Joey was the victim here. Hate and hurt wrestled with each other as Gabe stalked down the lamplit street, away from the house.

All thoughts of Gabe quickly vanished though as a meaty hand seized his collar and hauled him into the light of the porch. "How *dare* you cause such a disgusting scene in front of my house!" Joey's dad roared.

If Joey hadn't been so frightened, he might have pointed out that his dad's yelling was causing far more curtains to twitch than his and Gabe's argument. But he could smell the liquor on his dad's breath, and he shook Joey, hard.

"Let go of me!" Joey squeaked, trying to pull free.

His dad obliged, sending him flying against the wooden railing of the porch. Joey snatched a cold breath as his mom tried to rein his dad back in.

"Martin, no, please!"

Other than to shove her aside, his dad ignored her. "We've put up with enough of your fucking shit for long enough," he snarled, advancing on Joey. "You lay about all day, don't pay your way, bringing nothing but shame and embarrassment onto us decent, hardworking folks-"

"There's *nothing* decent about you!" Joey screamed back, not caring what the neighbors heard. "You're a hateful bigot who would disown his own son just because he's gay! You should be ashamed of yourself, you coward!"

The punch cracked across his jaw before he even saw it coming. Joey staggered, stars in front of his eyes and his mom's screams in his ears.

"You're *nothing*, you little shithead," his dad growled. "We'd all be better off if you did the decent thing and just fucking killed yourself."

Joey was mortified by the sob that escaped his lungs, but he couldn't help it. Instead, he dragged himself to his feet and stumbled down the steps into the front yard. *"Fuck you,"* he cried, not caring that the tears were dripping down his face. "I wouldn't give you the satisfaction." He wiped his eyes and glowered.

His dad was illuminated by the porch light and the light spilling out from the hall. His mom was sobbing silently by his side, her hands over her face. His brother and sister-in-law had come out to watch the show. Faintly, Joey could hear Michael crying from his crib.

"You're nothing but a little faggot," his dad spat. "I never want you in my house again."

Panic filled Joey. His bag was still in the basement. His laptop was in there, along with his few sets of clothes and irreplaceable sentimental items. Not to mention his wallet and his phone charger. But his dad stepped forward menacingly, his shoulders bulking as he raised his fists, challenging Joey to dare come near him.

"Fine," Joey said, trembling head to toe. The cold was already slicing through his thin jacket and the adrenaline was pumping through his veins. "I don't need you, I've never needed you!"

He turned on his heel and walked down the street, the opposite direction to the way Gabe had gone. He should have been far enough along the street not to have heard the humiliating exchange between Joey and his family, but he wouldn't take the risk of running into him, not after their argument.

Joey let himself cry, horribly, as his father's jeers and mother's weeping faded away. He could feel people looking at him through their windows, but he paid them no mind. Instead, he counted his blessings that he still had his earphones in his pocket if nothing else.

He sobbed in the darkness as the music consumed him, ignoring the rest of the world.

Now he truly had nothing.

CHAPTER

Twenty-Six

GABE

GABE WAS WALKING AIMLESSLY. SERIOUSLY, FUCK THIS WEEK.

What the hell had just happened? First, he got treated completely outrageously by Lewis, but stood his ground because he knew how much he'd come to care for Joey. He tried to tell Joey this, and the little shit breaks up with him? Which, of course, was his right if that's how he really felt, but did he have to be so nasty about it?

If Gabe had expected anyone to understand what it feels like to have your personal life twisted and demonized by the public, it would have been Joey. Except, he'd acted totally disgusted and didn't even want to give Gabe a chance to explain.

Gabe scrubbed his face again and took a deep breath of freezing night air. This hurt more than he could have imagined. He wanted to run back to Joey and demand he listen, that they hash this out properly. But his dad had come out looking like a raging bull, and Gabe just hadn't had the energy to deal with a homophobic asshole as well.

That caused him a twinge of worry. What had Joey had to cope with once Gabe had left?

Gabe scoffed and shook his head. He couldn't look after Joey too. He had to put himself first for once in his goddamned life. The sad truth was Joey had probably been eager for an excuse to run away and not even try to be a couple. He'd always made his views on a cozy, small-town life painfully clear. Because Gabe didn't want the hustle and bustle of a big cosmopolitan he was never going to be good enough for someone like Joey.

He angrily rubbed at his sore eyes under his glasses. He needed to stop crying, now. If this was how Joey really was, it was better to find out now rather than several months down the line. This was just a blip. Gabe had said when he and Lewis split that he wanted to work on how to be single. He never intended to fall so hard and fast for Joey.

For now, he just needed to focus on getting through these shitty accusations, keeping his job and then maybe in the new year he could consider dating again.

The idea of dating someone who wasn't Joey brought a fresh wave of tears, but he forced them back down. He was just sad for the imagined 'what if,' not Joey himself, he was sure. He didn't know Joey enough to be this fucking devastated.

He pulled his phone out. For the briefest of moments, he hoped Joey might have messaged to apologize, to ask him to come back. But of course there was nothing.

Gabe considered calling his mom and dad, but they wouldn't be able to help much. Plus, it was pretty late, they'd probably be asleep. Instead, he hit Mitch's number.

"Hey, son," he said on the third ring. "How's it going?"

"Hey, Mitch," Gabe said, hearing his voice catch. "Uh, sorry, I know this is a massive intrusion, and if you're busy no worries at all, it's just, uh-"

"Do you want to come round for dinner, Gabriel?"

Gabe stopped and smiled up into the falling snow. He

choked back a sob. "That would be awesome," he said emphatically. "I can grab some beer on my way."

"No need, we have plenty," Mitch insisted. "Just get your butt over here, okay?"

Gabe thanked him and made his way to the nearest bus stop. Normally, he'd walk it over town, but with the snow and bitter wind, he thought it best to get a ride most of the way instead.

He didn't look at anyone on the bus. He didn't want to risk seeing a look of recognition or disgust. He just kept his eyes down and his breathing steady.

It was amazing, he noticed in a detached sort of way, how much Joey's cruel words cut deeper than the man he thought he'd loved for five years letting him down completely. It was like he'd never known either of them at all, but Joey had felt like the missing piece to his heart. Now his heart was just in tatters, bleeding out into his chest.

He grimaced as he disembarked from the bus and decided to leave the full-on anatomical imagery for the medical dramas. His heart was just fine, pumping away like it always did. Just like Gabe would. He'd keep on with his life just as he had before.

Mitch and his wife lived in a nice part of town. Not the flashiest, but they had a three-story house and a newish car parked in the driveway that worked great. They even had enough left in the bank to go on a few vacations each year. So Gabe didn't feel too much of an imposing heel as he rang the bell.

Mitch pulled him into a hug as soon as he opened the door, then pressed an icy beer into Gabe's already-cold hand. "Come on in, son. Tell us all about it."

Gabe chuckled and let Mitch and his wife Mary-Lou fuss over him. Their house was toasty warm, making Gabe glad he'd left the heat on for Duchess back at his own place. Gabe was greeted not only by the Curtises but by their fat, old chocolate Labrador, Timmy, and purring black cat Lotus.

Mary-Lou had made spaghetti with meatballs and they'd waited for Gabe to arrive to serve. So he was immediately ushered into a seat in their dining room and presented with a huge bowl of beef and pasta.

Gabe moaned as he took the first bite. Mary-Lou's cooking was even better than his own mom's, although he'd never admit that out loud. This was just what he needed after such a terrible day.

Mitch allowed him to get through about half his plate without probing for answers. Mitch and Mary-Lou argued good-naturedly about feeding the dog at the table. Or rather, Mitch told Mary-Lou off every time she held out half a meatball for Timmy on her fork, and Mary-Lou raised her eyebrows as if she had no idea what he was talking about.

Lotus managed to climb on the table from every single route possible, hopefully sniffing at the cheese sauce on whoever's plate was closest. Mitch never paused or blinked each time he picked the cat up and placed him back on the floor, only to have to repeat the action thirty seconds later. Gabe guessed the only solution was for everyone to eat their meals as fast as possible. He was okay with that.

When Gabe started to slow down and his beer needed replenishing, Mitch pushed again. "Go on then," he said, leaning back and rubbing his own belly absently. "I'm guessing you're not all in a twist because of Debbie Slater's nonsense. Unless…has she done something else?"

Gabe sighed and looked between them. They'd always been there for Gabe in the years he'd been working for Mitch, even more so since his parents' retirement.

So he didn't feel he needed to hold anything back. After assuring them that Debbie hadn't upped her accusations, yet, he launched into recounting his god-awful afternoon and evening, all the while stroking old Timmy's head. From Lewis's pushiness to his downright deplorable change of heart once Gabe refused to try dating again. Then how hard it was to see Max and let him go again. His realization about his feelings towards Joey…then the gut-wrenching rejection he'd experienced on his front doorstep.

"I just don't get it," said Gabe, now on his third beer. He wasn't really interested in drinking it though as much as he was picking off the label. "I really thought we had something going between us. I…" he faltered, but a masochistic part of him wanted to say it out loud. "I thought I loved him. I think I love him." Because despite the vile words they'd exchanged, he did still feel like he was in love with Joey.

Urgh, that was annoying. Why couldn't he have just been a rebound fling? Gabe tore another strip of the label off.

Mary-Lou stopped his hand from fidgeting by placing a fork in it and a plate of tiramisu where he'd not even noticed his pasta had disappeared from. "Maybe you just need to talk with him again, when you're both a little more coolheaded?"

Gabe rolled his hands. "What else is there to say?"

Mary-Lou glanced at Mitch as he picked Lotus up and let him settle in his lap. "Sounds like neither of you said much at all," she said kindly.

"I think this boy is scared," said Mitch. "Terrified, actually. You come along and you're a damn fine young man. He's probably used to being treated like crap by everyone, not just his family."

Gabe sighed. "Yeah, I did think that," he admitted.

"Send him a text, at least," Mary-Lou urged, sipping her beer. "Tell him there's no truth to the rumors and that he means so much to you. Maybe he just needs time to hear it on his own."

Mitch was nodding. "Men can be stubborn creatures," he said with a chuckle, glancing at Mary-Lou. She poked his arm affectionately. "Obviously we don't want you getting hurt, and maybe this guy isn't the one for you. But, if you really think you love him, he might be worth trying again?"

Gabe wanted that so badly. He'd already missed Joey enough this week; it had been so wonderful to see his face when he'd opened the door earlier. Then it had all gone south so fast.

He nodded. "I want to text him," he said, reaching for his phone.

Mitch smiled and Mary-Lou nodded. "We'll give you a minute," she said.

Gabe was grateful. He watched them slip outside and share a cigarette. They'd been together forever, and they were still so happy.

It took him ages to work out what he wanted to say, with many drafts discarded and rewritten. In the end, he decided to be honest and keep it simple.

Whatever you heard about me being unfit for work isn't true, it's just homophobic bullshit, I promise. Please don't let this tear us apart. I've missed you so much this week. If you want, I'd really like to talk again. Gabe xxx

He had written and erased 'I love you' from the end so many times. But in the end, Gabe decided if he was going to tell Joey that, he wanted to do it in person, so he could see his reaction. So Joey could see how much he meant it. Those weren't empty words to be thrown around in an apology. The first time you said 'I love you' to a person was important.

Gabe hit send, then placed his phone down on the table to wait.

CHAPTER
Twenty~Seven

JOEY

Joey's phone died halfway through 'The Show Must Go On' by Queen, which he thought was somewhat ironic.

He knew he probably should have saved the battery and not used any apps until he worked out how he was going to charge it again. But his music was the only thing that could keep him calm, of that he was certain. It took him away from the miserable circumstances in which he'd found himself.

Six hours ago, he was on top of the world. Now he had no money, no home, no phone unless he got a charger, no way to contact Martha about the audition. Oh, yeah, and no fucking boyfriend.

He was stunned that Gabe had reacted so hostile towards him. Joey would have expected him to be at least be a little bit sheepish. He wished he knew what the full story was. Had Gabe been seeing Lewis this whole time? Or had they just reconnected because they missed each other too much?

He angrily wiped tears away from his face; he couldn't afford to get any colder than he already was. His hands were trembling badly as he shoved his useless phone and earbuds into his jacket pocket.

If only he had a hat or scarf, anything to cover his head. The snow was falling thicker now and his shoes were getting soaked. Earlier, he'd sat in one of the cafés he'd passed just to try and warm up a little. They'd let him stay and sip a glass of water. But after midnight he was the only patron and they'd had to close up, leaving him back on the street.

He just had to make it through the night. Then he could try and hitchhike into the city in the morning. There was bound to be a phone shop there that would let him charge his phone for a bit, or if not maybe a bar or a hotel?

Once he had a bit of juice, he was calling Blake, pride be damned. Joey had made it this far, but he had nothing at all now; he was at rock bottom. Blake wouldn't judge him. He'd wire him some money, maybe even get him a bus ticket to Cincinnati so he could stay with him and Elion for a while.

The thought of a friendly face brought a fresh sob from Joey's chest. He stumbled as he tried to wipe the tears away again. He'd been walking the streets for hours and his feet were aching. Maybe it would be a blessing if they went numb from the cold?

He desperately wanted to sleep, but he was too afraid to. Someone could hurt him if he just laid down on a bench in the park. Greenwich was probably a safer place to rough it than New York City, but he was reluctant to take his chances all the same. This town had been nothing but a vindictive bitch to him his whole life. He didn't trust it to leave him be, not even for a few hours.

He tried to guess the time. He'd sold his watch back in L.A., so generally relied on his phone for a clock. He'd not looked at it since he'd left the café at just past one, merely leaving his music to shuffle itself. He'd been walking a couple of hours at least before the phone had finally given out. So that put him at three, maybe four o'clock? The sun wouldn't rise until after seven.

"Fuck," he said out loud, his voice croaky.

Three more hours, without any music to coax him through it. Maybe he should head to the highway now? He really, really didn't want to risk getting in a truck with a stranger. It seemed like one of the most stupid and dangerous things he could do. But he couldn't stand the idea of asking anyone around here for help again.

Which way should he head? He seemed to have lost his bearings, but that was unlikely as he knew these streets inside and out. It must have been the snow throwing him off. But he couldn't decide which way was towards town, and which would lead to the interstate. He closed his eyes and tried to stop his whole body trembling so violently.

His hands were so cold they were painful in his pockets. He took them and cupped them in front of his mouth to breathe on before shoving them under his arms. Now he was no longer listening to constant music he realized how much his teeth were chattering in his head.

Keep walking, just keep going, he said to himself. The more he moved, the warmer he'd be. His head hurt, but that was no surprise given how much he'd cried.

He should have known this would happen eventually with his dad. The bastard had been itching to kick him out since the moment he'd come back. Joey suspected he'd only lasted this long because his old man had enjoyed tormenting him. But the scene on the porch had evidently shamed him one step too far.

It wasn't like all the neighbors weren't already fully aware Martin Sullivan had a little faggot for a son. Joey had to say he'd never really had that much hassle from them, aside from the odd stare. But he'd been a popstar, so part of him hoped their curiosity was from that too. Not just the fact he liked to fuck other men.

To listen to his father's drunken rants though, a person

would be forgiven for thinking all they did was laugh themselves silly over what a failure his dad was for having a queer kid. "At least we got one normal boy," he'd said to his mom more times than Joey could care to remember.

Even after everything he'd been through, Joey refused to accept that he wasn't normal. There was nothing wrong with him. Everybody had different tastes as to whom they were attracted to. As far as he saw it, liking men was no different to liking blondes, or women with big boobs.

He wouldn't let his dad influence him. He'd had people on social media telling him to kill himself almost every day for five years. That kind of thing was easier to ignore online, it was true, but his dad wasn't being as shocking as he thought he was. Joey could deal with it.

He just wished he didn't have to. He wished he didn't come from a family where hate was the norm. Where he was now fearful of what he'd left his own mother to face. Hopefully, his dad wouldn't take out his frustrations on her, or god forbid, the baby. If there was any luck in the world, his dad would feel victorious now he'd finally got rid of Joey for good, and leave it at that.

Joey wasn't an idiot, he knew most people had crappy folks. Blake's were no picnic, and TJ and Reyse were both estranged from at least one of their parents. Raiden's were actually okay, but out of five guys, it was only fair that one of them didn't get screwed by their families.

Joey rubbed his arms as his body was wracked with uncontrollable shivers. He needed to warm up, just a little. His eyes were drooping every other step now and he was fighting to stay awake despite being upright. He didn't know what to do though?

Nowhere was open. This wasn't like New York City where you could always find *something*. Greenwich was eerily quiet. The only sounds he could hear were his damp shoes squeaking in the snow and the wind rustling the branches whenever he found himself near any trees. There were no cars, no wildlife, and certainly no people.

It was no real surprise to him that in the bleakest moment of his life, Joey was alone and in the dark.

He was too tired to cry anymore. He'd been trying to walk to the highway, but he must have got turned around, because the same park where he'd seen Gabe and Lewis was looming up ahead.

Fuck it. The bench the two of them had occupied was under a tree. That meant that it would be relatively sheltered from the snow. It wouldn't hurt him to sit for a while; Joey had been walking for hours. Plus, he got a perverse sort of kick out of sitting where he'd learned the truth about Gabe.

He sank down on the cold, wet wood with a modicum of relief. At least his feet would get a rest, even if he wasn't much warmer. He touched the seat below him.

"Remember. This is what it feels like to trust other people," he whispered sadly to himself. Because he'd so wanted to have faith in Gabe, to give him his heart. But he'd let him down, just like everybody else.

Joey hugged himself and watched the snow fall around the branches of the big tree over his head.

He began singing softly to himself, struggling to keep his eyelids open. Murmurs of sunshine and loneliness.

He trailed off into an enormous yawn. Maybe it wouldn't hurt to rest his head for just a minute? Then he'd get walking again, make his way towards the interstate and thumb a ride.

The bench wasn't comfortable as he lay down, but it was slightly drier than the muddy ground at least. He pillowed his hands under his cheek and blissfully allowed his eyes to close.

GABE HUNG OUT WITH MITCH AND MARY-LOU FOR AS LONG as he could. If he wasn't alone, he was slightly better at not checking his phone every twenty seconds for a response from Joey. But come midnight, Mary-Lou had fallen asleep on the couch with a snoring Timmy, and he felt he'd outstayed his welcome.

Mitch insisted he'd only had a couple of beers before dinner, so was perfectly fine to drive Gabe back home. Ordinarily, Gabe wouldn't hear of it. The walk was only about half an hour and through several pretty streets. But the snow was coming down even thicker and piling up on the sidewalk. Gabe would have made the trek if he'd had to, but he'd be a fool to pass up a ride when it was offered.

He checked his phone again on the way. The message had been delivered, but according to the report, Joey hadn't read it.

He sighed and gave in.

Please, baby, talk to me. This is cutting me up. I don't want to fight. You mean so much to me xxx

He watched as the message sent. But after a minute

staring at the screen, it looked like this one hadn't even been delivered to Joey's phone. That meant it was turned off, or he had no signal. Fuck. Gabe began to worry even more.

Mitch patted his knee. "Give him time," he said gently. "He might be sleeping it off. Things will be better in the morning."

Gabe couldn't argue with that. In his experience, things were always darkest before the dawn. He had the morning tomorrow to himself before his shift with the fire department in the afternoon. Hopefully, Joey would reply back to him before then and they could sort all this out. He didn't think he could take another whole day of this.

Mitch waved him off and drove away. Gabe crunched down his drive, fumbling with his keys in the stiff, icy wind tearing through the air. With a sigh of relief he entered his hallway and flicked on the lights, just in time to see an orange, brown and white-striped tail disappear around the corner into the kitchen.

"Oh, Duchess," he said forlornly. He really could have done with a cuddle right about then.

Instead, he replenished her empty food bowl and changed her litter box. Despite her persistent shyness, Gabe reassured himself that her life was so much better now than it had been. She was warm and safe and lived in the quiet rather than that noisy shelter. If only she would allow Gabe to give her more affection. He wanted her to understand she was loved.

He fussed over his cat as much as he could, but eventually, he had to go to bed. No matter how many times he checked his phone, the last message to Joey remained undelivered.

Mitch was right. He'd probably fallen asleep and not plugged in his phone, so it had died on him. There was nothing Gabe could do but wait until the morning, and try again.

He pulled the comforter around him and did his best to sleep.

———

The alarm woke him several hours later, jolting him from an uneasy dream that he forgot as soon as he opened his eyes. He'd tossed and turned for most of the night, but he'd staunchly refused to look at his messages to Joey again, giving him time to charge his phone and react.

But now it was eight o'clock. The sun was shining blindingly through the cracks in the curtain, no doubt reflecting off of the freshly fallen snow. Gabe snatched his phone from the nightstand.

There weren't any notifications. Gabe's heart sank, but he still unlocked it and proceeded to check the messages he'd sent to Joey the night before.

The last one had now been delivered.

Gabe's heart jolted. Fine. If Joey was purposefully not looking at his texts, that was one thing, but the delivery report suggested his phone at least had power and/or signal now. He hit the call button before he could change his mind.

He didn't know how Joey was feeling after their argument. If he didn't pick up, he still wouldn't. But Gabe was much more clearheaded now. Mitch was right. Joey was anxious about trusting anyone and he'd probably been scared off by hearing whatever he'd heard about Gabe this week.

Although, it occurred to Gabe now that Joey had said he'd *seen* it, with his own eyes. Gabe wasn't entirely sure what that meant, but he was distracted as the call was finally picked up.

"Nurse Mullins speaking," the voice on the other end of the line said.

Gabe frowned and took the cell away from his ear for a second to double-check it was Joey he'd called. Sure enough, his name flashed up on the display once Gabe angled the phone enough away from his ear.

Dread shot through Gabe's whole body as he jammed the phone back against his ear. "Hello?" he said. "Is Joey Sullivan there?"

There was a pause. "Are you Mr. Sullivan's next of kin?"

Gabe leaped from the bed, panic propelling him forwards as he thrust his legs into the first pair of jeans he laid his hands on. "I'm his boyfriend," he said, not caring if that was still the case, or ever even had been. "Oh my god, what's happened, is he all right?"

"He's doing okay, Mr...?"

"Robinson, Gabe Robinson," he supplied.

The nurse paused, perhaps writing something down. "Mr. Robinson, Joey is doing just fine, now. He was brought in about two hours ago suffering from the onset of hypothermia. We hadn't been able to definitely confirm his identity until your call just now. Some of the staff thought they recognized his face, but it's good you contacted him."

Hypothermia. "Oh Christ," Gabe choked out. He'd managed to get into a sweater and was hastily looking for socks. "Where was he found?"

"One of the parks," Nurse Mullins confirmed. There was sympathy in her voice. "On a bench near the baseball field. Luckily an early morning jogger spotted him. Don't worry, Mr. Robinson, he came to us in plenty of time."

"Can I see him?" Gabe asked, already halfway down the stairs.

"Of course," she said. "But he's sleeping now. He needs the rest and time to heal. Visiting hours officially start at midday. But, if you came early, I could maybe sneak you in a little bit before if he's conscious by then."

Gabe pinched the bridge of his nose, trying to hold back

the tears. "Okay, thank you," he said, breathing slowly. "I'll do that, thank you, Nurse."

"My pleasure, hon. See you soon."

Gabe closed the call and let out a keening noise. He never should have left Joey with his dad. Gabe had been so mad, but obviously Mr. Sullivan Sr. had been madder. Joey had hinted many times that his dad was capable of throwing him out.

There Gabe had been fretting over his broken heart, and Joey had slept in a fucking park.

He let out a shout, no doubt startling Duchess, wherever she was hiding. But Gabe was so furious with himself.

Okay. Nurse Mullins said she could sneak him in earlier, so he'd aim to leave at eleven and wait. He'd sit by Joey's side until he woke up. That left him a couple of hours to get things sorted before he left.

He gripped the banister on the stairs and took a couple of deep breaths. "Shower first," he said out loud. He needed to wash yesterday's woes off. Start over.

Then he had a lot to do.

———

When Gabe arrived at the hospital with a bunch of flowers, he felt more nervous than he would have imagined. He was worried in case Nurse Mullins wasn't around. What if another member of staff didn't think Gabe qualified as next of kin and wouldn't let Gabe in? What if, once they'd had his identity confirmed, they'd called his family and his parents were there already? Gabe wasn't sure that would be likely, but Joey had said he got along with his mom well. What if she had come and didn't want to let Gabe in?

Worst of all, what if Joey was awake and he refused to see

Gabe? What if, despite the trauma he'd been through, he was still mad at him?

Gabe would just have to respect him if that was the case. He just really hoped it wasn't.

"Hi, there," he said convivially as he approached the reception desk on the first floor. "I'm looking for Joseph Sullivan? Joey. He was admitted this morning."

The elderly woman behind the desk smiled at him and began clicking her computer mouse. "Are you the patient's brother?" she asked.

Gabe shifted. "I'm his boyfriend, ma'am."

Just as he feared, the woman narrowed her eyes at Gabe. "I see," she said coolly. Damn it; he should have just said friend. But fuck it, the hospital website *specifically* said they didn't discriminate, and that same-sex couples had the same rights as opposite-sex and next of kin. Besides, Gabe had had enough bullshit this week.

So he simply smiled brighter and tilted his colorful flowers at her. "I'm awfully eager to see him, ma'am. He was rushed into the E.R. this morning, like I said."

She pursed her lips and looked back at her monitor. "Yes, he's still being held in the E.R., but visiting hours aren't until-"

"Thank you, ma'am," Gabe cried, already heading down the corridor. E.R. was one of the most obviously signposted units. He didn't need her help to find his way.

His heart was in his mouth as he approached the busy waiting area. The room was filled with people looking very sorry for themselves, and even a couple with an alarming amount of blood on their clothes. Gabe waited patiently at the desk for his turn.

"Hi," he said again, hoping he would have better luck this time around. "I was told my boyfriend is still here, Joseph Sullivan? He was brought in with hypothermia."

The dude behind the counter was grisly and somewhere in his mid-fifties, but he didn't bat an eyelid as he typed Joey's name into the system. "Yes, sir, he's here. They're waiting for him to regain consciousness before moving him to another ward."

Gabe glanced at the clock on the wall. Twenty past eleven. "Um, is Nurse Mullins still on duty? She said I could speak to her when I got here."

The guy nodded. "Take a seat, son, and I'll grab her when I next see her."

Gabe smiled, his relief probably obvious. "Thank you, sir."

Gabe found a place to sit between a girl sniffling with what looked like might be a broken arm, and a guy holding a heavy-duty bandage against his hand. The girl gave him a watery smile.

"Hey," said Gabe, glancing at her mom. She nodded at Gabe. What a relief, after the shitty week he'd had with all those rumors, not to be treated like a threat. He smiled at the girl again. She could only have been about six. "You look like you're being awfully brave. Would you like one of my flowers?"

The girl's eyes widened. "Can I?" she asked her mom.

"If the man says it's all right," she said.

Gabe showed them to the girl when she looked over again. "They're for my friend. But there's a lot here. I'm sure he won't miss one."

The girl hiccuped and cradled her injured arm. "Can I have a pink one? Please," she tacked on at the end.

Gabe fished her out one of the daisies. "Make sure you have your mom cut the end off the bottom and place it in some water. That way, the petals will open up and get even bigger."

The girl took the flower carefully. "Wow," she whispered. "Thank you, Mister."

"Thank you, Mr. Robinson," said her mom. Gabe raised his eyebrows at her, but she didn't say anything else. She just gave him a slight nod.

"Mr. Robinson?"

He turned around to see a middle-aged redhead nurse looking out over the waiting room. Gabe gave the mom and her kid a wave, then stood to his feet.

"That's me, ma'am," he said, walking over. The nerves were back in his belly. It hadn't even been a full day since he'd last seen Joey, but it felt like a year.

Nurse Mullins smiled at him, then rested a hand on his arm to guide the way. "He's still sleeping," she said. "But the doctors have done their rounds and I'm happy to let you sit with him."

"Okay," said Gabe, nibbling his lip. "Should I be worried he's not awake yet?"

Nurse Mullins shook her head. "He had a bad night, I would guess. Poor boy needs his rest. He'll wake naturally soon enough, I'm sure. We're doing quarterly vitals – so every fifteen minutes. We won't miss anything, I promise."

She showed him into a small private room. Joey looked so small in his gown under the pale hospital sheets. "Oh, baby," he whimpered. There were dark circles under his closed eyes and his hair was stuck to his head.

"We wrapped him in lots of blankets and gave him a warm saline solution through the I.V." She pointed at the almost-empty bag attached to the drip in his arm. "We're much happier with his core body temperature now, that's why most of the blankets are gone. Now it's just a matter of waiting for him to come round again."

Gabe nodded. "Thank you," he said, stepping closer. He brushed Joey's forehead with his fingers, sweeping some of his curls away. His breathing was steady and Gabe could see there was a little color in his cheeks now he was closer.

"We tried contacting his family," Nurse Mullins ventured. "They're the ones listed as his next of kin in his records."

Gabe raised an eyebrow at her. "And let me guess, they haven't come."

Nurse Mullins sighed. "I believe I spoke to Joey's father, and, no. He didn't sound eager to visit."

Gabe shook his head and blinked back the tears that threatened to fall. He needed to be strong, for Joey. "It doesn't matter. I'm here now."

Nurse Mullins squeezed his shoulder. "You sure are. Okay, hon. We're crazy busy here," she told him. "But someone will be in shortly to check him again. In the meantime, if you need anything, just ring the bell and I or one of my team will do our best, okay?"

"I'm sure we'll be fine now," said Gabe, giving her a grateful smile.

She nodded then rushed back onto the ward.

Gabe laid his flowers by Joey's neat pile of clothes. He should have thought to bring a vase. Joey's shoes were under the bed. They looked so tattered and damp.

Gabe let out a heavy sigh and took the plastic chair by Joey's bed. "I'm so sorry," he whispered, even though there was no one else around. He slipped Joey's limp hand between both his own. "I shouldn't have stormed off. But, I hope it counts for something that I'm here now."

Joey didn't respond, but his skin was warm to Gabe's touch. At least that was something.

So he settled in to wait. He'd already called to cancel his shift with the fire crew. He didn't have anywhere else in the world to be other than waiting patiently by Joey's side.

CHAPTER
Twenty~Nine

JOEY

Joey's eyes were stinging. He felt groggy and disorientated. This wasn't his camp bed?

"Joey?"

He groaned. His throat was dry. "Gabe?"

Someone was holding his hand. As he managed to crack one eyelid open, he wasn't that surprised to see it was Gabe. But everything else was a bit of a shock, he had to admit.

Gabe was sitting next to him, not lying like he might have expected. For a moment, he had thought they were still in Chicago. But that had been several days ago?

The argument.

Joey pulled his hand free of Gabe's and hugged himself. Was he in a hospital? How had he gotten here?

Oh fuck. The park.

He looked at Gabe, who was watching Joey pensively. "How are you feeling?" he asked.

Joey blinked and sat up. He was definitely in the hospital. "What happened?"

To his surprise, Gabe's expression turned cross. "I don't know. You didn't answer my text. But," he said with a sigh.

"I'm putting two and two together and guessing your dad kicked you out. Otherwise, why would you be out in the park at five o'clock in the morning?"

Joey pulled the covers up around him. "Yeah, okay, he did," he said. "Though I don't know why you're mad at me?"

"Because," Gabe said, his whole demeanor softening. "You never let anyone in. I wanted to help you. I would never have let you put yourself in danger like that if we'd just talked. If you'd listened to me."

There were tears in his eyes. But Joey could feel the lump growing in his throat too. "Look, I saw you, all right. In the park. I don't want you to string me along."

Gabe blinked. "What?"

"With your ex," Joey mumbled. "You didn't need to come to my house and explain your side, or whatever. It was pretty clear what was going on."

Gabe's eyes widened. "Jesus, fuck – Joey! Is *that* what you thought I was talking about?"

Joey looked down at his bed sheets as he pulled on one of the corners. "I don't want to be anyone's second choice," he said, managing to keep his voice steady.

Gabe seized his hand and sat on the edge of the bed in one motion, clutching Joey's hand to his chest. "Joey. Listen very carefully to me," he said. A smile was twitching at his mouth. "I asked Lewis to meet with me because I suddenly have some potentially serious *legal* troubles. He's a lawyer. I'm guessing you didn't stick around for long, because when he tried to get it on with me, I pushed him away and told him we'd had our chance. You know why?"

Joey was trying to digest his words fast enough. "Uh, no?"

"You. Because of you, you...*idiot.*" He laughed and cradled Joey's face. "Lewis was a total dick and told me if we couldn't try things again, he wouldn't take my case. And when that happened, all I wanted was to see you, to talk to you, like I should have just done when all this started on Monday."

Heat was flaring up Joey's body to his face. "So…you're not getting back together with him?"

"No," said Gabe in exasperation. He leaned forward, his lips only an inch from Joey's. "I'd like to get back together with you. If you'll have me?"

Joey surged forwards, clashing their mouths together. He was sure his breath was probably awful, but he didn't care.

"Oh god, oh fuck, I'm so sorry," he wailed. "I'm a terrible, awful person!"

Gabe hugged him tightly. "No, you're not. You just need to learn to trust people a bit more. Trust me."

Joey was embarrassed to find he was crying hard into Gabe's shoulder. But the relief was like a dam breaking. He may have lost everything else, but he still had Gabe. "He hit me," he said, feeling like a small child as he sobbed. "He told me to kill myself. I had to leave everything. Money, clothes, charger-" He pulled back to look at Gabe. "My phone died. How did you find me?"

Gabe pointed to Joey's phone plugged into an unfamiliar charger. Then he gently took Joey's chin between his finger and thumb, no doubt inspecting the bruise that Joey could feel on his jaw.

"I'm going to suggest something I should have weeks ago," Gabe said. He let Joey's face go and kissed him sweetly before pulling him to cuddle against his chest. "Can you please consider it?"

Joey swallowed and nodded. He wasn't sure what Gabe was going to say, but he was done running and hiding. He'd listen.

"I want you to move in with me. Just until you're back on your feet."

If Joey had been embarrassed before, he was utterly

humiliated by the sob that wracked his chest then. "Yes," he cried, clinging to Gabe's sweater and burying his face into his shoulder. "Yes, god, please Gabe, I'd love that."

For the longest time, Gabe just held him and rocked him gently until Joey felt like he could breathe again. "Tissue?" he mumbled hopefully, not wanted to face Gabe until he'd blown his nose.

Gabe chuckled and reached over to grab him one from the nightstand. Once Joey had mopped himself up and had a big drink of water, he felt much better.

"Are you sure?" he asked tentatively.

Gabe smiled and wiped his thumb under Joey's eyes, catching the last of the tears. "Absolutely. And I'll go to your parents' house and get your stuff back myself. I'll even bring some other big, scary firefighters too, in case your dad tries any shit."

Joey laughed weakly and took a deep breath. "You're amazing. I so don't deserve you."

"Don't say that," Gabe insisted. He turned around so he could sit beside Joey and put his arm around his shoulders. "You're very precious to me."

Joey didn't get why. But he was so sick of being dealt the worst hands that he was willing to grab a good one and hold on to it.

"You're very precious to me too," he said, snuggling against Gabe's side.

Joey listened as Gabe explained everything that had happened since they had come back from Chicago on Monday. He became more and more irate as Gabe told him all about the accusations.

"Do you know what?" Joey said. "I think I know who you're talking about. I ran into her at the fair that day. She's full of shit."

Gabe chuckled and rubbed his arm. "I thought as much,

but I'm worried the damage has already been done. And if it goes to court-"

"You need a lawyer."

"A lawyer that will work for free," Gabe said heavily.

Joey bit his lip. "I might know someone," he said.

Gabe looked down at him. "Really?"

Joey nodded. "I'd have to check, but I know his firm does some pro bono work. It's worth asking, right?"

The look on Gabe's face told him it was. God, it would be so amazing to give something back after everything Gabe had done for him. He kissed Gabe's shoulder and stroked his chest.

"Do you think they'll let me go home soon?"

Gabe broke into the biggest smile, and Joey realized what he'd said. But he didn't correct himself. He was starting to understand that home *was* where the heart was. And his heart belonged to Gabe. So settling down in his house didn't seem all that scary. In fact, it felt so right Joey almost got another lump in his throat.

He needed to get a grip on himself, but Gabe was kissing him softly again, so he figured it was okay to indulge in a bit of sappiness.

"I'll go see if Nurse Mullins is still on duty," Gabe said. "But I don't see why we can't get you home now you're all warm again."

With a final kiss, he slipped out the room to organize Joey's discharge.

———

Gabe didn't push. Joey sensed it was hard for him, but he gave Joey space to settle in.

They left the hospital not long after Joey woke up. Gabe told him sternly they weren't going to worry about the medical bill until they had things sorted out. It wasn't huge, all things considered. Once Joey started getting royalties from the Storm Sailor song he should be able to cover it in no time.

On the way to the house, Gabe pulled into a Walmart to get supplies. He insisted on buying Joey just some simple sweats, a couple of t-shirts, underwear and toiletries. Enough so he could get through the next few days in comfort.

Joey only felt a minor itch at letting someone else pay for him. But this was Gabe. He wasn't doing it to have one over on Joey, he was doing it because he cared. Besides, Joey knew he'd get a chance to pay him back in one way or another, and that was kind of wonderful.

Being with Gabe was like being part of a team. Even though Gabe was the one looking after him right now, it felt like they were in it together. He didn't make Joey feel like he was in debt.

Joey desperately wanted his stuff back, but as it was a Saturday, his dad and brother would almost certainly be at the house. So even with Gabe's offer of rustling up some of his big buddies to help, Joey didn't want to risk it yet. Part of him had already accepted that his laptop was probably already smashed or sold. As much as that destroyed him, he reminded himself that actually, he could have died on Friday night. Instead, he was here with Gabe. Safe.

Gabe let him go into the house first, promising they would get him a set of keys cut soon. Joey had only been there the one time before, but he immediately noticed things had changed.

"You've…rearranged?" he asked, unsure.

Gabe nodded and came inside after him, placing their bags down and shutting the door. "I thought it was time for a fresh start. So, some things have moved around. Other things are gone for good." He hugged Joey to him and cast his gaze around the front room.

Joey's heart swelled. From what he could work out, Gabe and Lewis had lived here for most of their relationship. The fact Gabe had shuffled everything around to make it seem new felt like he was making room for Joey in his heart.

Once they unpacked their shopping, Gabe gave Joey free rein in the bathroom. Joey had gotten accustomed to sneaking showers before anyone else at his parents' house woke up. Even on their Chicago trip, aside from the bath Gabe had run them, he'd washed as fast as possible so as not to waste time. Therefore, when Gabe kissed his nose and told him to take his time, Joey shut the door and filled the tub all the way to the top with hot water and bubble bath.

The hospital had warmed him up perfectly, but he could still feel the chill in his bones. It was probably psychological, but still, slipping under the suds was heavenly. He could just drift in the water, and he did his best not to think of much except how content he felt.

Dressed in his new sweats, Joey dried his hair so it was all fluffy then traipsed downstairs to find where Gabe had got to. The smell of sautéing onions and chicken suggested he was in the kitchen.

On his way down the stairs though, Joey spotted a little furry face peering around the corner at him. "Duchess?" he said in surprise.

The cat disappeared, almost as if she was never there in the first place. But Joey smiled to himself all the same. Slow progress was still progress.

Gabe had made them a late lunch or early dinner, depending on how you looked at it. Chicken in a creamy mushroom sauce served with rice and green peas.

Joey chuckled. "You put peas in your lasagna as well," he said, poking the pan.

"I put peas in everything," said Gabe cheerfully as he stirred the sauce.

"You're so weird," Joey said, grinning.

"Hey," said Gabe, pretending to be affronted. "I love them."

"I love you," Joey said, slipping his arms around Gabe's waist and cuddling to his side.

Then he realized what he said.

Gabe had frozen next to him and Joey was flooded with nerves. He looked up, not letting go of Gabe's body, staring into his wide eyes.

"Do you?" said Gabe in little more than a whisper.

Joey wasn't sure. Was this love? He felt complete in Gabe's arms. Safe and cherished and like he could accomplish anything. When they were apart this past week, it had pained him. Physically ached in his chest.

"I've never been in love before," Joey admitted, licking his lips to give him a second to think. "But…yeah. I think so." He took a deep breath and gazed into Gabe's beautiful brown eyes. "I love you."

It felt so right.

Joey broke into a huge smile and nodded. Gabe let out a cry and hugged him close. "I love you too," he said. "I realized last night. When…when we fought. It hurt too much to be anything but love."

Joey rubbed his back. "I'm sorry," he apologized again.

Gabe shook his head and kissed his temple. "I'm sorry too."

Joey cupped his face for one last kiss, then let him get back to cooking before something caught on fire.

He was in love. It did feel pretty amazing

Dinner was served on laps and they watched stupid movies throughout the afternoon and evening. Gradually, they slipped down until they were lying on the couch, spooning and snuggled.

Joey felt like Gabe was holding back, being extra cautious of where he put his hands and careful not to rub his crotch against Joey's ass more than was strictly necessary.

Joey was done holding back. He'd wasted too much time with Gabe being afraid of getting hurt, making sure he didn't give him too much of his heart away lest he might damage it. Now he was ready to give Gabe his all.

He closed his eyes and rolled his ass deliberately against Gabe's dick, lacing their fingers together and kissing his knuckles. "Baby," he whispered. The word alone sent shivers across his skin and got his heart racing.

Gabe moaned and nuzzled Joey's neck with his nose. "Are you sure, sweetheart?" he murmured. He kissed under Joey's ear then nipped at his lobe. Joey moaned back.

"Yes," he said. He turned his head just enough so their mouths could find each other. Gabe slipped his big hand under Joey's shirt and splayed it over his stomach, claiming him. Joey loved it.

"Here?" Gabe asked him. "Or upstairs?"

Joey grinned and caught Gabe's lower lip between his teeth. "Is it bad if I say I want you to take me in every single room in this house?" Joey was eager to banish any memory of Lewis and he wasn't ashamed at how he went about it.

Gabe groaned and turned Joey so they were facing each other, both hands under his sweater now. He gripped Joey's flanks possessively. "I like that plan," he growled between kisses. "But the stuff is upstairs."

"Stuff?" Joey repeated with a laugh. "What are you, sixteen?"

Gabe tickled him as punishment. "All right, the lube, condoms and toys are all in my bedroom."

Joey wriggled free from his fingers and looked at Gabe seriously. "Toys?"

Gabe licked his lips seductively. "Yeah, baby. Toys."

Joey whimpered. He wasn't sure he wanted to play around right then, he was too desperate to make love with Gabe. But the idea of using props very soon was immensely appealing.

"I just want you tonight," Joey said, cradling Gabe's strong jaw. "But sign me up for future fun."

Gabe gave him a wicked grin. "I'll hold you to that." He rocked them forwards and used his impressive strength to pick Joey up. With his legs wrapped around Gabe's waist, they kissed and walked their way up the stairs and into Gabe's bedroom.

Joey's sweatpants did nothing to hide his straining erection. Gabe lowered him carefully onto the mattress and kissed down his throat, palming his cock through the material.

By now, they'd had sex several times. But something was different between them tonight. The electricity crackled like a storm and Joey felt free in a way he wasn't sure he'd ever felt. There was no time limit weighing down on him. No sense that this was wrong or doomed to fail. He was going to fight to stay with Gabe with everything he had.

Gabe wasted no time pulling Joey's comfy clothes off, the elastic bands making it blissfully easy to get him naked as fast as possible. This being Gabe, he also took a moment to yank the comforter down and get them under the covers before hastily divesting himself of his own clothes.

"What do you want?" he mumbled into Joey's mouth.

Joey shook his head. "What do *you* want?"

Gabe laughed and kissed along his jaw. "We'll never get anywhere if one of us doesn't pick."

"That would be a tragedy," Joey agreed.

At present, Gabe was lying on top of Joey. His weight pressing him into the bed felt amazing, as did their thick, heavy cocks rubbing leisurely against one another. But Joey desperately wanted Gabe inside him, as deep as he could go.

"Like this?" He turned under Gabe and looked shyly over his shoulder. Gabe nodded, leaning down to kiss him.

"Perfect," Gabe told him.

Joey sighed as Gabe kissed down his spine, his big hands massaging Joey's ass cheeks. Gabe moved away for just a moment to retrieve lube and a condom, and Joey watched him with flutters in his belly.

He knew Gabe would take care of him. That was a thousand times sexier than all those guys Joey had let push him around in the past.

Gabe laid himself down beside Joey as he reached down and rubbed his hole with slippery fingers. Joey moaned into Gabe's mouth as he kissed him. He spread his knees out, giving Gabe better access to his ass.

Unlike previous occasions when Joey had been in charge of his own prep, Gabe took his time to ensure Joey was properly stretched for him. Joey kept Gabe hard by stroking his lovely cock and even stopped proceedings to suck him off for a little while. He didn't want to be passive and let Gabe do all the work, even though Gabe was probably happy with that. Gabe needed tending to as well, and Joey wanted to make that his job from now on.

Eventually, Gabe crawled on top of Joey and sank slowly inside his hole, kissing his neck and whispering how beautiful he was the whole time. Joey reached for Gabe's hand and was happy when they linked fingers again. Gabe slid his other hand under Joey's body and hugged his belly to him.

They kissed as Gabe began to move inside him, his cock stroking Joey's prostate and making him weep. He felt sublime. "Perfect," Joey managed to utter. "So perfect, fuck, Gabe, yes."

Joey moved in tandem with Gabe, their bodies coming together again and again. Now that their future was laid out before them like an open road, Joey knew they'd make love countless times. No doubt there would be occasions where they'd take it slow, eek it out and drive each other crazy. But tonight, there was no teasing.

Gabe pulled them up so they were both kneeling, Joey's back pressed against his muscular chest. He looked over his shoulder to capture Gabe's mouth for a kiss. Gabe hugged him tightly with one arm, then reached his other hand down to wrap strong fingers around Joey's bouncing, rock-hard cock.

"Come for me, gorgeous," he said.

Joey whined, his climax building deliciously. He dug his fingers into the arm holding him in place, gasping and uttering nonsensical noises. Gabe thrust inside him and worked his prick, making him delirious.

"Gabe," Joey cried. He bucked backward as his orgasm tore through him. Gabe rode him hard, chasing his own release as Joey spurted onto the bed and up his chest. Finally, Gabe clutched his hips, emptying his load into the condom deep inside Joey.

They gasped for air, tumbling back onto the mattress with happy sighs. Joey reached for the tissue box so they could both mop up. He could already feel his eyelids dropping as Gabe disposed of the condom.

"Let's get tested soon, yeah," he said sleepily, pawing at Gabe's arm as he nestled back under the comforter. "No more rubbers."

Gabe laughed at him and kissed his cheek. "My thoughts exactly."

Sleep took Joey easily after that, warm and sated in Gabe's strong arms.

He woke sometime in the night, briefly confused as to where he was. He'd slept in so many different places over the past week, it was understandable he got disoriented. But Gabe's solid form beside him soon reassured him he was where he was meant to be.

He felt a movement by his feet and froze. It was hard to see in the minimal moonlight filtering through the curtains, but Joey squinted at the shape at the end of the bed.

If he wasn't mistaken, he could have sworn he saw a pair of big, blue eyes.

"Duchess?" he whispered.

The cat let out a tentative meow and hunkered down by Joey and Gabe's feet, blinking slowly as she looked up at Joey.

He wanted to wake Gabe to share the moment with him. But he feared the movement would dislodge their visitor. So instead he watched her until he couldn't keep his eyes open anymore, hoping she might still be there in the morning.

CHAPTER

Thirty

GABE

Joey rubbed Gabe's back sympathetically. "It's just a town council meeting," he said, his green eyes wide. "The police aren't officially involved. It's not gone to court."

"Yet," said Gabe.

They were sitting in his car on the curb down the street from the town hall. It was an imposing building; three stories high with big, white Georgian columns standing out in front. Gabe had never been inside before. He'd never had to.

Two days after he had brought Joey home from the hospital, he'd got a call from Mitch saying the council was going to discuss Gabe's 'situation' at their next bimonthly meeting. Mitch had called on Monday; the meeting was Wednesday.

It was just a council meeting, so in theory, anyone could attend. Mitch had promised he and Mary-Lou would be there to speak up for Gabe. But in reality, Gabe had absolutely *no* idea how something like this worked. All he could imagine was a courtroom like you'd see on a TV drama, but he was pretty sure he wasn't going to be pulled up and cross-examined.

Pretty sure.

Joey took his hand and looked at him encouragingly. "Babe, you've done absolutely nothing wrong. They haven't got a leg to stand on."

Gabe nodded and tried to absorb some of his boyfriend's confidence. The only positive from being forced into taking vacation time from work was that it had happened to coincide with Joey moving in. Gabe wasn't sure what he would have done the past two days without Joey there by his side.

Not only had he been supportive and comforting, but Joey had also contacted his lawyer friend on Gabe's behalf. At such short notice, Gabe didn't hold out much hope anything could be done, but he appreciated that Joey tried.

Gabe's plan for attending the meeting tonight was simply to wait until they brought his name up. Then he would tell them that unless they had any proof of his wrongdoing, which they couldn't have, they were in violation of anti-discriminatory laws.

The thought of saying that out loud filled him with dread. He hated confrontation. He was still too hung up on how these people he thought were his friends could turn on him like this.

"Because they're assholes," Joey had told him several times. "They don't deserve your heart, so you need to stop giving it to them."

Gabe knew he was probably naive, but he still clung to some faith in his town. He'd told Joey about the Good Samaritan who had found him freezing to death on that bench and called 911. Also Nurse Mullins, who had gone above and beyond to care for them both. Joey had begrudgingly admitted that maybe not *everyone* was an asshole.

But some people were. Some people had decided that Gabe had to be treated differently, simply because he was gay. Gabe needed to forget the part of him that was hurt because of that, and seize the part that was fucking furious.

How dare they abuse him like this? This was no different to being judged by race or religion. He wouldn't stand for it. Couldn't.

With a resolute sigh, he nodded at Joey, and they got out of the car into the snow that hadn't let up since the weekend. Joey took his hand and they headed towards the council building together.

They were a little early, so they walked through the grand lobby by themselves. Their shoes echoed off the black-and-white-tiled floor. Both of them looked up in awe at the arched, pale pink ceiling, and white columns and banisters running around the room.

Gabe was aware you could get married in this room. The sweeping central staircase would certainly make a dramatic entrance for a bride. But for him in his current state of mind, it just seemed huge and impersonal.

He shook his head. Now was not the time to be thinking about weddings. He needed to focus on himself and the task at hand.

The council meetings were apparently held in an understated antechamber on the second floor. It was a simple room with white walls, grey carpet and wooden chairs with plush blue seats. The chairs were currently being set out like an audience for a play, all facing away from the door with a central aisle left down the middle.

A number of people were already in the room, either moving the chairs, sitting themselves down, or setting up with papers and notebooks at the table facing the seats where you might expect a stage to be. Gabe guessed the seven seats behind the table were reserved for the council representatives.

A few people glanced at him and Joey as they took a

couple of seats in the middle of the room. He tried to ignore them, but then he made eye contact with Debbie Slater, talking at the front of the room with a man Gabe presumed to be her husband. He was a weedy-looking man, but he gave Gabe a bold enough sneer.

Debbie, oddly enough, gave Gabe a pitying smile. That was pretty daring of her. Gabe would have expected her to cower away from him, considering she was actively trying to ruin his life.

Gabe hadn't realized how tense he'd got until Joey touched his arm. "Forget her," he said. "Don't let them get to you."

Gabe nodded and took his seat. He tried his best to ignore the Slaters after that, but he couldn't help but shoot them the occasional glare. Joey held his hand which was some comfort. Neither of them spoke much and Joey's knee didn't stop bouncing as the room gradually filled.

Gabe kept glancing towards the door. Where the hell were Mitch and Mary-Lou?

There were other faces Gabe recognized in the audience though, much to his surprise. Lara from the Goodwill store was there with her two almost-grownup kids. All three waved at him. He also spotted Brooke from the animal shelter, some of his buddies from the fire department, Maggie from the bakery, old Mrs. Turnell whose lawn he cut regularly, and a guy he took a moment to place as the dad of the little redhead girl with all the intricate questions about the fire truck at the fair. Every one of them gave him nods or smiles when he saw that they were there.

It wasn't quite the same as Mitch and Mary-Lou, but it was heartening all the same. And he had Joey beside him, which was the most important thing.

"All right, looks like we have a full house here tonight," a loud voice cut through the hubbub.

A portly man clapped his hands to get people's attention. He had a scruffy beard encroaching down his neck and a stain on the corner of his shirt cuff that he was obviously aware of by the way he kept pulling at his jacket sleeve. Mr. Tallis, if Gabe remembered correctly. He was a dentist or chiropractor or something. He rubbed his bulbous red nose and waved for quiet.

"Now we have several items on the agenda tonight. However, one is of a somewhat, uh, delicate nature. Therefore, I have been advised we start with that."

Gabe looked anxiously over his shoulder again. He couldn't believe his friends were late.

"Mr. Slater," said Mr. Tallis. "I believe you would like to address the council."

Skinny Mr. Slater nodded and stood up from his seat behind the table, allowing Mr. Tallis to take the central chair amongst the other five representatives. "Thank you," he said. His voice was slimy and ingratiating, grating on Gabe's nerves immediately. "As some of you are aware, my wife recently brought some concerns to the Greenwich public library about one of their employees. Specifically, questioning whether or not it was suitable for such a character to be operating in such close proximity to children."

Anger flared in Gabe's chest. Joey squeezed his hand tightly, keeping him sitting still. Although the look on Joey's face suggested he was even more livid than Gabe.

"As a father myself," Mr. Slater continued, placing a hand over his heart. "I can promise you that *nothing* is more sacred than the safety and protection of the innocence of our children."

"Of course," Mr. Tallis chimed in.

Debbie Slater beamed at her husband from her seat in the audience.

Mr. Slater nodded at Mr. Tallis. The whole thing was

sickening to watch. Gabe would have cringed if he wasn't so busy snarling.

But Joey's hand was warm in his, anchoring him. He reminded himself that he had to show them he wasn't a threat. He couldn't give them any excuses, so he managed to school his reaction back. However, Mr. Slater wasn't going to make that easy.

"I see Mr. Robinson is here with us tonight," he said, gesturing towards Gabe. Mr. Slater smiled, a grotesque thing that didn't meet his eyes. "Good. Hopefully, that will make things simpler." Mr. Slater turned his attention from the crowd to the head table. "My wife and I have a petition of over a hundred signatures urging this council to keep Mr. Robinson suspended from his job at the public library and the extracurricular activities he currently volunteers at. Until a thorough police background check can be run to assess his suitability to be around minors, he should not be in a position of authority around them."

"This is outrageous," Gabe cried. He shot to his feet despite Joey's protests. "You can run a background check all you like, I've got nothing to hide. But to stop me from doing my job because of your prejudices is just – it's-" What the hell was the law they were breaking? The word had gone clean out of his head and he began getting flustered and panicked. "It's not fair!"

There were murmurs of agreement around the room. "Hear, hear!" Lara cried.

"Not fair at all," said one of the guys that ran a computer course at the library.

Mr. Slater smirked. Mrs. Slater got to her feet. "This is nothing personal, Mr. Robinson. But when there are children involved we cannot be too careful."

"So why aren't you suspending all the staff at the library?"

Gabe demanded. "Doing background checks on them, too. Why have you singled me out?"

He wanted to make them say it.

Debbie Slater huffed. "Mr. Robinson, it has become obvious your lifestyle choices are far from family-friendly. We can't have our children exposed to such a destructive element."

"What choices?" he growled. Joey touched his arm.

"Keep calm," he muttered, looking around the room. Every pair of eyes was on Gabe.

Gabe took a deep breath and dared them to say it was because he was gay.

But Debbie gave him a sweet smile that didn't reach her eyes, then glanced at Joey. "Why, the company you keep, of course."

Joey's hand dropped from Gabe's arm. Fuck. Gabe had forgotten that Mitch had mentioned the Twitter pictures.

Mr. Slater laughed hollowly. "Mr. Robinson, you didn't think this was about your sexual orientation, did you?" Mr. Slater tutted. "That would be illegal, not to mention immoral, to suggest you were unfit to be around children simply because you are gay."

That was exactly what they were suggesting, Gabe was certain.

"I've had a boyfriend for the past five years," he said. He refused to mention Lewis by name. He could have been there, helping Gabe in his hour of need. Instead, he'd left him to the wolves. "Who I date has no bearing whatsoever on my ability to serve the community."

Mr. Slater frowned. "It does when that person is a known drug and alcohol abuser of questionable moral character, not to mention barely more than a minor himself."

Rage filled Gabe. How dare they drag Joey into this.

Joey leaped to his feet beside him, his fists balled. "I'm

twenty-one and have more life experience than you'll ever have, you piece of-"

Gabe yanked his arm before he could say something he'd really regret. Unfortunately, the people around them were looking at Joey and the tattoos that were visible on his arms and around his collar with raised eyebrows.

Fuck, this was not going well.

"Joey is not the one whose job and reputation is under threat here," Gabe said as calmly as he could. "If you have issues with him, that's your problem."

Mr. Tallis sighed from his position at the table. "Unfortunately, Mr. Robinson," he said to Gabe. "It is at this council's discretion how the annual budget is allocated. And as we come to review for next year's funds, it is fair to say that some of our members are uncomfortable supporting an institution that associates itself with such questionable behavior."

"That's discrimination," Gabe said through his teeth.

"That's good moral judgment," said Debbie Slater haughtily.

Gabe looked around the room. Some people were looking smug. Many others were looking stricken. But like him, they didn't seem to know what to say to that.

This wasn't fair, it couldn't be happening. He knew his job at the library wasn't as important as what he did with the fire department. He was hardly saving the world making sure the art club or parent-toddler group was set up and kept in good supply. But damn it, he loved it. He loved being connected to the community and helping it tick by every day.

Now these people wanted to poison the town against him. Him *and* Joey, which was totally unacceptable. Greenwich had treated him badly enough as it was.

But he didn't know what to do. Should he demand they

file formal charges? What would happen if this went to court? Surely they couldn't just get away with this because they didn't like Gabe and Joey for who they were.

He opened his mouth, desperate for something to say.

Instead, the door to the council room flew open.

Gabe, like everyone else in the audience, turned to see the group of people marching through the doors, brushing snow from their clothes and breathing like they'd just sprinted up the stairs.

Beside him, Joey gasped. Gabe risked a quick glance at him. His whole face was lit up.

"I do apologize for the late arrival," said the man at the head of the party. He smiled jovially at the room, totally at ease as he strode down the aisle. He was broad and blond, an expensive raincoat was hanging from one arm, an even more expensive briefcase swinging from the other hand.

Gabe realized people were suddenly whispering to each other like a nest of hornets. That was when he looked at the rest of the party following the blond man. He gasped too.

He identified Mitch and Mary-Lou immediately. Mitch had several sheets of paper clutched in his hands, and as soon as he met Gabe's eyes, he mouthed 'I'm sorry' to him.

The other two younger guys Gabe had never met. But he recognized them all the same.

"Blake," Joey squeaked, joy evident on his face.

Blake Jackson, star of Feet of Flames and formerly of Below Zero, was walking down the center of the room. He was stunningly good-looking, with pale blond hair like the man walking in front of him and had an athletic body that was visible even through his coat and sweater.

Beside him was a Hispanic-looking guy with barely contained glee evident on his face as he looked over the crowd, nodding to them until he spotted Joey. He grinned and gave him two thumbs up. That was Elion Rodriguez,

Blake's boyfriend, who had also been on the first season of Feet of Flames.

Gabe felt his jaw drop. What the hell were they both doing here?

"Can I help you?" Mr. Slater said to the blond man as he approached him at the front of the room. To his credit, he didn't flinch away like a lot of other people might have done. The blond guy was like a lion, perfectly at ease as he thrust his hand out, forcing Mr. Slater to shake it.

"Richard Jackson," said the blond man. "Of Jackson, Frazier and Pollak, Cincinnati. I'm here to represent Mr. Robinson."

Thirty~One

JOEY

"OH MY GOD," ELION HISSED FROM GABE'S SIDE. "THIS IS LIKE an episode of The Good Wife!"

Blake shushed him, but kindly. Joey had to agree. This was absolutely like something out of a courtroom drama.

While Mr. Slater stuttered and Mr. Tallis rose indignantly to his feet, Joey had shuffled down their empty row of seats so Elion and Blake could sit beside him and Gabe. Christ, it was so amazing to see them. It had been months, but they both looked so well. It was like a balm on Joey's shredded nerves.

At the front of the room Blake's dad, Richard, was completely unruffled. He placed his briefcase on the table at the front of the room and draped his damp coat over the seat Mr. Slater had left unoccupied.

"This is not a session in court, Mr. Jackson," Mr. Tallis said sternly.

Richard smiled at him, flashing perfectly straight, white teeth. "Of course not. But I am here as Mr. Robinson's legal representation all the same. Am I to understand you're currently blackmailing his place of employment into forcing leave on him with the threat of diminished funds next fiscal year?"

"No, no," said Mr. Slater, holding up a finger.

Mrs. Slater, the blonde with the earmuffs Joey already immensely disliked before all this, jumped to her feet. "We have the right to question Mr. Robinson's fitness as someone who interacts with children on a daily basis," she snapped, all but stamping her foot. Her two buddies from the fair were sitting next to her, nodding like the good lapdogs they were.

Richard arched an eyebrow at her. "Yes, you do," he agreed. "But as you have absolutely no grounds with which to cast these accusations, as Mr. Robinson's legal counsel I'm advising he sue this board for libel, slander and defamation of character, all of which could potentially affect his capacity to earn in the immediate and foreseeable future."

Gabe let out a small huff of disbelief, his mouth hanging open and eyes glassy. Joey slipped his hand into his, lacing their fingers.

"Holy crap, your dad is so scary," Joey whispered to Blake.

"Yeah," said Elion with no small amount of snark. "It's awesome when it's directed at someone else."

"Now, now," said Mr. Tallis, trying to regain control of the increasingly loud room. "There's no need for that, Mr. Jackson. We were simply concerned for the well-being of the community."

"A community which Mr. Robinson is actively part of." He turned and beckoned the bear of a guy with grey hair that had come in with him. "Gabe's employer, Mr. Curtis here, has some evidence we'd like to present to you."

"This *isn't* a court of law," Mr. Slater said with a scowl.

Richard winked at him. "Yeah, but you've got no grounds for dismissal, remember? How about we take a peek at some evidence just to put everyone's minds at ease?"

"What's going on?" Gabe whispered.

Blake leaned over Elion, who was watching the proceedings with such awe, all he needed was some popcorn. "Joey told us everything. My dad was in contact with your friend, Mitch. He's got twice as many testimonials to your good character as that witch over there has names on her petition. Hi, I'm Blake by the way. It's a pleasure to meet you."

Gabe shook his hand mutely, eyes darting back and forth between the people standing at the front of the audience. Voices hissed and whispered all around them. A man leaned over a whole row of seats to grip Gabe's shoulder.

"Well done, son," the guy said.

"This was a sham from the start," another woman chimed in. Joey recognized her as one of the waitresses that always gave him a sneaky slice of pie with his endless coffee refills.

"I wrote a few words for you," said another, pointing to Mitch.

Joey's heart swelled as more people in the room were nodding and calling out words of agreement. They'd not been brave enough to say more than the odd word before, but with Mitch's testimonials and Richard's unflinching attack on the council, they were finding their voices now. Joey smiled as he recognized the girl from the stall at the fair who'd given him a free turn, as well as the parents of the little Wonder Woman twins. So many people had come out to support Gabe.

"You did this."

Joey turned to find Gabe looking at him in a way he was sure no one had ever looked at him before. There was pride and happiness and gratitude and, of course, love. That word that Joey had been getting more and more used to over the past few days.

Joey so desperately wanted to kiss him, but he didn't want to aggravate the already-noisy crowd. The din was getting louder as more people tried to make themselves heard. Instead, he rubbed Gabe's thigh.

"We did this," he said. "It was a group effort."

Joey looked around again. Maybe people weren't all untrustworthy bastards, after all? Some of them could actually be amazing when you really needed them.

He suddenly stopped his wandering gaze, his eyes widening in disbelief. He'd spied a timid-looking woman standing at the rear of the room, a familiar backpack clutched in her hands.

"What?" said Gabe, reacting to Joey's stillness. Richard was still going at it with the council behind them.

"Mom?" Joey said, the word no more than a rasp.

She gave him the smallest of waves. He couldn't believe it. She was here, she was out of the house. She had his stuff.

Before he could properly process it, his attention was drawn back to the front of the room.

"It seems Mr. Robinson is, by all accounts, an outstanding member of the community," Richard said, pointing to the testimonials. "Furthermore, in the state of Connecticut, it is illegal for an employer to discriminate on the basis of race, color, religious creed, sex, national origin, age, ancestry, marital status, disability – learning, mental, intellectual or physical – sexual orientation, gender identity or expression." He looked out at the crowd. "Shall I go on?"

There were several cheers of support.

"Mr. Jackson," spluttered Mr. Tallis as Mitch handed him the testimonials he'd collected. "This is highly irregular."

"No," Richard shot back. "What is highly irregular is putting a man's livelihood and general well-being at stake because you have petty prejudices. Mr. Robinson will be allowed to return to work with immediate effect, and the Greenwich public library will receive the same funding as this financial year, or you will find yourself buried under a legal landslide. Do I make myself clear?"

Mr. Tallis clenched his jaw. "Yes, sir," he said.

Mr. Slater slunk back to the audience to sit by his sour-faced wife.

"Excellent," Richard said cheerfully. He tapped the testimonials in front of Mr. Tallis. "We have our own copies of these. So I'll just leave those there." He deftly picked up his coat and briefcase and walked back down the aisle. "Come on," he said to Blake, his face stony. Joey blinked in surprise at the sudden change in demeanor.

Blake didn't seem all that surprised though. "Let's go," he said, rising to his feet.

They weren't the only ones. As Mr. Tallis shakily called the next order of business – something to do with parking regulations – half the room must have stood to follow Joey and the others out.

Amidst the throng, Joey craned his neck looking for his mom. She wouldn't have left without talking to him, especially as she had what looked like all his possessions with her. But it was such a shock to see her on top of what had just transpired, Joey wasn't sure what to think.

"That was…" Gabe said as they got buffeted from the room.

Richard was up ahead, already on his phone. People were clapping Gabe on the back as they swarmed downstairs, telling him congratulations. Joey recognized some from the firefighter display as they hugged him. A little girl came running up. One arm was in a sling, but her free hand clutched a pink daisy in a Coke bottle to show Gabe. Her mom told him she'd been coming to classes at the library for years and wrote a testimonial without hesitation.

The man and woman who had come in with Elion, Blake

and his dad pushed through the crowd to engulf Gabe in a hug. "We got stuck in the snow," the guy, Mitch, bemoaned.

"He wouldn't put the chains on the tires," the woman said. Joey guessed they were married by the way he just rolled his eyes and smiled at her. "Are you all right?"

"Great," said Gabe, slightly dazed. People were still waving at him and patting him on the back as they left.

Mitch and his wife said they had to run because they had one of their grandkids staying over. They gave Gabe another long hug before they departed. "See you at *work*," Mitch said pointedly, tapping Gabe's cheek fondly.

Joey couldn't quite believe this was his town. Sure, there had been plenty of shitty people in there trying to tear Gabe down. And fucking hell, in the end they'd tried to pin it on *Joey*, which given his track record with this place, wasn't all that surprising. But damn, if the room hadn't mostly been filled with people there to support him. All those testimonials. Joey would have to ask Blake for a copy from his dad. After all this unpleasantness, he wanted to read the wonderful things that people had had to say about his boyfriend.

Joey was pulled from his musings as he saw his mom standing to the side on the first floor, letting the crowd go by. "Wait up, guys," he said. Gabe, Blake and Elion stopped, then followed him as he pushed his way through the throng to her. "Mom?" he said again. "What are you doing here?"

He hugged her carefully. Her slim frame wouldn't withstand the bear hug he wanted to give her.

"I heard about your Gabe's troubles from Cathy," she said. Her tone was a little sheepish, no doubt because Joey's sister-in-law was probably over the moon to hear about a 'fag getting justice' as she saw it. "I – I wanted to support you both. And, well, you left this behind."

She held out Joey's bag and he had to fight the lump in his

throat. Gabe slipped his arm around Joey's waist and watched over his shoulder as Joey opened the backpack. As far as he could see, everything was in there. His laptop, wallet, clothes and the irreplaceable keepsakes in the front pocket. He placed the bag on the floor.

"I hid them," said his mom, a tear rolling down her cheek. "So he couldn't find them. He was so…so mad."

Joey looked back at his friends, then to her again. "Mom," he said, wishing they were alone. At least most of the townsfolk had left now. It was just them and Richard talking on his phone in the hall's grand lobby, with the occasional person walking past. "Did he lose his temper with you?"

She didn't like it when he asked directly if his dad had hit her. It was too blunt. Joey had learned years ago to dance around the subject to a certain extent. But the way she tried to stop her lip trembling told him pretty much all he needed to know.

"I tried…" she said as he let go of Gabe and hugged her again. "Oh, baby, I'm so sorry. I let you down so badly." She was choking back her sobs now. Joey's heart ached.

"No, no," he said. "You did great. I can't believe you saved my things."

"Where did you go?" she asked. They pulled apart enough for her to wipe her eyes. She glanced warily at Gabe and the others then back at Joey.

Joey pulled Gabe to him and smiled. "I'm staying with Gabe at the moment." She didn't need to ever know about his brief jaunt in the E.R.

"For as long as he wants," Gabe interjected. "I'm taking care of him, Mrs. Sullivan."

Joey took his mom's hand, feeling Blake and Elion come a little closer. "Who's looking after you though, Mom?" he said. He could feel his voice cracking, but he tried to keep it steady. "Don't you want to get away from him?"

Her eyes widened and she drew her hand back. This wasn't the first time he'd suggested such a wild notion to her, but he meant it more than ever. She needed to get the fuck away from that asshole.

"No," she said, shaking her head. "No, I, uh. I couldn't."

Gabe squeezed Joey's side. "Is that what you want, Mrs. Sullivan?"

She rubbed her neck, blinking rapidly. "Tess," she mumbled, shaking her head. Joey couldn't help but smile a little, despite the awful circumstances. She only let people she trusted call her Tess. She'd never once asked Cathy to call her that.

"Mom," Joey said. "I'm not coming back, not ever again. You need to do what's best for you now."

"But Michael," she said with a hiccup. "I don't want to lose him."

"So you're willing to put up with Dad's bullshit?" Joey asked. He was pushing her, he knew. But he had to try. "Patrick and Cathy are going to move out soon. Then it'll just be you and Dad again. Is that what you want?"

She looked between him and Gabe. "He needs me," she said, her voice small.

"No, he doesn't," said Joey firmly. "That's just what he says to keep you there. Please, *please* Mom. At least think about this. Are you happy with him?" Her lip trembled and more tears leaked from her scrunched-up eyes. Joey hugged her again. "I can help you get out," he promised.

"How?" she said. "How do you unravel twenty years with someone?"

"Um, Mrs. Sullivan."

Joey let his mom go and they both looked at Blake.

"Hi," he said warmly. "It's lovely to finally meet you. I'm Joey's friend, Blake."

"Oh," she said, a twitch of a smile on her lips. "Joseph's told me so much about you."

Blake smiled. "He's told me lots of lovely things about you too. I'm so sorry to intrude, but I think I might be able to help. If a divorce is what you really want, I think I could introduce you to a lawyer. He's taking on some pro bono cases right now."

She blinked. "What?"

Elion rose up on his toes in obvious glee. "Blake's dad got caught saying some of his usual homophobic bullshit on camera." He rolled his eyes at Blake. "You'd think he'd have learned by now?" Blake shook his head. "So his firm and Blake's mom have got him doing all these goodwill cases."

"He's an amazing lawyer," Blake assured her. "Despite his narrow views on...certain things."

Elion raised an eyebrow, but said nothing.

Joey's heart was beating fast. He turned back to his mom. "What do you think?" he asked gently. "You could stay somewhere else while it's going on, if that's worrying you."

"You can stay with us," Gabe said, rubbing Joey's shoulder. Joey felt fit to burst with love and pride. Gabe had only just met his mom, for heaven's sake.

Joey's mom was shaking her head, looking between them all. "I couldn't..." she said uncertainly.

"You can," Joey said. "That's Blake's dad, right there." He pointed to Richard, pacing the tiled floor several feet away. "You don't even have to go back tonight. You can talk with him now, then come with us after."

She bit her lip. He couldn't believe it, but he saw hope blossom in her eyes.

"I never thought..." she said slowly, "he'd really hurt you like that, sweetheart. Or throw you out into the snow. I...I don't think I can stay with him any longer."

She was trembling all over, but Joey hugged her again. "You can do this. I believe in you."

Because sometimes, you really did need other people to believe in you. Joey thought maybe he understood that now.

He held Gabe and his mom while they waited for Richard to wrap up his call. His best friend stood by his side, his own boyfriend holding his hand in support.

Joey had friends. He was loved. These people thought he was important.

From now on, he was going to work harder to show them that he was worthy of their love, and do his best to let them know it was returned. Trusting others was pretty terrifying, but actually, being alone was worse.

He looked at Gabe, and made a vow to try and never push anyone away again.

GABE WAS AMAZED HE'D BEEN ABLE TO FIND A SPOT FOR HIS car this close to the park. It was a positive omen for what he hoped would be a good day.

The spring sunshine was beaming down overhead, making even the grumpiest of New Yorkers smile. Despite it being a Saturday, the drive down from Greenwich had been bearable thanks to such lovely weather spurring him on. Gabe twirled his keys before dropping them into his pocket and pulling out his phone.

Joey had given him specific instructions on where to meet him. He only had so long for a lunch break and wasn't really supposed to slip out of the studio in costume, but since the show hadn't aired yet, Joey argued that people would be less likely to recognize him.

Gabe was glad. He would be fine to do this by himself, but he would rather share it with Joey.

Joey waved from the subway entrance as Gabe approached. It still made his breath catch sometimes, to see the happy man Joey had transformed into from that troubled guy he'd met last fall. Joey was so full of optimism and light these days.

Gabe had to admit his outfit wasn't immediately recognizable as being from the eighties. It still brought a smile to his face, thinking how much Joey screamed the house down when he found out he'd got the part on Beat It. Gabe had helped him read through the scripts as he'd got them, and he knew with absolute certainty it was going to be a huge hit once it aired on Netflix.

When he reached Joey, he greeted him with a kiss and a hug. "You ready?" he asked.

"Oh hell yeah," Joey replied, green eyes sparkling.

They walked hand in hand. Gabe always felt a bit nervous doing that, but today he wanted to be bold. People might have stared or sneered. He didn't notice. All that mattered was Joey by his side as they entered the park.

Unlike last time, Gabe felt like he had the upper hand as he approached Lewis and his beloved Max waiting on a bench. Lewis had screwed him over, but it hadn't mattered in the end. Joey had stepped up and saved the day, and that was all that Gabe cared about.

Sure enough, Lewis looked sheepish as they approached, his eyes darting back and forth between Gabe and Joey. "Hi," he said.

"Hi," Gabe replied to be polite. Joey didn't say anything, just raised an eyebrow. Gabe did his best not to chuckle.

"So, um, thanks for this," said Lewis.

He handed over Max's leash.

It turned out that Lewis loved the *idea* of having Max a lot more than the reality. When Gabe found out the poor dog was being cooped up in Lewis's apartment for most of the day and only being walked a couple of times a week, he'd lost his shit. That wasn't the agreement they'd made, and if Lewis couldn't keep up Max's care, then he needed to give him back to Gabe.

A year ago, he wouldn't have made such a demand. But Joey had taught him it was okay to put himself first from time to time. In fact, Gabe had cut back on several of his weekly activities since Joey had moved in. He'd taken a good, long look at what really made him content after that nasty business with Debbie Slater. Gabe had come to realize that a lot of what he'd done had been to make other people happy, telling himself that made him happy.

To a certain extent, that was still true. For example, he still volunteered at the homeless shelter. Joey even came with him when he could. That work was important and Gabe loved seeing the people they helped getting back on their feet.

But some of the library groups he was only doing because he'd told himself there was no one else to step in if he didn't give his time. That might have convinced him when he was with Lewis, but he wasn't going to leave Joey neglected for the sake of people that Gabe now knew might not always appreciate him.

He had to look after his own heart as well as those around him.

Joey had made it so much easier for Gabe to love and care for him since moving in. Once he'd got the part in New York, Gabe had taken a risk and suggested Joey not get his own place. He could commute from Gabe's house and they could continue building their relationship together. Building their home.

He'd been stunned when Joey had agreed immediately. Gabe obviously wasn't the only one learning how to care for himself better. Joey had opened his heart and trusted him.

As Gabe smiled at Lewis and took the leash, he said a silent thanks that they had broken things off when they had.

Gabe now knew they hadn't been in love. It had all been very nice for a while, but love was what he had with Joey.

He watched Lewis's gaze linger just a bit too long on Joey. Gabe didn't care if he still thought they'd been fooling around while he and Lewis were still together. Lewis's opinions no longer mattered to him. Especially after he'd failed to look after Max properly for all these months.

Gabe crouched down. "Come here, boy!" he cried.

Max had been playing with another dog, but at Gabe's voice he charged over and threw himself into his arms. He and Joey laughed. Lewis sighed.

"Well," he said, his voice strained. "Good luck."

With that, he shoved his hands into his pockets and marched off.

Gabe shrugged. He got the feeling Lewis would get over it. He'd never been the most caring man in hindsight.

"Joey," Gabe said, looking up at his gorgeous boyfriend. "I'd like to introduce you to the other man in my life."

"Oh no," said Joey in mock horror. He dropped to his knees and buried his face in Max's soft, golden fur. "I don't stand a chance!"

Gabe chuckled and kissed his cheek, stroking an excitable Max as he wriggled about.

"What do you say, buddy?" he asked. "Do you want to come home?" Gabe was a little worried what Duchess might make of him. She was doing so much better these days, often coming to him and Joey for petting and sleeping in their room or on the end of the bed. Hopefully, she and Max would be the best of friends.

Max barked and wagged his tail. Gabe's heart ached. He was so happy to have him back he almost couldn't stand it.

Joey sighed as they both stood. "I'll come home as soon as I can," he said, glancing back towards the subway station.

Gabe hugged him close and placed a sweet kiss on his

lips. "Your family will be waiting for you when you do," he promised.

Joey got a strange look in his eye as he looked between Gabe and Max. "Family," he said.

Gabe knew he was still getting used to the idea. His mom's divorce was almost finalized, much to his dad's fury. But Tess had her own apartment across town now and saw Joey and Gabe all the time. Joey's brother was still being an ass about letting either of them see baby Michael, but maybe with time things would get better.

Joey had been on his own for so long, it made Gabe's heart soar to see their little family growing. For now, that was just giving loving homes and second chances to their cat and dog. But perhaps one day…

"Yeah, family," he said, giving Joey's shoulders a squeeze. "You're a great dad."

Joey rolled his eyes. "It'll be a bit different with actual *kids*," he said. He then paused. Gabe loved it when he accidentally blurted out what was really on his mind. Especially when it was something so wonderful.

"We can start with pets," Gabe said. "Work up to babies."

Joey looked at him, his eyes wide. And…Gabe spotted a mischievous glint there too.

"Well, I am a traditional boy at heart," he said, a smile creeping on to his face. "You'd have to marry me first."

Gabe wrapped his arms around Joey. Max ran around them both, his tail wagging so hard it was smacking their legs. "Is that so?"

Joey swallowed. "Yeah."

Gabe licked his lips. He already thought this was where they were headed, but he'd imagined planning some great romantic gesture a year or two down the line. But why wait? He knew he loved Joey more than anything else in this whole world.

"Okay then. Would you, Joey Sullivan, marry me?"

Half of Central Park probably heard Joey's scream as he leaped into Gabe's arms, throwing his legs around Gabe's waist. Max barked and hopped around like a maniac.

"Are you sure?" Joey asked between kisses, tears in his eyes.

He'd never been more sure of anything. "Yes," Gabe said. "We can wait and make it official with a ring if you like-"

"No, no," said Joey. He shook his head, the tears spilling down his face. "I don't need a ring. I don't need things. I just need you."

Gabe let out a sob and clutched him so tightly he was probably leaving bruises. "You make me so happy," he said. "I love you so much."

"I love you too," Joey said.

They kissed until Gabe couldn't hold him up any longer. He didn't want to let him go, but Joey had to get to back to work.

It was okay though, because they had the rest of their lives to spend together. Despite what Joey said, when Gabe got back to Greenwich he was going to fetch his grandfather's ring from the attic and prepare the most romantic dinner he could.

Because Joey deserved the very best. And they were going to have a lifetime of happiness together.

Bonus Epilogue

JOEY

Joey bit his lip as he switched lanes on I-95. Traffic wasn't terrible, but this was his first commute back from work since he'd started filming the new season of Beat It. He was suddenly wishing he could click his heels like Dorothy and get home in an instant.

The drive wasn't all that bad, especially when there hadn't been any accidents. But Joey's anxiety was clawing up his throat. He couldn't be late, not today.

Today set a precedent. He had to be back on time, so the days he couldn't avoid being late wouldn't seem so bad.

He drummed his fingers on the steering wheel and turned his Spotify playlist up, but he couldn't concentrate on singing along to the track like he usually would to pass the miles. The words just slipped through his brain like water.

As he slowed the car to a stop yet again, he made himself take a deep breath and exhaled slowly. He was fine, he still had time. Besides, Gabe was at home already.

His work had been more flexible about paternity leave.

God, even just thinking the word made Joey's stomach flip. It wasn't like it had come as a surprise in the end. They had fought and worked so hard to get where they were today. But still, it didn't seem real.

Joey was a dad.

He rubbed the back of his neck and tried to swallow down the nervous lump in his throat and blink back the tears that sprung in his eyes. He was so filled with doubt it was crippling. How could he be a dad? He could barely look after himself.

But then Gabe's strong, soothing voice materialized inside his mind. *"You just do the best you can,"* he'd told him over and over. *"You're so full of love and kindness. We'll work it out. Together."*

Joey took another breath as the traffic started moving again and reminded him of the promise he'd made himself when they'd committed to this process. The only thing he had to do, the one and *only* thing, was to be a better father than his own. And since his dad had been a homophobic and abusive alcoholic, the bar really wasn't that high.

It was *good* Joey was terrified. That meant he *cared.* He couldn't stop thinking about what they had to get at their weekly grocery trips and what supplies they had to make sure they never ran out of. He'd watched a zillion YouTube videos on how to change diapers and what the hell to do with a time-out and what games to play to best stimulate little minds. He and Gabe must have found all the parenting books at the library and checked them out one after the other, taking notes on sleeping patterns and teething. Their drawers and closets were overflowing with tiny clothes that had been gifted by friends and family, and the spare room had finally been decluttered and freshly decorated.

Yet...Joey still felt underprepared. The first few days had been an exhausting, confusing blur as everyone recovered from the flight back from China. Joey wished he'd had a couple more weeks before he'd had to go back to work. But the show had accommodated his shooting schedule as best they could around his newfound parenthood. Besides, this was the start of a new life, not anything temporary. It made sense to get back into a routine as soon as possible.

Finally he turned off the interstate, heading back toward Connecticut. Not long now.

"Daddy's nearly home," he murmured to himself, making him believe the words were real. He *was* Daddy now.

And he was going to make it home for bedtime.

———

As soon as Joey stepped through the front door, the wailing hit him like a brick wall. His stomach dropped as he shrugged off his coat and kicked away his shoes, careful not to step on any of the toys that had spilled out into the hall.

"I'm home!" he called as he petted the head of their dog Max. The poor thing seemed pretty distressed as to what was going on. Joey stuck his head in the living room, but there was no one there. The crying seemed to be coming from everywhere.

"Up here!" Gabe's strained voice traveled down the stairs. Joey took them two at a time.

His heart swelled at the sight of his husband with the chubby baby in his arms. Gabe was pacing what used to be their cluttered spare room. Now it contained a crib and a small bed, the walls painted light green with decals of dinosaurs, fire trucks and ballerinas. The room was dark, the only illumination coming from a night-light projector in the corner which shone slowly spinning multicolored stars onto the ceiling. A lullaby played softly as the stars gently twirled.

Gabe was pacing back and forth with nine-month-old Hai bawling in his arms. In the small bed sat his sister, four-year-old Jia Li, with all the covers pulled up around her little frame. She was in her new unicorn pajamas with a storybook about a bunny rabbit open beside her, but she was looking wide-eyed at her crying brother.

"I don't know what to do," Gabe said, his voice croaky. "I've fed him and bathed him and changed him and rocked him, and he just won't stop."

Joey immediately walked over and wrapped them in his arms. Even though Gabe was the bigger of them both, he still leaned into the embrace with ease, resting his temple on top of Joey's hair and sighing. Baby Hai sobbed and squirmed between them, but at Joey's presence, he turned and pawed at his new daddy's face, calming a little. Even if it was only from confusion at the appearance of another person, it was at least a little respite for them all.

"It's okay," Joey said in a soothing voice. He drew up every last bit of confidence he had. He didn't have to get this *right*. He just had to be *kind*. "It's all right, baby boy, shh."

Hai hiccuped and sniffled.

Jia Li said something in her native Mandarin. The orphanage where she had been living had done their best to teach her some English as well, but she was so timid she hardly spoke at all. They only had a limited family background on the siblings, but Joey knew enough to appreciate Jia Li was fiercely protective over her little brother.

"Why don't you walk with Hai a bit," Joey said to Gabe, rubbing his back. "I'll do story time with Jia Li. Has she brushed her teeth?"

Gabe leaned down and kissed Joey's cheek gently. "She's all ready for bed," he said, the relief clear in his voice. "I didn't want her to feel ignored, but Hai-"

"It's *fine*," Joey insisted. Hai was already crying less. "Go walk with him a bit. Or maybe rock him in the stroller?"

Gabe's eyes lit up. "Oh, yeah. He likes that."

Joey watched the two of them head out the door, Gabe

bouncing Hai in his arms. "I'm not scared of you, baby boy," Joey heard him murmur fondly as they slowly walked down the stairs. "You cry all you like. Papa's not going anywhere."

Joey smiled, then turned back to Jia Li, who was sitting patiently in her bed. She looked so small, but there was something resilient about the way she looked back up at Joey. She was a tough little cookie, Joey knew already.

"Hey, princess," he said cheerfully, sitting down beside her. "How's Daddy's favorite girl?"

Jia Li chewed her lip and looked at Joey with a frown. "Daddy?" she said, as if she was trying the word on for size.

Joey nodded and pointed to himself. "Daddy," he repeated.

They had also read up as much as they could on how best to teach her English. Down the line, they planned on all taking Mandarin lessons, too. It was very important to Gabe and Joey that the kids didn't lose touch with their heritage. But for now, they were focusing on making sure Jia Li learned enough words to start communicating her needs as soon as possible.

She frowned and pulled at the comforter, her brown eyes narrowing as she looked around the dark bedroom and frowned deeper. "Daddy...gone," she said after a moment's thought.

Joey's heart sank. "I know, hon," he said sadly. But then he smiled. She had to get used to this idea. "But Daddy came back. Daddy will *always* come back."

Jia Li pulled at her long hair, tied back in a braid to keep it from knotting overnight. "Daddy back," she repeated. "Daddy home."

Joey nodded. "Yes, that's it. Daddy home to say 'night night'!"

He watched her think that over. Then, in a blur, she

launched herself at him, hugging him surprisingly tightly for a child. "Daddy home!" she said with more conviction.

Joey smiled, a lump in his throat that came from a mixture of pride, happiness and disbelief. "Can Daddy have a big hug?" he asked.

She let go of his waist and nodded, opening her arms for him. He carefully picked her up and stood, resting her on his hip with her small legs wrapped around his waist. She snuggled against his chest, sucking her thumb.

Joey kissed the top of her hair and walked over to the framed photos they had already mounted on the wall. Downstairs, Hai's cries had become grumbles.

"Who's that?" Joey asked.

He pointed to the first photo they had received of the siblings from the adoption agency that was now framed on the wall. He would never forget the moment he had laid eyes on the two tiny people he and Gabe were being trusted to invite into their lives, to care for forever more. Jia Li was sitting on a wall with Hai protectively wrapped in her arms as she grinned at the camera.

"Jia Li!" she cried happily around her thumb, looking at Joey for praise.

"That's right," he said proudly. "Jia Li is happy, isn't she?" She nodded with such enthusiasm it jolted her whole body. Joey shifted his grip, making sure she was held tightly against him. "And who's that?"

"Hai!" said Jia Li, taking her thumb out and smacking Joey's chest lightly with her damp hand.

"Yes, well done," he said warmly to her with another kiss on the head.

He didn't have many fond memories from his own childhood. Right from the moment he'd been able to walk and talk, his dad had made it pretty clear he was not the favorite son. But he remembered his mom's hugs and the way she used to whisper to him that he was brave and smart and talented. He never wanted his kids to feel touch-starved. He always wanted them to know they were loved down to their very bones.

"Who's that?" he asked, moving to another photo. It was Joey's favorite one of him and Gabe, from their first Christmas together. Gabe's friend Mitch had snapped a candid shot while they'd snuggled in their ugliest Christmas sweaters, oblivious to the rest of the world around them.

Jia Li looked between the photo and Joey. "Daddy," she said after a moment.

He jiggled her and grinned. "Yeah! You got it! And who's that?" She frowned as he pointed at Gabe, then glanced downstairs, unsure. "Is it Papa?" Joey asked.

She raised her eyebrows and smiled. "Papa," she repeated happily.

Joey wandered out into the hallway where just a lamp was on, so the light wasn't too bright. They could still make out the other framed pictures on the walls, though. "Look," Joey said, tapping on the glass. "That's Grandma and Grandpa Robinson."

"Robison," Jia Li repeated uncertainly around her thumb. She hadn't met them yet, but they were traveling up from Florida next week, beyond excited to meet their grandchildren.

"And Grandma Sully," Joey said, pointing to a lovely photo of his mom. It was funny, but she looked so much younger now she'd divorced his dad and moved away from him. Technically, his dad had moved away with Joey's brother, sister-in-law and their son, leaving Joey and his mom in peace in Connecticut. Good riddance. Needless to say, there were no photos of them on their montage wall.

Jia Li kicked her legs and excitedly pointed down.

"Duchy! Duchy!" she said, bouncing around as the cat wound her way around Joey's legs.

Duchess wasn't the friendliest of cats until you got to know her, but for some reason she had warmed to Jia Li immediately, allowing her to pet her head and stroke her tail. Jia Li was more wary of their big golden retriever, Max. He was undoubtedly by Gabe and Hai's side, wagging his big tail. It was funny how each pet had picked a child to watch over.

Joey moved down the hall to some more photos. Jia Li picked out the one from his and Gabe's wedding day impressively fast. She was a smart kid, he could tell. There were a few pictures of Gabe's friends – now both their friends – from around town, as well as a cast photo from Beat It's wrap party last year. But Joey went to a collection at the end of the hallway.

"Jia Li, look. Here are your uncles. These are Daddy's best friends in the whole world. They can't wait to meet you." He tapped at the glass to get her attention. She sucked her thumb and looked at the various frames. "There's Reyse, Blake and Elion, Raiden and Levi, and TJ and Ashby. Look, isn't Ashby pretty?"

Like a lot of little kids, Jia Li was naturally drawn to shiny, pink and sparkly things. So Ashby's makeup in the photo made a change from the rest of the guys and caught her eye. "Pretty," she mumbled happily around her thumb.

She was getting heavier, so Joey slowly walked back into their bedroom. Once the kids were settled and Hai was a bit older, they'd already decided they needed to think about moving to a bigger place or getting an extension. But, for now, Jia Li was happy to share with her brother.

"Once upon a time," Joey murmured, taking her back to the photos of him and Gabe and her and Hai, "there was a little princess and her brother, the prince. They lived in a faraway land. But when two kings heard the prince and princess needed a new home, they flew *all* across the world to find them. They battled the dragons at the adoption agency and bargained with the knights at the kingdom borders."

He crossed the room and placed her gently back on her bed, lifting the rabbit book out of the way so she could snuggle under the covers. Then he sat beside her, wrapping his arm around her small shoulders.

"After a long time, the kings were victorious. They brought the prince and the princess back to their castle where they would live happily ever after. The end."

Jia Li looked up at him with sleepy eyes. "The end," she repeated. He wasn't sure how much of the story she followed, but he would keep telling it to her every night until she understood it all.

He slipped off the bed to kneel beside it, encouraging Jia Li to lie down. She watched him, her eyes slowly blinking as she sucked her thumb.

"Who loves Jia Li?" Joey asked, stroking her hair back.

"Hai," she said, taking her thumb out and rubbing her face.

"That's right. Who else?" Joey asked. "Does Papa love Jia Li?"

She nodded. "Papa," she murmured, her eyes closing and opening.

"Who else?" Joey asked, pointing at his chest.

She smiled and reached out with a fumbling hand. "Daddy," she said into her pillow, her eyes almost totally closed now. "Daddy loves Jia Li and Hai and Papa."

He smiled and kissed her cheek, a lump rising in his throat. "He loves you all so much, princess," he promised.

He stayed for a while, watching on as her breathing evened out and she fell into a deep sleep, safe and secure in her new home.

———

Joey's legs were stiff when he emerged from the kids' bedroom. He stretched and jogged down the stairs. Max was waiting for him in the entrance hall, wagging his tail slowly, like he still wasn't quite sure what was going on. All he knew was that his pack had almost doubled in size the last couple of days and he had to look after them all. Even if one of them was especially noisy.

Hai was still crying and flailing in Gabe's arms when Joey walked into the den, but at least he wasn't outright screaming. Gabe looked up at Joey with tired eyes, his shoulders sagging as he cradled their small boy to his chest.

"I'm sorry," he whispered tearfully. "The stroller didn't work this time. I don't know what I'm doing wrong."

"Hey, no," Joey said firmly. He marched over and cupped Gabe's cheek with his palm. Even though Joey was shattered from his first day back at work, the commute, and putting Jia Li to bed, he suddenly felt a fresh wave of energy for his husband and his son. "None of that. You've done an *awesome* job. This place would look like a war zone if I'd been home alone with them all day."

Gabe gave him a small smile. "They were good as gold, honestly. We had lunch and played in the yard and the den. Jia Li did numbers with me while Hai had his nap and then they had dinner – Jia Li isn't keen on peas, either," he added with a chuckle.

Joey laughed, too. "Just like her Papa," he said.

"Then Hai got in a mood and he just won't stop crying," Gabe said, shaking his head.

"Give him to me," Joey said, already slipping his hands around Hai's small, rotund body. "You go take a bath, okay?"

"Do I smell of puke that much?" Gabe asked, a twitch of a

smile on his lips as he allowed Joey to take the squirming, hiccuping Hai.

"No, baby," Joey said patiently, even though Gabe did maybe have a bit of vomit lingering on his back where he must have burped Hai earlier. But Joey didn't care about that. He was so full of love, seeing how much his husband was worrying himself into knots over their kids after just a couple of days. "We installed that big tub for a reason. Go make the most of it without anyone asking to play Lego or needing their diaper changed."

Gabe laughed and rubbed the back of his neck, making it click loudly. "I love you, gorgeous," he said, kissing Joey's cheek. "And you, chubba buba," he said with a lopsided grin, stroking Hai's hair. Hai looked around, blinking at his Papa as he snuffled his cries down for a moment.

"There we go," Joey said, pleased at such a small victory. "We're going to be asleep in no time, aren't we, champ?"

Hai's lip wobbled.

"Run while you still can," Joey said with mock urgency. He and Gabe grinned at each other, before Gabe bolted up the stairs.

Joey walked with Hai into the kitchen as he began to cry again, Max following by his knees. Joey fetched one of the facecloths off the side that had already gone through the wash – he was going to have to get used to the levels of laundry they had to do now – and wiped away Hai's tears and around his nose. Hai arched his back and kicked his legs, gearing up to start wailing once more.

"Hush, little baby, don't say a word, Daddy's gonna buy you a mockingbird," Joey began to sing.

His voice was tired from recording on the show today, but Hai didn't need a Grammy award-winning performance. In fact, at Joey's croaky effort, he calmed and blinked his big, brown eyes at Joey's mouth.

"Oh, you like that, huh?" Joey asked with a smile. He bounced Hai on his hip and started walking back toward the stairs. *"And if that mockingbird don't sing, Daddy's gonna buy you a diamond ring. And if that diamond ring turns brass, Daddy's gonna buy you a looking glass."*

Hai leaned his head onto Joey's chest, then surprised Joey by popping his thumb into his mouth. He thought it was only Jia Li that did that, but it seemed her brother took after her.

As Hai had already had his bath, Joey walked them into his and Gabe's bedroom, Max dutifully trotting along by his legs. He seemed happier now the small, pink pup was no longer bawling. Joey glanced around for Duchess, but he could just make out her outline on top of the dresser in the kids' room, watching over Jia Li. He smiled, feeling relieved.

"And if that looking glass gets broke, Daddy's gonna buy you a billy goat." Max whined and tilted his head. "Not really," Joey whispered, sitting on the bed and winking at Max. "I think this house is full enough for now."

Max grumbled in agreement and laid himself down on the carpet.

"And if that billy goat won't pull, Daddy's gonna buy you a cart and a bull," Joey continued to sing, even though the lyrics were kind of nonsense.

He'd learned them by heart weeks ago on the off chance one of the kids would actually respond to a lullaby. He rested his head on the pillow, lying on top of the comforter with Hai snuggled on his chest. Joey straightened out Hai's onesie covered with little sheep, hopping over fences.

"And if that cart and bull turn over, Daddy's gonna buy you a dog named...Max!"

Max lifted his head and wagged his tail with a small, doggy grin.

"And if that dog named Max won't bark, Daddy's gonna buy you a horse and a cart."

Joey closed his own eyes, turning so Hai was on the bed, cuddled up to him, safe and sound. Hai's breathing was light and steady. Joey stroked his impossibly soft hair, inhaling that particular baby scent that he was still getting used to. Tiredness washed over Joey, but he was also happy. It was the kind of contentment that he'd first experienced when he'd first met Gabe, and was only growing now as they continued on their life journey together.

Joey was a dad. This was a no-takesy-backsy sort of deal. And yet…Joey found he was becoming *less* terrified. He wanted this with everything he had. More than fame and fortune, more than a big, beautiful wedding, even though he had been lucky enough to have all those things.

Knowing that he was going to be a parent until the day he died was unimaginably thrilling and daunting and the most wonderful gift he could imagine. He was never going to stop trying every single day to try and be the very best dad he could be.

Of course, some days were going to be awful. Some days they were going to scream that they hated each other, and there would be tears and slammed doors. But as sleep began creeping over him, Joey had faith it would be okay. That he and Gabe were in this together.

Forever.

"And if that horse and cart fall down," Joey mumbled with a happy sigh, *"you'll still be the sweetest little baby in town."*

In the quiet of the house, Joey drifted off to sleep, never forgetting to be careful of the precious little one cradled to his side. When the bed dipped with a heavy weight, Joey stirred, but Gabe shushed him, urging him back to sleep. He smelled of their shower gel and something spicy that was always Gabe.

Joey felt him shift around, thinking he was angling himself next to Hai. But then another little body dropped down on the mattress. Joey cracked his eye just enough to see Jia Li worming her way next to her Papa in the dark.

Joey smiled as Gabe pulled a blanket over them all. Joey expected some fuss from one of the kids, but all he heard as he slipped back into a light sleep was a chorus of soft breathing.

Then some purring by his head.

Then he felt the bed dip for a final time as a big, fat golden retriever hauled himself up to join the rest of his pack at Joey and Gabe's feet.

This was why they'd gotten the super king-sized bed, Joey thought with a soft chuckle.

For so many years, he'd felt so alone. Like he didn't belong anywhere. Now he had so much family his heart was overflowing with happiness.

He kept hold of that thought as sleep finally claimed him for good, his most treasured loved ones snuggled around him.

This was his idea of heaven.

———

To see Gabe and Joey's first night together from Gabe's point of view, sign up to my newsletter here: hjwelch.com/subscribe

The next book in the Homecoming Hearts series is Raiden and Levi's story, Burn. Turn the page to learn more...

BURN

Scary stalker. Bratty client. But can chemistry this explosive lead to true love?

Raiden Jones never thought he'd need a bodyguard. Now he's back home, his life as a songwriter has been tame to the point of boring compared to his pop star days with boy band Below Zero. But when a malicious hacker starts destroying his career and threatening his life, he finds himself desperately in need of protection.

After leaving the Marines, Levi Patterson takes a place with his uncle's private security firm. The last thing he expected was a dumb babysitting job for the bratty, privileged Raiden. However, the two men have no choice but to get to know each other as they are forced on tour with one of Raiden's remaining clients.

Levi has never told anyone of his secret, occasional hook-ups with guys from his unit, and Raiden's never thought about going with another man before. But it's obvious the increasing chemistry between them is burning to become more than physical, and there's only so long they can resist.

As the hacker gets bolder, Levi finds himself in a race against time before Raiden is taken from him forever. He's no stranger to combat, but with his heart on the line, he finds himself in the fight of both their lives.

Burn is a high heat, low angst standalone MM romance. It's the third book in the **Homecoming Hearts** series, where these former pop stars swap the limelight for happy ever afters. This book features frenemies who become lovers, a surprise bachelor party, perky morning runs, so much UST, a terrifying fire, and a guaranteed HEA with absolutely no cliffhanger.

Acknowledgments

There are so many people who I have to thank in helping me complete my first series in MM romance. Heck, my first ever book series! It's been a fair old journey and whether you've been here since the start or have only just discovered Below Zero and Homecoming Hearts, I couldn't have done this without you.

Thank you to the people who have been here all the way, behind the scenes, keeping me going and bringing these books to life with me: Ed Davies, Amelia Faulkner, Conrad Rivers, Meg Cooper, Cate Ashwood, Aria Tan, Tanja Ongkiehong, Leslie Copeland and LesCourt Author Services.

Thank you to my incredible husband, whose support I simply couldn't have done without. You believed in me when I didn't believe in myself and cheered on every milestone and accomplishment. Thank you for giving me my own happy ever after.

Thank you to my friends who make *me* feel like an international pop star!

Thank you to my fur babies for keeping Mummy company in her writing cave.

And finally, thank you to every single one of *you* who has enjoyed Blake, Joey, Raiden, Trent and Reyse's stories. Thank you for all the loving reviews, for the encouragement in our Facebook Group, <u>Helen's Jewels</u>, the emails you've sent saying how moved you were by a book, the excitement for each new release, everything. Without you this series wouldn't have come to life. You're the best and I have so much love for each and every one of you.

PINE COVE BOX SET BY HJ WELCH

Welcome to Pine Cove, where true love lives happily ever after! **This 2000 page box set contains all six novels as well as all five companion short stories.**

Safe Harbor

Robin Coal needs a fake boyfriend for his high school reunion. He asks his housemate: a gorgeous, totally straight ex-Marine. What could go wrong? There's only one bed, and Dair might not be so straight after all... When Robin's past threatens their future, only Dair can save him.

Sweet Spot

It's Halloween and Robin has prepared a sexy little surprise for his boyfriend Dair when he gets home from work. Hold on to your horses, Marine!

____

Troubled Waters

Bodyguard Scout Duffy doesn't know what's worse: the fact that his scorching one-night-stand, Emery Klein, is his bratty new client, or the fact that he doesn't even remember Scout. But Emery's life is in danger thanks to his out and proud charity work, and once he finally recognizes Scout, their chemistry in undeniable.

____

Homeward Bound

Swift Coal just found out he's a father, and his daughter (and her cranky cat) are coming to stay. His best friend's younger brother, Micha Perkins, has nowhere to go and a wrongfully tattered reputation. He's relieved when Swift asks him to be a live-in babysitter. He just has to hide his lifelong crush. Easy, because Swift is straight—right?

____

Bright Horizon

With sixteen years between them, baker Ben Turner and lawyer Elias Solomon have no idea their crush is mutual. But when Ben inherits his long-lost family's estate and becomes an overnight millionaire, Elias swears to protect the innocent younger man from the vultures circling him. To unravel the mystery of the inheritance, they must go to England to confront Ben's estranged relatives…and their feelings for each other.

____

Crossed Paths

Raj Bhat is done living in the shadows. It's time for him to take charge of his own destiny and tell the man he's fallen for how he really feels.

———

Midnight Sky

It's the night before New Year's Eve. Taylan Demir is all alone, and he's just lost his dog. Except when his handsome customer, Hudson Perkins, comes to his rescue, Taylan doesn't just get his dog back. He's suddenly got a hot date, and maybe someone to kiss when the clock strikes midnight.

———

Memory Lane

Angel Shields saved Jay Coal's life in high school, and Jay has secretly loved his straight best friend ever since. Now Angel's back in town with amnesia after a suspicious work accident and it's Jay's turn to rescue him. He pretends to be Angel's fiancé to see him in the hospital, but with his scrambled-up memory, Angel's not sure it's fictional after all. He just knows he loves Jay more than ever.

———

Thin Ice

Kamran's ex broke his heart, tricked him into aiding a bank robbery, and now he wants him to do one last job. There's only one way to say no: seek the protective custody of the biggest, grumpiest FBI agent ever, Lee Marshall. And pretend to be his boyfriend for a week-long family reunion in their giant mansion. Wait, what?

———

Calm Shores

Gorgeous, sophisticated Dante walks into Oliver's bar and orders…a boyfriend?! Dante needs a man to keep his mother from setting him back up with his awful, cheating ex, and Oliver is up for the challenge.

———

Fresh Snow

Emery Klein is throwing the best Christmas party ever, but his fiancé, Scout Duffy, and all their friends have something more exciting in mind.

———

Each Pine Cove book can be read as a stand alone and has its own happy ever after. But if you read the whole series, you'll see a lot of familiar faces!

Available as an ebook or audiobook.

I've spent almost four years trying to get my captain Seth to notice me. He's hot as hell and knows how to boss a guy around, even one as big as me. To him, though, I'm just the team clown. But when he drags me into this graduation bet, it's no laughing matter. So why shouldn't this little cherub Gabe tutor me as well? In fact, I don't see why we can't share him in all *kinds* of ways. Seth is clearly a natural Daddy, Gabe thrives being doted on, and I'm happy to Daddy *and* be Daddied. Win-win, right?

GABE

Somehow, I've found myself standing up to the guy whose family pretty much owns Paddle Creek and put my neck on the line for two of the college's star players. Now we're spending every day together as I try and save their grades, and I don't know if I'm crazy but it's like they both *want* me. I've never had a boyfriend. I'm not even out to my overbearing parents. How could I choose between them…or do I actually have to when they *both* want to be my Daddies? After my life comes crashing down, it's their turn to come to my rescue. Maybe what me and these god-like men have isn't just a fling after all?

Heaven Sent is a steamy, standalone MMM romance. It's the first book in the **Paddle Creek College** series, where it's always the quiet ones who get up to the best kind of trouble. This book features a geek tutoring two hot jocks, two hot jocks tutoring a geek in a completely different way, a trash panda with a heart of gold, a human ice cream sundae, a revenge curse, and a guaranteed HEA with absolutely no cliffhanger.

PADDLE CREEK #2: YES, SIR BY HJ WELCH

Two men. Two secrets. Can true love set them free?

BENEDICT

Just one more year, then I can go back to my beloved Oxford University and leave this tiny town behind me. Teaching is my passion, but I have other desires that I know would get me fired if anyone found out. The only trouble is, my new TA is pushing all my buttons and I'm not sure he even realizes what calling me Sir does to me. That's nothing, however, compared to when he starts calling me Daddy.

JACKSON

Have I got hots for teacher? Oh, yes. Messing around is off the table, though, so in a way it's safe to flirt with him and see him lose that stiff upper lip. It's not like he'd be interested in me anyway if he ever discovered what I love wearing under my clothes. Tough guys like me shouldn't like satin and lace. They shouldn't want to feel pretty. But Sir makes me feel gorgeous, and I want to be *such* a good boy for him.

__Yes, Sir__ is a steamy, standalone MM romance. It's the second book in the __Paddle Creek College__ series, where it's always the quiet ones who get up to the best kind of trouble. This book features two people learning they don't have to be ashamed of who they are, a sassy brat who really wants to behave, a master in the bedroom who's a caring Daddy at heart, role playing so good it could win an Oscar, and a guaranteed HEA with absolutely no cliffhanger.

PADDLE CREEK #3: LITTLE PLEASURES BY HJ WELCH

One jaded Daddy. One brand new boy. A fake relationship that becomes all too real.

XANDER

It's bad enough I have to move back to Paddle Creek with my awful stepmom, but now my half-brother's best friend has decided he has to look after me—even pretending to be my new boyfriend for a family wedding to keep my stepmother off my back. What Ruben doesn't know is that I've been in love with him for as long as I can remember and spending so much time with him is torture. Until it isn't. I can't believe that he's interested in me and even wants to be my Daddy, unlocking something in me I never knew was there. But when my stepmom goes too far, can I rely on Ruben to be there for me seeing as no one else in my life ever has?

RUBEN

When my life-long best friend asks me to keep an eye on his half-brother, of course I agree. Except he's a young man now, not a kid, and he's tugging at every single one of my Daddy heartstrings. Xander has just moved back into town and between finishing his degree, part-time work, and hellish stepmother, he's stressing himself into knots. It's a long time since a boy interested me, but I just want to protect Xander from the whole world. No matter the cost.

Little Pleasures is a steamy, standalone MM romance. It's the third book in the **Paddle Creek College** series, where it's always the quiet ones who get up to the best kind of trouble. This book features a Daddy introducing a boy to his inner little, the most loyal doggy best friend, a lot of dinosaurs, a heart-stopping rescue, and a guaranteed HEA with absolutely no cliffhanger. CW: Age play but no ABDL.

After my husband and I swapped military life for married life, we quickly met our sweet baby boy who we'll do anything for. When Brady says he's found a sassy little lamb for the three of us to stalk, I'm happy to indulge him. But this broken young man swiftly captures all of our hearts, even though he says he can walk away any time. There's a difference between walking and being taken, however. Now I have the scent of a fool who's about to discover what happens when he's stolen what's *mine*.

Four Play *is a super steamy, standalone MMMM romance. It's the fourth book in the **Paddle Creek College** series, where it's always the quiet ones who get up to the best kind of trouble. This book features exhilarating primal play, one hell of a paint ball match, an underwater themed motel, so many smooches, an obsessive ex-boyfriend, and a guaranteed HEA with absolutely no cliffhanger.*

BEARS-4-U (MULTI-AUTHOR SHARED UNIVERSE): KEEP ME BY HJ WELCH

Snowed in for a second chance at love...

BECKETT

It's been over two years since I lost my darling husband, and my best friend is taking matters into her own hands. She's signed me up to a dating app for bears and those that love them, even encouraging me to attend a weekend mixer. I go to humor her, not expecting to rescue the most adorable boy...twice. But I'm not ready to open up my heart again, am I?

LAURiE

My last Daddy was bad news. It's taken a lot of courage for me to reach out on Bears-4-U and go to this mixer, only to find that the new Daddy I've been talking to is just as awful. That's when Beckett swoops into my life like a hero in a story book. I know he's not looking for love, but I want to mend his broken heart so badly. When a scary snowstorm blows in and strands us, I trust he'll keep me safe and warm. I want to be in his life, in his bed, in his heart…forever.

__Bears-4-U__ is a MM Daddy romance multi-author series, featuring a host of delicious Daddy pairings. The Bears-4-U dating app is all about putting Bears and Teddy Bears together for their honey-sweet HEAs. Psst, no real bears involved. Each book can be read as a standalone, but why not snuggle up with all the bears?

DADDY'S FAIRY TALES BOX SET BY HELEN JULIET

Experience Goldilocks and the Three Bears, Little Red Riding Hood, The Three Little Pigs, and Puss in Boots as you've never seen them before in this box set of contemporary adaptations! Available together for the first time, each stand alone book features a caring Daddy finding his HEA with a loving boy (or boys!)

––––––––

Golden

When Goldie's ex-boyfriend leaves him in serious debt with the adult entertainment company he works for, Goldie gets the chance to work off the money…in front of the camera. The idea excites him, but then his favourite throuple—Daddy, Papa, and Baby —*demand* he comes to play with them. No matter how scared he is, he can't miss this opportunity, not even when his past comes back to haunt him.

Wild Ride

When Red is chased into the woods, he seeks sanctuary at his estranged grandma's house. He doesn't expect to be rescued by his older brother's best friend, the man he was always madly in love with. Could Hunter be the Daddy of Red's wildest dreams? Especially when he unlocks a secret passion of Red's for beautiful lingerie. There's still a threat lurking in the woods, though, and Hunter realises he'll do anything to protect his beautiful boy.

Three

When three shy best friends sign up to a dating app to finally get some by the end of the year, they don't expect to all fall for the same gorgeous, slightly scary-looking Daddy. The only solution? Let him choose who he wants to bed. Except he doesn't. Daddy Wolf wants to spoil each little piggy, one after another. But when danger comes calling, will their love for each other be enough to save them all?
Includes Halloween bonus scene!

Nine Lives

When Charlie suddenly finds himself homeless and penniless, he decides to sell the only thing left he owns. Himself. For the very first time. Lucky for him he stumbles across Miller, the own of a London kink club, who saves him from those who would take advantage of him. As Miller discovers his inner Daddy, he also unlocks Charlie's kitten alter-ego. But with both their families meddling, will new love be enough to keep them together?

Available as an ebook.

HJ Welch is an author of contemporary MM romance series, including the international bestselling Pine Cove series. She lives just outside of London with her husband and two balls of fluff that occasionally pretend to be cats. She began writing at an early age, later honing her craft online in the world of fanfiction on sites like Wattpad. Fifteen years and over half a million words later, she sought out original MM novels to read. By the end of 2016 she had written her first book of her own, and in 2017 she achieved her lifelong dream of becoming a full-time author. When she's not writing she's usually dancing, singing, filming music videos, taking long walks, working on jigsaw puzzles, drinking prosecco, or talking about Eurovision.

She also writes contemporary British MM fairy tale adaptations as Helen Juliet.

———

You can contact Helen via the following:
Newsletter: https://www.subscribepage.com/helenjuliet
Website – www.hjwelch.com
Facebook Group – Helen's Jewels
Instagram – @helenjwrites
Twitter – @helenjwrites
Book Bub – @HJWelchAuthor
Facebook Page – @HJWelchAuthor